Take Me Home to You

MIRANDA LIASSON

MIRANDA LIASSON, LLC/HAWTHORNE HOUSE

Published by Hawthorne House Press

Miranda Liasson, LLC

P.O. Box 13707

Fairlawn, OH 44334

www.mirandaliasson.com

Print ISBN 978-0-9986346-6-1

E-book ISBN 978-0-9986346-5-4

Cover by The Killion Group, Inc.

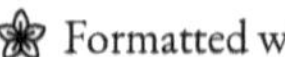 Formatted with Vellum

Also by Miranda Liasson
(www.mirandaliasson.com/bookshelf):

The Doctors of Oak Bluff (Take Me Series)

Take Me Home for Christmas

Take Me to the Wedding

Take Me Home to You

Seashell Harbor Series

Sweetheart Series

Angel Falls Series

Mirror Lake Series

Kingston Family Series

Ani is one of my favorite characters because she has the courage to act. May we all be inspired to do good in the world.

Chapter One

Adam

The woman next to me in first class wore dark sunglasses, a Packers sweatshirt, leggings, and mismatched tennis shoes. The mismatched shoes, one white and one navy, should have been a warning that something was seriously wrong and definitely a clue to change my seat ASAP.

Her blond hair was askew in a way that seemed to indicate a bird had gotten stuck and flapped its wings hard on the exit. The first thing she did was reach over me, breaching my personal space, to flag down the flight attendant for a drink.

Was she high? On drugs? By the way she kept swiping at her eyes, she appeared to be seriously upset, but her Anne Hathaway à la *Princess Diaries* sunglasses obscured the full story.

The flight attendant brought her a Bloody Mary with a celery stick jutting out of the glass. She took a sip and choked, which made me turn quickly from the medical journal I was trying to read.

I was an ER doctor from a busy Chicago hospital, trained for emergencies. I just wanted to make sure I wasn't sitting next to one.

"Sorry," she said, patting her chest until the spasm stopped and then sucking down the rest like she was pre-gaming for a frat party. "I don't usually drink."

Sure, you don't, was what I thought, but I gave a polite smile and a quick nod and went back to my reading. Before I left, my mom had handed me a sack of food, which I was still holding, sort of like I was still in grade school even though I was thirty-five years old. Unfortunately, the bag she'd chosen featured Santa bending over to set a giant bow-tied present under a Christmas tree. And the sack was *big*. Did she think there was no food in Turks and Caicos?

Apparently, my aunts had been power cooking Mediterranean food this morning, and I could tell from a quick whiff or two that inside were homemade spinach pies, cheese pies, and also probably baklava. Their well-wishes for a nice trip. I shoved the bag under the seat in front of me.

"I'm glad you're going," my mother had said as she kissed me goodbye, "but I wish you weren't going by yourself. Remember, no reading medical journals or listening to those educational podcasts, and don't sleep with any strange women just because you're lonely." Final advice from a lifelong social worker on the brink of retirement.

"Thanks, Ma." I'd kissed her on the cheek and taken the bag, even though it was embarrassingly large and also...the Santa. And did I mention that it was ninety degrees in mid-June?

I heard sucking sounds as my seatmate hit the bottom of her glass, which was suddenly being waved in front of me. "May I please have another?" she asked the flight attendant, who, in first class, was only an arm's length away.

"This is my first time in first class," the woman said, apparently to me. "How about you?"

I was afraid to make eye contact. I had my own stuff going on, and being functional over the past two years had taken every ounce of effort I could muster. "Yeah, me too," I said without turning to face her.

This was adding up to trouble. And I was here specifically to avoid that. To have a peaceful, quiet week not working, the opposite of what I'd done almost constantly since my wife died two years ago.

Two years! How was that possible? It seemed like yesterday in some ways, yet in others, our entire relationship was all a dream. Much to my chagrin, I was forgetting—the sound of Liv's voice, the way her hair used to fall forward, and she'd reach up to tuck it back behind her ear, the outlines of her precious face that I once knew so well. I felt like someone hanging off the edge of a cliff, clutching desperately at anything—rocks, branches, handfuls of dirt—anything not to forget.

"Why are you here?" my seatmate asked, the liquor clearly loosening her tongue.

"I—um, haven't had a vacation for a while." And I wanted the privacy and space. Which I clearly wasn't going to get with her next to me.

"I signed us up for first class even though Tyler said it was a waste. But I told him that it was our honeymoon, so why not? I'm usually frugal, but I mean, *honeymoon.* Come on."

Do not turn your head, my inner self warned. *Do.Not.Turn.Your.Head.* I made it a point not to get involved with women in general. Women on the edge were a hard no.

"I should've known from the way he was so predicable—no surprises, you know? Predictable isn't good—it's boring. And he was so careful about money." She dropped her voice. "Did you know that I have my own Amazon Prime account, so he wouldn't get on my case about buying too many pairs of underwear? 'Do you really need all of those pens?' he asked me once." She smacked her head. "How could I have been sooooo stupid?"

If I hadn't put two and two together before, I did now, even without seeing the big rhinestone *Bride* spelled out in scrolly letters on her bright white sweatshirt. Her hair was in some kind of fancy updo. Well, apparently it used to be, because half of it wasn't, and there were a couple of random pearl pins holding that sad half up. Her earrings were dangling drop pearls—in our wedding pictures, Liv was wearing nearly identical ones.

I'd gone a whole fifteen minutes without thinking of her. I blew out a breath and tried to distract myself from the ever-present ache in my chest. While Liv used to accuse me of having a savior complex, I wasn't about to swoop in and indulge it today. Because today would have been our five-year wedding anniversary.

Except she'd been gone for the last two. During the last few months of her life, she'd been obsessed with my getting to Turks and Caicos.

She'd visited there before we were married and once afterward with her friends. She made me promise to go on this anniversary. Even though we'd never been there together, and she knew she'd never make it back there herself.

I think she sensed what a train wreck I'd be and believed the trip would be good for me.

My best buds knew that I wasn't going to handle this well, so they'd bought me this nonrefundable ticket and told me specifically not to come back until I got laid. I promised no such thing, but they practically forced me to go—even called me an Uber to make sure I didn't back out.

I was about to Venmo them their ticket money back when something weird happened. I'd scrawled my Venmo password on a sticky note and stuck it somewhere—I know, dumb move—and was rummaging through my desk drawer when I found an old postcard. It was from the year before Liv died, from what turned out to be her final girls' trip.

I don't usually keep old things around, but I do of Liv's. Photos, grocery lists in her handwriting, a bit of yarn she'd half-crocheted into a granny square. Little pieces of her I haven't had the heart to let go of. The postcard was one of those things. The front showcased the aquamarine waters and the long stretch of pure white sand of Grace Bay Beach.

On the back she'd written, *You've got to see this place! Promise me someday! It's too beautiful to miss. xoxoxo*

I don't believe in omens, but this felt like one. Her gently nudging me to go and experience a place that had felt reviving and rejuvenating for her. Maybe she was telling me what I desperately knew—that I needed it. That I was leading a zombie life, dragging myself through, working myself to death to not feel the pain.

So I got on this plane despite being terrified about what I was going to do with myself for an entire week at the beach. All that time to be alone with thoughts I spent most of my waking hours trying to shut out.

I heard tiny sniffling sounds coming from next door. I squeezed my eyes shut, as if that would block out the noises. Seconds passed.

She was still crying. *Aw, hell.*

"Are you okay?" I asked my neighbor. This time, I fully turned.

I saw her swallow hard, as people do when they are trying hard not to cry but failing anyway. She had a nice, elegant neck. She seemed very pretty, despite the fact that most of her face was shrouded behind her big dark glasses. Big black mascara trails from her full wedding makeup scrolled down her cheeks.

Her straw made yet another sucking sound as she drained drink number two. She looked my way but didn't answer. "I don't know," she said, then punched her call light. "May I please have another?" she asked another flight attendant who'd appeared as suddenly as a genie from a bottle and acquiesced to her request.

I cleared my throat. "We haven't even taken off yet. Do you think you should—ah...?"

A fine crease appeared between her brows. "Surely, you aren't going to do that."

I lifted my brows in surprise, taken aback that she would give me some pushback at a time when she was so...distressed. "Do what?"

"Actually tell me what to do when you literally just met me." She frowned. "Are you like Tyler too? Are all men like Tyler?" She paused. "And if the answer is yes, I am going to drink that third drink. And maybe a fourth too. Whatever. It. Takes."

"Whatever it takes to...?"

She shrugged. "To get drunk as quickly as I can." To prove it, she worked hard on downing number three.

"Look," I said carefully, "do you want to talk about it? I mean, clearly, you've been through something."

"How do you know that?" she asked in mock surprise.

I pointed to her feet. "Because you're wearing mismatched shoes."

She looked down. "Oh *no.*" She smacked her head and looked back at me. At least I think she was looking at me. "Did you know that my almost-mother-in-law wouldn't be caught dead with mismatched anything? And she refused to wear any of the colors I suggested. Guess which color she chose?"

"Um, I don't know. Black?"

"Do you *know* her?"

"Just a guess." Seemed to me that the woman was a whole lot better off without Tyler and his mother, but I decided not to share that.

She sniffed again. "My nose is running. You wouldn't have a tissue, would you?"

I didn't. But I was good in a pinch. I emptied out half my food bag, came up with a napkin, and passed it over to her.

She blew her nose loudly and pointed to my bag. "Do you own a restaurant? Whatever's in there smells great."

"My aunts made it."

"Your aunts made you food? For your journey? Aww. That's so sweet."

I smiled. Mainly because she was right. I had a great family. "In my family, food is love."

"In my family, our hometown is love." She laughed.

"I'm not sure I understand."

"My parents were retired, living in Fort Myers. My dad golfed every day and was thinking of buying a boat. My mom belonged to three book clubs."

"And?"

"And then they moved back home. To Wisconsin. To be near *me*!" she said in an exasperated tone.

"Well, that's nice."

"My mom and I don't see eye to eye." She paused and gestured to herself. "I'm not the daughter she wanted." She rubbed her forehead. "Obviously."

"I'm sure your parents are very proud of you regardless of what happened today," I said because...well, what do you say to that? Besides, it would be better for both of us if she stopped crying.

Just then, the loudspeaker crackled as the captain signaled our takeoff, and the plane began to cascade down the runway, gaining speed.

The woman, whose name I still didn't know, clutched her chest. "Oh my goodness, I think I feel a little sick."

I touched her arm. She felt cold, despite the sweatshirt. But even worse, her face had gone as white as her sweatshirt.

"Try deep breaths." I went into ER mode. "Keep your head down."

She inhaled deeply. "You were right," she whispered. "Three was too many."

Her hand came up to her mouth, which I recognized as the universal vomit sign. I quickly dumped out all my homemade goodies just in time to hand Santa over for his ultimate sacrifice.

And then she hurled.

People around us freaked out. "Ew, gross," I heard from

behind us. "Henry, did someone just *puke*?" came from the woman in front of me.

Despite being mid-takeoff, the flight attendant was on us in a flash, handing over wipes, tissues, a glass of cold water, and a brand-new barf bag. My seatmate's face quickly went from pale to bright red as she wiped her mouth, shakily accepted the water, and thanked the attendant profusely.

All this before we hit 30,000 feet.

A minute later, my new friend sat back and lifted up her sunglasses. When she turned to me this time, I saw that her eyes were a clear, pale blue, lined like a raccoon with watered-down mascara, but still stunning. I immediately saw something in them that I was no stranger to—pain. "I'm really sorry," she said. And then she started to cry.

❧

Ani

On my way back from the bathroom, I paused in the aisle in front of my seatmate, crossing my arms to hide the fact that I was freezing. I also felt incredibly sober. "I want you to know that I'm normally a responsible person. I'm actually a pediatrician. I'm saying this because I've never been more embarrassed in my life."

"What's your name?" the man asked after I'd excused myself, climbed over his long legs, and lowered myself back into my window seat. "I mean, I think we should be on a first-name basis after working together to avert a greater disaster, don't you?"

He punctuated his statement with a winsome grin, which told me that with looks like his, he was probably used to being charming. The fact that he was joking did wonders for my embarrassment, which was painfully acute. He was nice and was clearly trying to help a woman who surely appeared to be losing it all around.

For the first time, I noticed that he had a head full of thick wavy hair and enough lean muscle to be an easy contender for a name-brand underwear ad. My looks were a completely different story. While I'd managed to finger-brush my teeth, it was impossible to make my hair look normal after the stylist had sprayed an entire bottle of intense-hold hairspray all over it this morning, giving it the consistency of frozen leaves.

"My name is Ani." I handed him a clean plastic bag I'd procured from our saintly flight attendant. "For your goodies." Which were now tucked into the seat pocket in front of him. Also, he'd taken off his black quarter zip and left it on my seat. Out of necessity, I'd pitched my sweatshirt in the bathroom trash and was now so cold I had to grit my teeth to prevent them from chattering. But surely he couldn't be offering me, a complete stranger, his jacket. I picked it up as I sat down.

"Your name is pronounced *Oni*?" he asked. "Not *Annie*?"

"That's right." Why was he even talking to me? I looked like I'd stuck my finger in a light socket. And I'd barfed in his Santa bag. *Geesh.*

"I'm Adam," he said, extending his hand. When I grasped it, he squeezed with a gentle but firm pressure. Comforting. He had nice hands. And they were warm. Which I definitely wasn't.

"Listen, Adam. I'm so sorry. I—I don't usually drink and I—"

He scanned me, taking in all my disarray. And my white camisole. I quickly crossed my arms over my chest to hide what I was sure was even more of a show.

"You're clearly having a bad day, he said. "No apologies necessary."

"A *really* bad day," I emphasized. "I'm sorry about...Santa."

"He was irreplaceable."

"Oh no—" I stared at him in horror and pulled out my phone to make a note about searching for the bag on the internet.

He stopped me by touching my arm. "I'm kidding. I saved the food. Now *that's* valuable."

That made me smile a little. Then I remembered his jacket. "Here." I held it out to him, secretly hoping that he'd meant to leave it there for me. *Please, God,* because this plane was now the temperature of Antarctica.

He pushed it away. "I don't need it. Just put it on."

With a grateful nod, I did and felt instant relief. It smelled clean and spicy, like guy soap or deodorant but not as nose-stinging as strong cologne. As a doctor, I noticed these things because in the hospital, we didn't wear strong scents. No one wants to smell pungent cologne when they're sick.

As I drank more water, my stomach rumbled loudly.

From the seat pocket in front of him, he pulled out a little plastic-wrapped triangle from his stash. "Try one."

As I accepted it, I cataloged my diet for today. A cup of coffee over hair and makeup. Two mimosas. Half a bagel before I was interrupted for pictures. I didn't even count the Bloody Marys. I bit into the triangular pie. It was wrapped in soft, homemade bread dough and stuffed with a lemony mixture of chopped spinach and pine nuts. And it was spectacular.

Wow. "How wonderful to have aunts who feed you."

"I take it you don't?"

"Only child, small family. No one cooks." What I didn't say was that we had staff for that.

"You want to talk about it?" he asked.

I snorted. "About my sad childhood?"

He smiled that nice smile again. I knew it would get to me if I were in any condition to feel anything, which I obviously wasn't. "Okay, fine. I didn't really have a sad childhood. But I did stop my wedding. Literally a minute before I had to walk down the aisle. The boyfriend of one of my best friends had to go tell our two hundred and twenty guests that everything was off and to go home." I rubbed my forehead, as if that would erase the memories. "It was horrifying."

He was still looking straight at me, listening intently, which made me wonder what his job was. An air traffic controller, maybe, with that sharp focus? "But not as horrifying as marrying your fiancé, apparently."

"Exactly." The word came out in a choked whisper. "He's not terrible. The worst thing he did was want a future completely different from the one I envisioned." I lowered my head and sighed. "I don't think I should have gotten on this plane. But I just...couldn't stay. It's all a blur."

I'd left a mess behind—reception food that would never be eaten, gifts that would never be opened, and a man I should never have said yes to in the first place. Why had I waited so long to break things off? This was a pattern in my life. Talking myself out of the hard truths in relationships.

"Who thought it was a good idea to put you on this plane alone?" My seatmate's tone made it clear that he thought that was the dumbest idea on the planet.

"I think—I think my parents were embarrassed. Maybe they thought it was best for me to escape all the questions, the people, the *mess*. I don't really know. I'm not sure *I* knew exactly what I was doing."

I'd said way too much. I pondered in a raw panic what on earth I was going to do in a tropical paradise alone for seven whole days? This really had been the worst idea ever. As soon as I landed, I vowed to book the first flight back the next day.

I needed to change the subject fast, before the tears started falling again. "You're meeting someone?" I mean, he had to be. The guy was gorgeous. He was going to a coveted, romantic destination, definitely not one you'd associate with a typical guy trip.

"My wife passed away two years ago," he said. "Turks and Caicos was one of her favorite places, and she'd always wanted me to see it. My friends bought me a ticket because they were worried about me." He paused, but before I could ask why, he said, "I haven't taken any time off since it happened. Frankly, I'm not so sure this is such a great idea either."

I suddenly felt even more awful. It was one thing to dump someone at the last second, and another to lose the love of your life. Honestly, I cared for Tyler, even loved him, but not in the absolute way I should have to marry him. Now that things had gone down this way, my predominant feeling was not sorrow. It was relief.

"I'm sorry about your wife," I said. "My problems seem very small compared to that."

I thought of the hassles awaiting me on my return—the roomful of unopened gifts that needed to go back and all the wasted money my parents had spent on the reception. Additionally, I'd bought an adorable house with Tyler that I would now never live in and would have to put back on the market.

My bigger problem involved wondering if I'd made the right choice moving home to Oak Bluff. Now that my parents were back, I'd have to confront the issues my mom and I had that we both tended to sweep under the rug. I'd signed with a local pediatric practice to fulfill my dream of practicing in my hometown, where I could truly know and care for my patients. But my partners and I couldn't have been more different.

All I'd wanted was to settle in, and yet everything I'd done recently had been very *un*settling. Except my worst disasters were nothing compared to Adam's.

He shook his head. "No. I mean, either case is—well, it's giving up something that you thought would be forever."

"Now that I'm actually thinking about it, I always panicked at the *forever* part. But I kept telling myself that it was just normal nerves."

"My mom keeps telling me that recovering from any shock or tragedy takes time." He had soft brown eyes that easily showed compassion. And while I didn't exactly take comfort in his words, I gave him major points for trying.

"Do you think she's right?" I asked before I stuffed the last bite of the tasty spinach pie into my mouth.

Maybe I'd recover, but I was never dating again. I would sell the house and do my job with my unusual partners until I could afford to return to Milwaukee, where I'd trained, and lead a quiet life off the radar. No *Ani-you're-just-too-much*, which was what my mom was fond of saying.

"Not sure." He held out another pie, but I shook my head, not wanting to risk adding to my still-queasy stomach.

I settled my head back against the seat, suddenly suppressing a yawn. "I've been up since five a.m.," I said. "Hair and makeup." I lifted my hand up to my hair, but feeling the hopeless scope of the disarray and the strange, crunchy texture, dropped it back into my lap.

"You should take a nap."

I glanced sideways at him. Maybe he was an angel, sent here expressly to prevent me from completely losing my shit. In any case, he was the best thing that had happened to me on this awful day. "Thank you for the food. And for being nice."

The soft, warm jacket, the good food, the kindness—it all helped to settle my mind and brought me to a place where exhaustion finally overtook me.

Adam

"How long does it take to get a cab to the airport?" Ani, standing at the reception counter, asked the concierge.

It was the next morning, and I sat in an open lobby surrounded by potted palms, tropical-colored sofas, and bright parrot prints on the walls. As I sipped my coffee, I pretended that I hadn't been hanging out waiting for her—*Ani*—to show.

I was *not* stalking her. Being the sole person who knew of her crisis, I felt a responsibility to check on her and make sure she was okay. But now, apparently, she was leaving and going back to face the chaos she'd left behind.

Good, I told myself. I was absolved of responsibility. *Now go out there and get some sun.*

I waited for relief to wash over me. After all, she was someone in the middle of a massive emotional crisis, and I was here for rest and relaxation, not to help a stranger who didn't have anyone. Instead, I felt a strange twinge of disappointment.

Maybe I'd somehow gotten myself too wrapped up in her

plight. Maybe I was sitting here because this woman, whom I didn't even know, had done something for me that no one else had been able to do in the two years since Liv passed—woken me up from the dead in some supercharged manner.

Either way, I had no further obligation to help her. Even though that look in her eyes had haunted me, causing me to toss and turn all night. I sensed her absolute aloneness—because that was what I also had inside of myself.

The woman standing at the counter looked a lot different from yesterday. Petite in stature, she wore a navy sleeveless shirt, jean shorts, and sandals. She had a halo of blond curls—I never would have guessed that her hair was naturally curly—and no bird's nests today. She looked appealing and pretty, like someone ready to enjoy a week in the sun.

Plus, she had a really cute butt.

Which really startled me. Because I'd been fairly dead below the belt since Liv died.

But I swear, I was *not* interested in her that way.

"Could I please schedule the cab for two p.m.?" she asked.

Okay, she was definitely leaving. My heart sped up as it often did in the ER, and I found myself reacting before I could think. I stood up and intercepted her as she turned away from the concierge desk.

That was when I saw her face. She wore no makeup, and her eyes were puffy. But she was *stunningly* pretty, far more so than with the cakey, heavy makeup she'd worn yesterday.

I should have known right then that I was in over my head.

"Oh hi, Adam," she said in a friendly tone. "You don't have to check on me—I'm fine."

She'd called me out in her first sentence. "Great to hear it," I said. She'd been blunt, so I would be too. "You're leaving?"

She bit her lower lip in worry. "I've got to go back and deal with the mess I made."

"That's the physician in you talking." *Be careful*, I cautioned myself. *Don't interfere. You don't even know her.* Yet I couldn't seem to stop myself.

"What do you mean?"

"Responsible. Never giving up. That kind of thing. Most of us are like that."

She narrowed her eyes. "Those aren't bad traits."

"No, but maybe sometimes it's okay to let other people take care of things. After what you've been through, some might say it's okay to take a few days off."

"Wait." She flicked her gaze up at me. "Did you say *us*?"

"I'm an ER doc."

"Oh." She took that in. "Well, thank you for checking on me. But I'm absolutely fine."

"You look much better than yesterday," I said. She looked amazing, *period*.

"In appearance maybe." She tapped her head. "But in here, it's still pretty wild."

I laughed. I liked her self-deprecating humor. And the fact that she was able to joke after all she'd been through. It spoke of resilience, something I always respected in anyone because of my own situation. "Hey, you're dressed, and your hair looks really nice. I mean, not like a bottle of glue got stuck in it."

She almost laughed at that. But not quite. Instead, she smoothed down her curls and said, "Well...guess I'd better go pack up." But she didn't move.

Before I could think about what I was doing, I seized the moment. "Did you—did you have breakfast yet?" I could feel myself turning red, but I kept rambling. "Because I haven't. You should have breakfast—with me. I mean, so that you don't eat alone." I couldn't believe what I'd done. But something in me just couldn't let her go.

Again, I heard that warning voice in my head. *What the hell are you doing, Adam?*

I didn't really know. But before I could beat myself up more, she said, "I am a little hungry, now that you mention it."

We walked toward an outdoor restaurant surrounded by palm trees and took a seat overlooking a sparkling aquamarine ocean. The water was calm, the breeze gentle, and the warm sun felt wonderful on my skin. I told myself I was doing this for her, but who was I kidding? Even knowing her such a brief time, I felt captivated, wanting to know more about her, not wanting to say goodbye forever.

Someone filled our cups with coffee. I looked over the menu but saw that Ani was staring off into the distance.

I shut it and set it down. "Not hungry?"

She smiled a little, but I could tell from her eyes that she was doing that on my behalf. "Coffee's okay. Breakfast might be wasted on me."

"Did you have dinner last night?"

"No."

"Okay, I'm going to order us some things. And you can eat or not eat."

"Honestly, I hope you don't feel responsible for me—your basket-case seatmate on the plane." She flicked her wrist dismissively. "I'm fine, really."

I studied her carefully. "My guess is that you don't like being fussed over."

"Normally, I don't *need* anyone to fuss over me."

Independent. Strong. Those traits were coming out despite her crisis. But I needed her to understand something. "Look, I—I feel a little lost here. Helping you is giving me a little bit of purpose." Or I'd be headed straight back on that plane today too. "So I'm just going to go for it, okay?"

She flashed a real smile this time, and it was a stunner. "Go for it."

I went ham on breakfast and ordered crepes, eggs, fruit, yogurt, and a banana protein smoothie that she took a couple of sips of. I distracted her by telling her random stories about how I chose medicine, how my mom raised me as a single mom, and how all I wanted was to see her retire and enjoy herself.

Ani looked at her watch. "Almost time to go."

I didn't know what to say. I'd just met her—who was I to want her to stay? But I did.

"I see it both ways," she said.

I frowned. "See what?"

"I see a lot of chaos when I get back. And crying—not only from me. And friends trying to help me. Which means I'll have to think about everything all the time. But here I have a lot of time to think too. So I don't know what to do."

"Exactly my problem."

She assessed me carefully. "You're really nice, but how do I know you're not a serial killer?"

I opened my wallet. Handed her my hospital ID, my Fellow of the American College of Emergency Physicians, my driver's license, my Giant Eagle card, and my library card.

She flipped through everything until she found the bright orange one at the back. "You have a library card?" She flipped it onto the table. "Then you must be okay."

That made me wonder what kinds of books she liked. I found myself wanting to ask and felt guilty about it. Because I hadn't been interested in anyone since Liv. But also because I shouldn't be interested, of all women, in a runaway bride in the middle of a crisis.

"If I stay," she said, "I don't want to talk about Tyler, but I want to say one thing. He's not a bad person, and I do love him. But he wasn't *my* person. And he didn't share my idea of a happy life."

"What's your idea of a happy life?" I couldn't help asking.

"Happy chaos—you know, like, kids and dogs and...everything. That's what I want someday—to be in the middle of the fray. Tyler envisioned our life as the kids having nannies and babysitters so we could have couple time over drinks every evening before we kissed our freshly bathed children goodnight."

A cold sense of remorse hit me because I used to want that kind of happy chaos too. But not anymore. I could never give myself to anyone like that again, much less to a child. I was dead inside. Empty. I wasn't exaggerating—that was the truth. But of course I kept that horrible fact to myself.

"Did you and Liv have any kids?" she asked.

"We were trying for a baby before Liv got sick, but it never happened." Month after month when Liv found out she wasn't pregnant, she'd cry. That was heart wrenching, but even worse, the very day she was diagnosed with cancer, she'd looked up at me tearfully and said that it wasn't ever meant to be. That was an awful moment, the first of the heartbreak. With a bitter taste in my mouth, I couldn't help thinking that all our dreams and plans— our life together—was never meant to be.

I thought I was managing to keep my expression neutral, but Ani saw right through it. She reached over and squeezed my hand, her eyes filled with compassion. "I'm sorry."

Her touch felt so good. No one had touched me in a long time. People comfort you, but no one touches you—it's just a line that most people don't cross. I didn't realize how much I missed it. "It's funny, how you believe you know how life is going to go. You fall in love, you get married, you expect things without even thinking about it. A house, a dog, kids. You don't expect that the girl you knew since eighth grade would be gone forever by the time you were both thirty."

Ani nodded and added, "Or you meet someone, and you decide to get married, but for whatever reason, something feels off. And that feeling keeps eating away at you. Except in my case, I kept pushing those feelings away until it was almost too late." She gave a thoughtful pause. "I don't know what that must feel like—to love someone so much that it rips you apart to lose them."

"Yeah." I looked out over the water. "It would have been our fifth anniversary this week. Liv made me promise to take this trip. Somehow, she knew I'd try to work myself to death after she was gone."

"We don't have to talk about this anymore."

"No—I—it's okay." I blew out a held-in breath. "I haven't talked about Liv to anyone—I mean, after a certain point, you start to feel like you're dragging people down, taking advantage of your friendships. You're afraid that everyone will label you as a downer and avoid you, so you don't talk about it. And everyone is sympathetic, but no one can *really* know what you're going through. So you keep it to yourself and keep going. But it's felt really good to say her name."

Ani smiled. "Thanks for telling me all this, Adam. It's made me feel less alone. I'm eternally grateful for your kindness."

That pleased me far more than I could admit. "I have an idea. Let's explore and see things, get moving. That way we don't think about anything. That is—if you stay."

She gave a little smile. "I'll stay—for today. One day at a time, right?"

"Right." I nearly fist-pumped. I had her for one day, and that felt thrilling. Honestly, I needed for us to get busy ASAP. Because despite all my good intentions and my rotten mental state, I found myself thinking about *her*.

~

Ani

On Tuesday, I said I'd stay until Wednesday, and on Wednesday, until Thursday. Then, in the blink of an eye, it *was* Thursday. By then we'd explored all the beaches and Chalk Sound National Park. We'd seen the underwater coral gardens at Bight Reef and taken an adorable Potcake dog for a walk at Potcake Place K9

Rescue. We ate at least two meals a day. I was starting to see the light of day. And I was feeling stronger.

We'd both booked flights to return home on Friday, which seemed reasonable if daunting. Except there was one problem—I was starting to really like Adam.

Which may have been turning into a bigger issue. I consciously tried not to look directly at him, because there were these strange moments when we just...connected. When our gazes would snag, and it was hard to look away. I know, I know, it was simply... hormones. Attraction, which I was pretty shocked to feel in my current state. I knew not to trust it, and did my best to steer clear of it.

Maybe our friendship was so raw and honest because I didn't have the bandwidth for pretending. Whatever I felt, I said. I didn't have the strength to hold back or cover anything up. While we didn't talk about my wedding fiasco at length, Adam accepted my many silences, my sudden wanting to be alone, and my need to sleep like the dead. Once, he got emotional when we visited Grand Turk Lighthouse because he said Liv had described that iconic spot. In general, I felt that we could just be ourselves. The self that he got was probably close to me at my worst, but somehow, he made me feel okay with that.

By Thursday evening, I was also realizing that it would soon be time to say goodbye.

"We've seen a lot these past few days." We'd hung out all day on Grace Bay Beach, and then drove to Providenciales for the iconic Thursday Fish Fry, which featured local food, music, and dance performances. It had been a feast of the colorful local culture.

And here I never thought I'd leave my room. I'd forced myself to get up and go each day because going was my lifeline. For that, I'd be eternally grateful to him.

"Today you ate breakfast, lunch, and supper." He seemed very pleased with himself. And his nose was a little sunburnt, which was kind of cute. He looked healthy and happy and not weighted down with his cares, which I felt I'd had some influence on.

"I'm going to write your aunts and tell them you're a natural auntie too," I said. "A caretaker."

"Ha. Maybe."

"Well, you've made sure I've eaten and showered and kept me busy so I didn't think about things. I'm starting to actually think I can handle going back now."

Our eyes met, and I felt a sudden flush of heat. Improbable as it was with me being such a mess of emotion, I became aware that we were on a beautiful island with a gentle breeze and a full moon. He was nice and funny, and I loved his kind brown eyes. I also knew that it was past time to say goodnight.

I would not want to become swept away by the magical beauty of this place. To use it—and him—to forget what was really going on in my life.

Yet being with him these past few days had saved me—from loneliness, from despair, from myself.

I was at a sudden loss for words because I was thinking awkward things. We'd chosen not to say things like, "What do you want to do tomorrow?" We'd sort of made it a rule to live in the moment, not look too far ahead or too far behind. Except that I was noticing the way he walked, long-legged strides, confidently. I was noticing how big his shoulders were, how lean his waist was. He was naturally curious. He kept up with current events. He read books. We sometimes ran out of things to say, but the silence was never awkward.

In other words, I was liking him way too much. But I was wise enough to know that anything I was feeling couldn't be trusted.

"I'm going to say good night," I said.

"Good night." He made a theatrical bow with accompanying hand motions. Then he reached down and lifted my hand. Held it. Brought it to his lips and gave me a quick peck. "We had fun today, Ani Green."

"Imagine that." Despite his joking manner, heat flushed through me. I felt alive, like I wasn't dead. Which was a miracle. Even the past six months with Tyler, I'd done a lot of faking, a lot of trying, a lot of hoping things would get better. Somehow, these days away had made me feel like there was hope for me to move forward, away from this terrible time.

Adam was staring at me. Our gazes met and held again. The firm but gentle grip of his hand, the soft touch of his lips on my skin; it all awakened something deep inside of me. My heart began a slow knock in my chest that kept accelerating. I knew what was happening. I couldn't believe what was happening. But the sensible part of me had to stop it.

My hand was tingling from where he kissed it. "I-I don't do one-night stands," I blurted, and immediately wondered if I was completely off base. Even if I was, I had to let him know how I felt.

He looked around. "Did...did someone ask you to have one?"

"No! I mean, I'm sorry." I could feel my cheeks heat up. "I must be getting my balance back because it seems that I just now noticed that you're really hot."

That was a mistake. Why hadn't I toned it down, said *cute* or *attractive* or *good-looking*? At least I hadn't said *perfect*, which he totally was, with those warm brown eyes and that strong jaw and that I-need-to-shave-twice-a-day five-o'clock shadow thing going on.

"You're beautiful," he said with a slightly crooked smile that was very endearing, "even if it was questionable whether or not there were live birds involved in your hairstyle the other day." I rolled my eyes at that. "I don't either," he added, "have one-night stands, that is."

"I'm in no condition to do something I'd regret. I mean, I can barely deal with putting one foot in front of the other. I can't add another bad decision on top of everything else I regret." Although it was questionable if I could ever regret him.

"Agreed," he said. "I'll see you tomorrow. We'll say goodbye before we catch our planes."

"Okay," I said, pulling my keycard out of my purse. "Thanks for walking me back. The day was fun." I opened my door and turned to him. "Can you believe I just said that? 'It was fun.'"

"It *was* fun. Everything these past few days was fun." He paused, his gaze controlled and neutral. "Good night."

Maybe it was staring in at my bungalow and suddenly feeling so heartbreakingly alone. Or the fear of returning to reality, only a day away.

Or maybe it was the feelings that had been awakened out of nowhere that kept tugging on me like the tide. Or the warm, salt-tinged breeze. Impulsively, I turned and grabbed his hand. "Don't go."

He took a sharp intake of breath. He stared at where I clasped his hand, then up at me, his eyes full of struggle.

My pulse pounded out a quick, steady thrum. My hand was still tingling. Heck, all of me was.

"I'm sorry." I released his hand. "I—I guess I'm a little afraid of being alone. You know, saying goodbye. You were a nice person to lean on these past few days. I guess reality is just hitting me again." I turned back to my door to go in.

This time, he grabbed my hand. With a gentle tug, he pulled me to him. I landed in his arms, staring up at him, his arms wrapping around me. We were so close, I could see the way his Adam's apple moved when he swallowed. The arch of his brow, the set line of his jaw. A warm breeze teased us, ruffling his hair. The moonlight emphasized the heat in his eyes.

He let go of my waist and said in a throaty voice, "Ani, I think you're really fun and really special. But I don't want—I don't think this is a good idea. We're both too—"

I don't know who kissed whom first, but I found his soft, warm lips on mine. My arms tangled around him, my hands skimmed the long, elegant planes of his back, his neck, the thick silk of his hair. Our kisses grew deeper, more fervent, desperate. He traced a trail of them down my neck, making me gasp, before we both somehow managed to stumble through the doorway. We ended up against the wall, his body pinned against mine, all hard muscle, soft murmurings, and featherlight touches as he reached his hands under my blouse and stroked my back.

We made love on that bed, under the beamed ceiling, with the A-frame glass overlooking the full moon and the ocean, and it was tender and passionate and playful. Maybe I was trying to make a quick, impulsive decision mean something deeper, but that night, Adam made me feel like I was worth loving.

That despite my mistakes and missteps and whatever I'd done or hadn't done that had led me to that preacher in front of all my friends and family before I'd finally found the courage to say no—despite everything—I was going to be okay. He gave me understanding and comfort and acceptance. Support when I'd needed it most. Laughter over silly nonsense we shared that I'd never told anyone before. I trusted him completely.

And afterward, I fell into a deep, drugged sleep.

Adam

A phone was ringing and ringing. I startled awake, disoriented, taking in the room. Beams of moonlight slanted over the bed, the sounds of the tide entering through the windows along with the balmy air. Finally, my gaze landed on the woman next to me, covered by a sheet, her shoulders bare.

For a moment, it was a dream—the moonlit night, the surf, Ani next to me. And everything was good, it was happy, it was exactly the way it was supposed to be.

But as I became more awake, I remembered the frantic coming together, the act of comfort and caring—the desperation.

I rubbed my forehead. *What had I done?*

There was no further time to think. I groped around on the floor until I found the offending device. Ani's phone told me it was 11:45 as I walked over to the bed and gently shook her shoulder. She lifted up her head from the pillow, her blond curls spilling everywhere.

"Someone named Mia's calling," I said, handing her the phone.

"Hello?" she said, sleep in her voice. "Mia, hi! I—um—fell asleep early. Wait—what?" She sat bolt upright, clutching the sheet to her chest. "In *this* lobby?" More pause. "Oh my gosh, you didn't. Sam too? I-I'm speechless." She stood, sheet and all, and hopped around, gathering her clothes. "Give me a few minutes. I'll be right down."

She hung up the call and tossed the phone onto the bed. "My best friends are in the lobby."

"This lobby? Like, *here*?" None of my advanced degrees appeared to be helpful in making the truth penetrate my thick skull.

"Yes, here. They somehow got time off. They flew in after work!"

"Oh." I sounded disappointed, which, I have to be honest, I was. I rubbed my neck. "I mean, yeah. You have great friends." But I didn't mean it. Because those friends were going to make me give her up sooner than I'd expected.

"I do have great friends." She grabbed my arm. Her touch was light and warm, and I wanted to grab her hand and kiss it, kiss her arm, kiss every part of her over and over again.

I grasped her hands tightly. Her gaze searched mine. I tried not to look agonized, but that was exactly how I felt. "Ani." I took her in—her wide-open eyes, her heart-shaped face, her halo of hair that caught the light in so many different ways. My voice came out strained, serious. "We created a bubble here. One that we knew would eventually have to burst."

She nodded in agreement. "We'd be fools to think that this was anything more than two people seeking comfort at a time when we both really needed it." Then she smiled brightly. "Because of you, I reduced my uncontrollable crying from ten to five times a day. Big improvement. Huge."

"And I've actually gone and seen this beautiful place instead of staying in my room reading my journals."

"Neither of us is in a good place." She was right, of course.

"I would never want to be a regret."

I could feel both of us mulling that over. Tension lay heavily in the air, which smelled scented and tropical and felt like a warm caress.

A last one.

"You could never be a regret," she said softly.

"You deserve the best." We stared at each other for a few long heartbeats. I couldn't breathe. My pulse was skittering. My body flooded with a warm heat that I recognized as desire. It felt wonderful because I was actually feeling something other than pain. And it felt bittersweet because we'd only just begun, yet it was time to end.

She teared up because we both knew that this was it. This was goodbye.

"Maybe we'll meet again when—when things are different," she said. "I mean, Normal Me is kind of nice. You'd like her."

I tried to smile, but it was hard. I'd thought that getting to know her these few days was harmless, that it would leave no scars. Suddenly, I wasn't so sure. "I like you now," I said, gathering her into my arms one last time.

When she looked at me, she was tearing up.

I tipped up her chin, made her look at me. "No matter what happens next, you're going to be fine. You're going to go out there and make a huge splash in the world."

She nodded, lips pursed, trying not to cry. "How do you know that?"

"Because you're not afraid to follow your heart when things feel wrong. You were bold enough to act."

A tear rolled down her cheek, but she was smiling. "Your friendship these past few days has meant everything. You prevented me from drowning in my sorrow."

"Same."

She reached over and touched my cheek. I squeezed my eyes shut, wanting to remember her touch. I grasped her hand and held on.

"I'll never forget you," I whispered.

Then I kissed her one last time and forced myself to leave.

Chapter Three

Ten Months Later

Ani

"The new head of the ER is a real hunkadoodle." Angie, the head staff nurse in the Oak Bluff ER, waggled her brows and nudged me with her elbow as we walked at a steady clip down a corridor of the emergency department.

"I haven't met him yet." I'd only been doing ER shifts for a few months, and it was a little nerve-wracking, but Angie always had my back. Just so long as her poking meant she wasn't secretly trying to fix me up. That was the very last thing I wanted.

I vowed to take at least a full year to focus on getting used to my practice, getting settled back in my hometown, and learning not to hate the ER shifts that I had to do four times a month, like all the other primary care docs who worked in our small community. We helped out because there simply weren't enough ER docs to go around.

"He's coming in to work tonight," she said. Who? Oh, the hunkadoodle. "So you'll get to meet him. Except…"

I halted. "Except?"

Angie stopped before a closed exam room door and handed me a rectangular plastic package containing a sterilized set of tweezers. "Except he's a teeny tiny bit grumpy. The staff's started calling him Dr. Grumpenstein."

I didn't care about the hunk part, as I was off hunks since my failed wedding last summer. (Well, except for the angel hunk I'd met on my honeymoon trip—but he was too wonderful to be real.) But the grumpy part gave me cause for concern. A grumpy boss could make life hell, and my new life in Oak Bluff already felt like that in some ways.

My life was still so unsettled, and one thought kept tugging on my brain: Coming home had been a huge mistake. I just wasn't gelling with my partners. My mother was troublesome—I still didn't think she'd forgiven me for all the wedding headaches. The house I'd fully bought out from my ex was still a war zone of remodeling.

And while my two best friends had met their forever people, I was convinced that I would never meet any eligible men under the age of sixty in this small town. Not that I wanted to date right then, but someday. Maybe. So my move home was adding up to my making another big whopping mistake.

I frowned. "How grumpy is he?"

"He's a stickler for rules. And he's all business."

"That's a good thing," I said carefully. I didn't need a boss who noticed me in any way except as a colleague. No matter how messed up my personal life might be, I was a good doctor. And I worked damn hard at it. That was the only thing I wanted to be noticed for—being good at my job.

I was just about to ask his name when Angie adjusted the band of the high-intensity lamp on her forehead. "How do I look?"

"I hear coal miner chic is all the rage for ER nurses now."

It was near midnight on a blustery April 14th, and it was snowing, which was not unusual for central Wisconsin at this time of year. Above our heads, paper tulips hanging from the ceiling tiles twirled in the breeze from the heat. Lights salvaged from the ER Christmas stash flashed gently as they looped around colored Easter eggs.

Spring should be on the way, but winter was lingering forever.

Plus, the ER was a little scary. I was a pediatrician, not an ER doc. I didn't like the scary stuff that could walk through the door at any moment, even though the staff was very nice and always competent. Crash and dash simply wasn't my personality. I loved talking with families, teaching new moms, and dealing with little kids, but I hated knowing that anything could walk in the door at any time—an infected hangnail one minute, a full cardiac arrest the next.

Despite my ER fears, I'd always dreamed of practicing in my hometown, in a small practice where I actually knew my patients and could spend time with them. My mom had said that no one should make any major life decisions within a year of a crisis, so I took that to heart and kept hanging in there, hoping for all my feelings of dread to turn around.

Angie was adjusting the settings on her headlamp. Except she accidentally turned on strobe mode, nearly blinding me. "Sorry," she said in a sheepish tone, quickly hitting the off switch. "When there's a foreign body up a toddler's nose, you need all the help you can get. It's like a cave in there. Especially when you're working through snot and tears."

I laughed. Angie had been working the Oak Bluff Hospital ER way before med school was even a twinkle in my eye. She always managed to make me laugh, regardless of my worries.

"You ready?" she asked, seeming to sense my fear.

"I know *you're* ready," I countered. Angie had been born ready. Being an ER nurse suited her no-nonsense, adrenaline-fueled personality.

I opened the exam room door and walked in. A mom and the rosy-cheeked toddler on her lap both looked up from a book, where the little girl was studiously pointing at farm animals with her finger.

The mom happened to be my practice partner, Penelope Pendergast. She was sweet as could be. The moms in our practice loved her, because she always took time to talk with them. Her only problem was that she sometimes had difficulty making decisions and often sought reassurance from the other two of us. Most of the time she made good choices, but she was low on confidence.

Except right then, she was simply a stressed-out single mom sitting in the ER with her kid, her three-year-old Taylor, who just so happened to have shoved an unknown quantity of leftover Christmas M&M's up her nose.

"Oh, Ani. You're here," Pen said with a slight hint of desperation, then quickly checked herself. "Taylor," she said in a more excited voice, "look who's here."

"Hi, Tay," I said as I sat down on the stool and wheeled myself over. She immediately burrowed into her mom's chest.

I met Pen's gaze. "If this blows the fact that I'm her number one favorite person, I'm going to be really upset at you."

Pen shrugged. "I'm really glad it's you working tonight and not me. Besides, you're the best." She peeked at her child. "Right, Tay?"

"Thanks for that." I ruffled Taylor's hair. "Hey, Tay-Tay girl, why in the world did you put M&M's up your nose?"

She gave me a look that was half blank, half mischievous. Which made me understand that sometimes there was no why. The answer was simply that she was three, and anything was possible.

While I originally spotted two candies, one in each nostril, experience told me that there might be even more. I mean, if you're going to shove M&M's up your nose, might as well go for it.

"Just get them out," Pen whispered to me. "Her snot on the

left side is bright yellow and gross." Hence the late-night visit. "I mean, it's practically fluorescent."

The purulent drainage meant that the candies must have been wedged in there for at least a few days, and a bacterial infection was starting up from the blockage.

I rubbed Taylor's arm. "Aunt Ani's going to get the M&M's out of your nose, okay? Easy peasy."

Judging by the fact that they were wedged waaaay up there, it wasn't going to be easy. I really wanted to tell her that it wouldn't hurt, but I couldn't promise that. I just knew that I would do everything possible to make this quick, painless, and positive. So I spoke the language that only she and I understood. "If you hold still and let Aunt Ani get the M&M's out with my special tool, I'll take you to Target on Saturday, okay?"

She lifted up her head and peeked out at me. "Fwench fwies too."

A girl after my own heart. "You bet, girlfriend." I did a fist bump that involved a little dance and a kiss on the top of the head. At least my antics got me a small smile.

But not from her mother, who preferred to feed her daughter better food.

"I couldn't let my her grow up without McDonald's French fries, could I?" I said.

Angie cleared her throat, which I took as a subtle reminder to get going.

"Okay, baby girl," I said. "Can I carry you over there to the exam table?"

I know, pediatrics can be horrifying. I was always aware of this. I was anxious about extracting the discs, but I also knew that I had a good shot at getting this done. Maybe I hated ER shifts, but stuff like this was my forte.

As soon as I delivered her to the exam table, Angie reached into her pocket and pulled out her phone. "Want to see my pet squirrel?" she asked Taylor.

Angie was the queen of distraction. Maybe I could borrow her as a grandmother one day. Except I doubted that being a mom would ever be in the cards for me. I'd already had a long-ago divorce and a recent left-the-groom at the altar scenario behind me. What could I say? Relationships weren't my strongpoint.

Honestly, I didn't know what my strongpoint was. I was totally confused. At a crossroads. But for right now, I focused on doing my job.

I peeked over to see what was causing Taylor to become totally focused. Sure enough, there was an up-close video of a squirrel stuffing his cheeks with round dark objects.

"Are those *blueberries*?" I asked.

"Yep," Angie said. "This is video from inside my bird feeder. Taylor, can you count how many that little rascal popped in his mouth? Twenty, twenty-one, twenty-two…"

Meanwhile, I suddenly had a brilliant thought. "Ang, I need a Katz extractor."

"A what-whozit?" she laughed. "Okay, you go, Dr. Green. We'll be looking at my pet opossum."

I popped out into the ER and walked up to a wall of supply cabinets. There was a nurse in scrubs loading one of them. I thought I would try to find it before I had to ask, so I peeked in a few doors and drawers.

Someone cleared their throat. "Can I help?" I froze, immediately recognizing a baritone that had re-played many times in my fantasies over these past months. But no. That would be impossible. Thinking I must have been mistaken, I slowly turned to find a man in dark navy scrubs. With amazing biceps, by the way. But not just any man. I was eye-level with a breast pocket that read *Adam Lowenstein, Hunkadoodle.*

Actually, it read *M.D.*, not *Hunkadoodle*, but it was *him*. Adam. *My* Adam. The Adam from the airplane, the Adam from Turks and Caicos. Fantasy Adam that I'd slept with that last wild night of insanity.

And oh, he looked...scrumptious. The same nice brown eyes, that same pure dark brown color that I liked my coffee to be in the mornings. The thick wavy hair, the shadowy shadow of stubble that was just that way—indicating that he wasn't trying to be hot, but rather that his facial hair just grew fast enough to be really sexy.

He was a *definite* hunkadoodle.

And I *knew* him. How was this possible?

His eyes widened with recognition. But he definitely did not seem shocked or startled to see me.

I gave a little gasp. "You're stalking me," were my unfortunate first words. "How did you find me?"

He cleared his throat. Glanced around to make sure no one was around. "Dr. Green, I am the head of the ER." He dropped his voice. "And I am definitely not stalking you."

No smile. No barely turned up tip of the lips. Nada. *Nothing.*

"*You're* Dr. Grumpenstein?"

His brows shot up in surprise at the nickname, but he recovered quickly. "I was coming to find you to discuss some protocols so that we're both on the same page when an emergency arrives. Being that you're a pediatrician and not an ER doc."

Wait. *Dr. Green?* A man whom I'd seen in all his naked glory had just called me *Dr. Green?* Had he suffered a bout of amnesia since we'd met? Was I so forgettable?

I would say that, judging on how he'd cried out *Ani* at a certain particular critical time that last night, I was definitely *not* that forgettable.

"But—but why are you here? In Oak Bluff? You—you work in Chicago." I might possibly have known that from stalking him online. Northwestern, to be exact, about three hours from here.

"My mother lives here," he said matter-of-factly. "I moved to be closer to her."

The whole thing sounded strange and suspicious and really answered nothing. I was so distracted that I forgot to be insulted by his "not an ER doc" comment, which was borderline insulting.

But right then, my partner's trusting daughter was down the hall waiting for me to get the things out of her nose that didn't belong there, and Angie had only so many birdfeeder videos on her phone.

"Oh, okay," I said as I continued to rummage through the cabinet. "I—uh—I'm looking for a Katz extractor. I know you're new, but would you happen to know where they are?"

"We're a fully staffed ER." He stood beside me, reached above my head, and rummaged through the part of the cabinet that I, all five-foot-two of me, couldn't reach. His arm grazed mine, which reminded me of when his entire body had grazed mine, and it sent all those memories flooding back—his kindness, his care, his ability to joke. The tender way he'd kissed me.

Could this be his evil twin? I side-eyed him when he wasn't looking. He was very tall, I'd bet six-two, even taller than I remembered. And he smelled like oranges. Everything else was the same except for the personality transplant.

Plucking out a package, he said, "Here you go. What are you planning to use it for?"

"I have a toddler with a couple of M&M's up her nose, and I need to get them out quick and easy."

He frowned. "You think that this is the appropriate instrument?"

"Yes, I think it will work quite well." Was he actually challenging me?

"Maybe you should consult ENT instead?"

Okay, enough. I'd already thought this through—calling a consultant would mean having to wait until tomorrow, and Pen would have to miss work, and the pus drainage would get worse and... "I think it's worth taking a shot."

He pondered that, cupping his chin with his hand and tapping his jaw. Then he looked up. "Would you like some assistance?"

"No, thank you, *Adam*," I said. Then I plucked the package out of his hands and got out of there as fast as I could. The rest could wait until I'd taken care of my patient.

The whole interaction had been so strange.

Back in the room, Angie and Taylor had moved on to cat videos, and Pen stood behind Angie watching them too. Angie seemed as enraptured by the videos as Taylor was. "And that's my Floyd. He's so lovey-dovey. All he wants is to be petted."

"Do you give him kisses?" Taylor asked.

"All the time," Angie said.

I smiled, pushing all thoughts of Adam to the back of my mind.

Maybe I'd hallucinated that he'd been so distant. That was the last time I'd eat kombucha for dinner the day before an ER shift for sure.

"Let's do it." Angie gently held Taylor's arms while Pen held the phone and gently sneak-held her legs so she wouldn't move them.

"Okay, sweetie, you just keep watching the kitties, and we'll get that stuff out of your nose," Angie said, keeping up a steady stream of commentary as I very gently inserted the instrument into Taylor's right nostril and past the M&M. It was as thin as a wire with a tiny little balloon at the tip that inflated with water when I pressed the syringe. I inflated, I pulled, and out tumbled a green M&M.

I quickly repeated the process, and a red one tumbled out too.

I addressed Pen. "What kind of person are you that has M&M's in your house from Christmas?"

"One with self-control?" Pen answered.

That made me think of Adam again. And our lack thereof last summer. Hard to believe this rigid, by-the-book person was the same charming, fun-loving guy who had been there for me when I'd reached the brink of the abyss.

I was starting to feel cocky when I approached the other nostril. But the offending candy was lodged a little further back, plus it was the one with the gross drainage, meaning that it must have been really stuffed up there. But I chickened out. There was a lot of drainage. And I didn't want to hurt her.

I swallowed, thinking that there was a fine line between being a hero and knowing when to throw in the towel.

Medicine was like that. Sometimes more art than science.

I smiled at Taylor, who was being so amazing. So trusting. I never wanted to give her any reason to lose that. "Tay, I'm going to try again. So here I go. Maybe we'll go see the Disney princess exhibit at the art museum too, what do you say?"

Someone cleared their throat. I looked up to find that Dr. Grumpenstein had stealthily entered the room. *My* exam room. Without knocking. And of course he'd seen my hesitation. I did what any good doctor would. I ignored him and focused on my job.

"Dr. Green, may I have a word?"

I made eye contact with Angie, who shrugged. I set down my instrument and followed him out into the hall.

"We could call ENT." He lowered his voice. "I don't want to risk traumatizing the child."

I rolled my eyes. "Trust me, that's the last thing I'd ever want to do."

"It's hard to be objective when you treat people you have a relationship with," he said in a calm, logical voice. "I'll be happy to take over for you."

"Absolutely not." He'd be happy to take over? How about when reindeer fly, I wanted to say. Or on the thirtieth of February. Or how about when hell freezes over. "I'm going to give it one last shot."

"I'm not sure that's wise."

I shot him my most deadly glare. "And I don't think it's wise to enter my exam room without knocking."

"Can we please just work together on this?"

Anger was brimming inside of me like an overheated kettle. I forced myself to think of Taylor. So I didn't say anything, but I let him follow me back into the room. He said hi to Pen and asked if it was okay if he took a look. He quickly assessed the situation, then turned to me. "Let's suction the pus first."

"Okay." I blocked my outrage at him stepping in, my even more fierce outrage at him pretending that he didn't know me. I only thought of the job ahead of me.

Luckily, I'd always found that a healthy dose of outrage always went a long way. I returned to my task with renewed determination, filled up the balloon and tugged.

A red disk dropped onto Taylor's upper lip, and Angie whisked it away.

"All done?" Taylor asked.

"Almost." I somehow got beyond the last green one and quickly tugged it down too.

"I need to make sure there's nothing else up there," I said. "Sure you didn't put any more candy up there? Buttons? Money? Barbie shoes?"

She shook her head, smiling. I loved that she was smiling. "No, silly Ani. Can we spend the whole day together on Saturday?"

"Yes, my love." I was shaking a little with relief. I caught Adam looking at me. He wasn't gloating or angry; he was relieved. His eyes were...twinkly. Like that Adam I'd known. And like maybe he was proud. Or maybe he was lost in remembering all that great sex we'd had until my friends showed up.

I did my checking, hung up the otoscope, and pronounced, "All done. You were amazing!"

Taylor sat up and beelined straight into Pen's arms.

Pen sighed audibly. Then she hugged me. "Ani, thank you." She bent down and spoke to her child. "Give Dr. Aunt Ani a hug." And she did.

"Want a Popsicle?" I asked.

She nodded.

"Can I take her to get one?" I asked Pen.

"Only if you bring me back a drink," she said.

"Sorry, we've only got Popsicles," Adam said. I couldn't tell if his mouth was curved up in the tiniest smile. Or not. But then he left.

"That was Dr. Grumpenstein," Angie whispered.

"More like *Dr. Hunkenstein*," Pen said.

More like a complete mystery to me.

Chapter Four

Ani

I carried Taylor down the hall to the break room, using her three-year-old positive energy, which she had in spades, to push away the confusion that was building inside of me. Adam Lowenstein, the man who'd been so loving and caring at a time when I was at my rock-bottomest low, was kind of a...jerk. A cranky, joy-killing pain in the eardrum.

On the way down the hall, Taylor entertained me by singing a song about germs that she'd learned in preschool. She was wearing blue tights, a blue top, and a blue tutu that bounced as she moved her arms and sang. I headed toward the refrigerator. The fridge part contained everyone's lunches, but the top exclusively held magical boxes of Popsicles.

"Red, purple, or blue?" I asked, inspecting the stash.

"Bwuu," Taylor said.

"Great choice." I grabbed a pack and put it on the counter to snap it in half. Then I unwrapped it, giving each of us half. "I'm getting the vibe that your favorite color is blue. Is that right?"

"Bwuu," Taylor said as she enthusiastically took a lick.

"Remember," I said, "M&M's taste better when you eat them. Right?" We walked together to the nursing station. She grinned, displaying blue teeth. Cathy, the charge nurse, was sitting behind the large desk area, crocheting what looked like a baby blanket. Tom, our medical assistant, was playing a game on his phone. Ivy and BethAnn, two of the staff nurses, were flipping through a Pampered Chef catalog. Angie walked over to join the group at the same time we did.

"Hey, everyone," I said. "Meet a very brave patient, who's just set a record for the number of Christmas M&M's up her nose. Whoever guesses how many gets a Popsicle."

"Oh my goodness," BethAnn said, walking over.

Cathy guessed first. "Um, three?"

Taylor shook her head and held up five fingers.

"What?" Cathy exclaimed. "That many?"

Taylor shook her head. Pulling her Popsicle out of her mouth, she said, "No, thix." And laughed.

"Six?" Cathy said. "That's unbelievable!"

"I want a 'nother Popsicle."

Pen walked up to the desk with her purse and paperwork and gave a quick wave to everyone. "Taylor Marie, you are a storyteller. Time to go home."

"Bye," I said, kissing her on the head and handing her off to her mother.

"Say thank you," Pen said, accepting her daughter and trying to keep the Popsicle from dripping on her sweater.

"Fank you," Taylor said and leaned forward to give me a big wet Popsicle-y kiss.

"Love you," I said.

"Target, McDonald's, and Disney princesses," Taylor said, counting out our Saturday activities out on her fingers.

"The girl is brilliant," I said proudly as I finished off my own Popsicle.

"Do you always share the treats with your patients?" a voice behind me asked.

I stopped mid-lick and turned to find Adam standing there, hands behind his back. His absolute handsomeness took my breath away. That thick, dark hair spilled chaotically over his forehead. Those dark chocolatey eyes. That impossibly square jaw. Even with his white coat on, the breadth of his shoulders impressed. I knew for a fact that even more wondrous muscles were hidden under that white coat.

He was kidding, right? Any second now he was going to break character and say he'd been clowning around. But he didn't. Apparently, that stunningly handsome shell hid an awful interior.

"You're eating on the job," he said.

"Of course I'm eating!" I said, not disrespectfully but not exactly calmly either. All I'd had since lunch was an Oreo Tom reluctantly sacrificed. I refused to explain how busy we were, how hard we worked at the sacrifice of human comforts. Geesh.

"Well, we have a new rule," he said, speaking not only to me but to everyone gathered behind the desk. "No eating in the work areas."

I looked around. Literally everywhere was a work area. "So where do we eat?"

He tossed me a sideways glance. "That's exactly what I was about to discuss, Dr. Green. We're about to have a little impromptu staff meeting. Why don't you have a seat?"

He was still acting like he had that massive branch up his butt, and the staff was offering no pushback. Why?

Well, I was going to offer lots of feedback. Starting with him barging into my exam room and trying to take over. I felt like I'd fallen asleep and awakened in a dystopian nightmare, where the hottest guy of my life didn't remember me. Did *he* not remember the hottest sex of his life?

I mean, come on. *Spectacular* was the word that had passed his own lips. I was not making that up.

"We have new guidelines," he said in a cheery voice. "Food is only allowed in the break room."

Eating was literally the only fun we had between patients. We all took turns bringing our newest recipes from home for everyone to try—so as we sat together waiting for the next onslaught, we often fortified ourselves with delicious snacks. Every ER I'd ever worked in had food. Lots of it. We shoveled it into our mouths when we could, sometimes as fast as we could—especially on the days when there was no time to pee, let alone seek out food in a room waaay down the hall.

"Are you sure?" I was being insolent now. In front of the staff. I warned myself to curb my anger. I was always professional. But right now, I was so angry. And, to be honest, a little hurt.

"Dr. Green, I'm very sure."

"It's *Ani*. Remember?" I gave him a cold, hard stare. I didn't care how cute he was. I hated him for being...different than before. Where was *my* Adam? I wanted him back now.

Angie's brow immediately quirked up as she glanced from Adam to me.

He turned red. Okay, good. So he *did* remember.

How I wished that he'd stayed my dreamy fantasy, untouched by this reality. I'd used his memory as an escape when the pain of last year threatened to take me down. He'd been a quiet, invisible hug during my most alone times. Someone who'd cared for me when I'd needed it most. Who'd given me his jacket and food and who had made me laugh and who had done even more—I couldn't even think about that now.

To think that dream man was an actual human—and a grumpy one at that—was sort of devastating.

"We just ordered a pizza," Angie confessed.

Stella, our unit clerk, violently shushed her.

"Pizza can be enjoyed in the break room, Angela." Everyone was now sitting straight upright, wide-eyed. "A few more things.

Everyone has to remember to clock in and out. And there will be no romance novels, no catalogs, or...crafts."

Everyone stared at Cathy, who suddenly froze in the middle of a stitch. "What, this? She held up a foot-long piece of soft, pastel colored baby blanket. "This is for my brand-new niece. It's not a craft. It's a...work of art." She grinned expectantly.

"Sorry, Cathy," Grump said. "Any activity that doesn't have to do with studying or learning ER skills is now banned. We want the highest rating from the Joint Commission on Accreditation. We want the best stats—less wait time, quicker treatment times, faster discharges, better care. And to do that, we have to be professional. At all times."

He took in a final glance at all the employees, still sitting there, slack-jawed but silent. "I'll be in my office until the next patient arrives," he said. "Meeting dismissed."

I waited until his footsteps faded and his office door closed with a definitive click before I turned to my colleagues, whispering, "Isn't anyone going to say anything?"

"Maybe you're not afraid of losing your job," Ivy said. "But my husband got laid off last week."

"I'm speechless," Tom said. "I mean, I don't even know where to begin."

"Poor guy thinks we can have great stats if we pay attention one-hundred percent of the time," Angie said. "He's forgotten all about having fun too."

"We do pay attention," Cathy said. "When it counts. If we were like that all the time, we'd burn out from stress."

Poor guy? "Angie, why do you cut him slack?" I could barely contain myself.

"He's not bad," she said, "just misdirected. He just needs time."

"And to get laid," Tom said.

I looked around at our little group. "No one's going to fight this?"

"Not right now," BethAnn said. "The hospital's helping me finance my nurse practitioner degree."

I shook my head incredulously. Then headed straight down the hall to his office.

~

Adam

I loved the ER, but it had to run tight, like a ship. Because here, every second counted. You had to be sharp 100% of the time, or someone's life could be at stake. It didn't matter who walked in—every single person got treated the exact same. Even if that woman was Ani Green.

Tonight was finally the night our paths crossed. And I'd done everything wrong.

In the quiet of my office, I pinched the bridge of my nose, hard. A reminder that my priority was to do my job. Period. I opened my center desk drawer and slid out the photo that sat right on top. Liv was leaning against me, her smile radiating from her eyes. I'm displaying what I call my happy dumb grin. Happy to be with her, nothing else really mattering. Thoughts of sickness and death were as far away as our old age.

I ran my eyes over all her features that I knew by heart: her great smile, the little crinkles around her eyes. Her sweater was cabled and black, her hooped earrings gold. My shirt was a blue button-up, still my favorite. How could I possibly still have that shirt and not her?

After almost three years, I was slowly forgetting what she looked like. What she sounded like. How she felt. I didn't know how to stop that from happening, and it made me frantic.

I felt a lump rise up in my throat like it did every single time. I would never fall in love again, never subject myself to being so helpless and out of control in the face of disaster. *Never again.*

I used the photo as a reminder of my ultimate mission: to be a wall. It was an expression ER doctors used that meant to do everything possible to not overwhelm the floors with admissions, to treat people and try to send them home instead of admitting them. But in my case, it meant being sturdy. A leader. Impenetrable to nonsense.

I glanced up to see a shadow cast over my doorway, just outside my door. A second later, Ani Green stepped into my office.

Her hair was up in a ponytail, no nonsense. "May I have a word?" And was that her shoe tap-tap-tapping impatiently on my office floor?

I'd been expecting this day, wanting it and fearing it, the moment she would walk back into my life.

"Of course." I gestured her in, warning myself to keep it to business. "Have a seat."

I spied her earrings—dangling hummingbirds. My mom always said that hummingbirds were spiritual messengers, evidence of reassurance from loved ones who have passed. *Ugh*. Also, a tiny fuzzy koala bear was attached to her stethoscope. *These pediatricians.*

She sat down in one of the chairs opposite my desk, where staff members came to complain, cry, or, rarely, to celebrate. She rubbed her forehead. Opened her mouth then shut it. Then simply stared at me for a beat or two before she finally spoke. "Did you lose something, Dr. Lowenstein?"

Her question threw me. I glanced around—my desk was nearly cleaned off and impeccably neat. Everything else was spotless and in perfect order. "I don't think so," I said.

"Oh, *I* definitely think so. I'm thinking that it was your sense of humor." She folded her arms. "You must've left it in Turks and Caicos. Along with your sweater."

"I *gave* you that sweater," I said somewhat indignantly.

"Aha!" She stabbed the air poignantly. "So you *do* remember."

As if I could ever forget. "Of course I remember." She kept drilling down on me with those eyes, a perfect clear blue, like the sky in Grand Turk. And right then, they held anger. Lots of it.

"That's all you're going to say?"

"For right now, with my entire staff probably crowding to listen at the door, yes." I got up and checked the hall in both directions, just in case. No one there—yet. Then I walked back and leaned against my desk in front of her.

"Why..." She pressed on her temple. "Why would you..."

"Why would I what?"

She threw up her arms. "I have so many questions, I don't know where to begin. How did you come to take this job? There is no way we'd 'coincidentally' end up in the same ER, in a small town that's barely on the map. No. Way." She did air quotes on the *coincidentally*. "Did you—did you follow me here?" Her eyes grew wide. "Oh, my God, you did, didn't you?" She smacked her forehead. "*This* is why you should never have one-night stands. Because you don't know who the person you sleep with really is!"

"Shhhh," I said, which made her even more angry. "Relax, Ani. My mother lives here. She's about to retire. Would you like to meet her? She can assure you that I'm not a criminal." But I also knew from the moment I googled Ani last summer that she was living in Oak Bluff, of all places. And soon as I was hired, I knew that one night, she'd show up in my ER and walk back into my life. I'd worried about it, anticipated it, replayed it in my head, and dreaded it, all in equal measure.

"I don't believe you," she said weakly. Like she was trying to process how my mother could actually live here.

He snorted. "Believe what you want. But this is a place of business. And I'm in charge. I can't—"

"Express emotion? Say hi to an old friend?" She got up and paced my office, which held a desk, two chairs, and all my diplomas and board certification certificates on the wall. Seemed like all the degrees in the world couldn't tell me what to do now. She spun around. "At least, I *thought* we were friends. But even a one-night stand deserves some recognition, don't you think?"

I tried not to flinch. "Regardless of how you define our relationship, now we're colleagues. Professional colleagues."

Under her scrutiny, I felt like a jerk. But I could not make her a distraction. I had to draw a clear line. "I liked you," she continued, making me further feel like a pile of steaming bird guano. "You were really nice. You stood out. And you were a lot different than —this." She waved her hand over me, as if wishing I would disappear into thin air. *Poof.*

She wore her heart on her sleeve. She seemed incapable of deception. I didn't know how to handle such honesty. And I definitely couldn't give it back or tell her that she'd stood out to me too.

I reminded myself of my number one goal – *keep everyone safe.* Make my ER the safest, best ER in the state. Hell, on the planet, if I could have my way. I couldn't save Liv, but by God, I'd use every brain cell in my head and every muscle in my body to save as many people as I could.

A dead, loaded silence filled the room. She curled her hands into fists. I waited for her to pummel me—physically or mentally, I wasn't sure. How could I possibly befriend her when I was essentially her boss, at least in the ER? And I was not going to say that I still thought of her, still wondered what might have happened if we had met at a different time of life. That standing before me, angry as she was, she was even more beautiful than I remembered. I absolutely could not allow anything personal to spill over into my professional life.

She narrowed her eyes, and I saw something else in them. Her anger I could take, but this...this was disappointment. *Hurt.*

The man I was before Liv died wouldn't have let her feel that way. He would have been honest too. But I wasn't that man anymore.

"Wow," she finally said, her tone even and with deadly aim. "What...happened to you?" It was a punch in my gut.

What had happened, indeed. I could ramble on about the randomness of life, the unfairness of tragedy. How happiness could turn to grief in the space of a heartbeat. But no one wanted to hear about that.

Strange, that she was more concerned about our friendship—or whatever it was—than the fact that I'd hovered over her during her procedure. Which I shouldn't have done.

I knew her qualifications, her recommendations. By all accounts, she was an excellent clinician. I hadn't needed to check in on her.

So why had I done it? To scare her away? To make her angry? Or was it that if I made her angry, I didn't have to deal with other, more complicated emotions?

I flicked up my gaze and tried not to notice her disappointment. "What happened is that I am in charge of a place that deals with life and death. Every. Single. Minute. It's my job to ensure that everyone is doing all they can to never, ever forget that. Our, um, *relationship* would put my ER at risk."

She snorted. Snorted! And crossed her arms. *The defiance.* "I'd hardly call extracting a couple of M&M's from a child's nose a life-and-death procedure."

"One minute it might be M&M's, but the next it might be someone being rolled through that door dying. Which reminds me, I wanted to reassure you that you'll always have the backup of the ER doctor you're working with. So never hesitate to call on me if you need help with anything."

I reached onto the floor near my desk, pulled out a huge binder, and set it on the desk.

She stared at it with loathing. Opened it. "What is this?"

"Our protocols. You can read them at your leisure. It's how we handle all the main emergencies, including a contact list of specialists who are on call twenty-four seven."

"Oh." She shut the binder. As she leaned over my desk, my heart accelerated. I smelled her clean powdery scent, and it took me straight back to that hotel lobby on that bright, sunny, warm day, with the humid heat and the sound of the ocean waves lapping in the background.

Staring into her eyes close up, I remembered the very first time I'd seen her, when she was a terrible mess, those eyes red and puffy and mascara-streaked, but I had seen everything about her—her openness, her kindness, her heart. Her strength.

Her curls fell forward. I could reach up and touch one. Cradle her cheek like I had done once upon a time and admit to the strong connection between us that maybe hadn't quite gone away. Ask her how she was doing—did she get over what's-his-name? Did she ever think about me too?

"I'm not an ER doctor," she said, "but I am a board-certified pediatrician. And I will not work shifts in this ER if I can't have autonomy. That means no barging in on me when I'm treating patients. Okay?"

"It's my responsibility to make certain that you're a good doctor."

She threw up her arms. "I *am* a good doctor." And then she glared at me. "You have a real problem with control, don't you?"

She had no idea. "I work with all kinds of community doctors with different levels of rigor in their training. I have to make sure we're all on the same page."

"I'll tell you when I can use the help. When I'm out of my league. When an emergency comes in that I can't handle by myself. You're going to have to trust me on that."

I nodded. "You'll always have backup. You have my word."

"Okay. You don't dog me, and I'll do my best to ask for help when I need it."

"Deal."

She extended her hand, and I took it.

Big mistake. Touching her—the warmth of her hand, the

smoothness, the softness—made me realize that we were finally together again, through luck, serendipity, or fate. All the dust kicked up in my old soul and blew away, replaced with a brand-new feeling of hopefulness, of excitement. I tried like hell to tamp it all down. But if I had any doubt that the attraction, the chemistry, the *heat* from last summer had faded the least little bit...I was dead wrong.

I found myself lost in her eyes. Feeling the familiar undeniable pull between us. Remembering that brief but intense time when we'd both needed someone desperately and had found comfort in each other.

I never thought I'd see her again. But I *had* looked her up. I knew who she was, where she'd gone to school, and that her mother was the head of the women's board for the hospital.

We were still awkwardly staring at each other, and I was still struggling to find words, any words, which were all muddled up with my swirling thoughts, when footsteps sounded down the hall, getting louder by the second. The hair on the back of my neck prickled. Footsteps with that amount of urgency meant that a staff member was coming to tell me something important: *Someone's had an accident. Someone's bleeding. Someone's in cardiac arrest.* It all boiled down to a patient needing help ASAP.

Sure enough, Angie, out of breath, burst into the room. "Dr. L." Angie was the real force in this ER, my right-hand enforcer and the best nurse I'd ever seen. She was never out of breath, and she was never panicked, but now she was both. I immediately started for the door. "We've got two coming at once." She glanced first at me and then at Ani.

Ani was already right behind me. We followed Angie straight into the ER, in time to see Cathy toss her yarn into a drawer and slam it shut. Tom stood at the front desk, ready for action. Ivy and BethAnn gathered around the desk for assignments.

"We have a fifty-eight-year-old male in cardiac arrest and a teenager in labor," one of the triage nurses said.

"I'll take the cardiac arrest," I said to Ani. "You take the teen."

Her face blanched.

I turned to Angie. "Is Dr. Cardiff on the way?"

"Already paged her," Angie confirmed. "She's the OB doc," she said to Ani. "She's twenty minutes away."

"Oh good." Ani blew out a breath.

Angie looked hesitant. "Not sure this baby's going to wait. The teen is two minutes out and the EMT said she's crowning."

"I'm a pediatrician, not an obstetrician," Ani said, her voice slow and steady. "I haven't delivered a baby since med school."

"Once the baby is born, you can practice your pediatric skills," I said. "But for right now, Dr. Green, you're in charge."

She flicked me a pissed-off look, which I took as a positive sign. Defiance was always better than fright. I felt a little bad not being more encouraging, but this was an ER, not a kindergarten. She turned to Angie. "Which room?" she asked.

"Room 2." Ani immediately headed that way.

"Dr. Green." My words stopped her in her tracks.

She turned, her brow creased. She was already deep in thought.

I put my hands together, palms touching, fingers out.

"What is that?" she asked, irritation in her voice.

"Just catch the football."

"And don't drop it," Angie added, chuckling.

Ani looked at Angie. "Wait, Angie, aren't you going to..."

"Sorry, Dr. G. Life and death first." She patted Ani's back. "You'll be fine."

The old me might have offered Ani more than a stupid football joke. Maybe even reassured her that I'd be right next door if anything went wrong. Or that I knew my staff of very experienced people would help see anything through.

But that wasn't me anymore. I wasn't here to coddle anyone, and I wasn't here to resume an impulsive relationship that had happened by accident. Ani would have to sink or swim, just like all of us.

Chapter Five

Ani

Like a football, I kept repeating to myself, mimicking the hand position Adam had just demonstrated. *It's easy. Just catch it.* And the obvious corollary: *Whatever you do, don't drop it.*

I hadn't even gotten to tell Adam what an insufferable, rigid, strange dude he was. But now I had much bigger problems.

I'd never heard of anyone in a hospital actually dropping a baby during birth. Of course, I could be the first. I examined my hands. They weren't big. Definitely not the size of Adam Lowenstein's big paws.

What was I doing here? Why did I ever come to this in-the-sticks, out-in-the-boonies place where I needed skills I hadn't used in years?

Calm down, Ani. You can do this. I tried to cheer myself on. Before I applied to med school, I'd been a nurse who'd floated on various different floors for several years. I'd seen a lot during that time, and it had made me adaptable. I called upon that adaptability all the time, especially when confronted by difficult situations.

At the big teaching hospital where I did my med school rotations in Milwaukee, there were teams that rushed in and took care of this kind of stuff. The OB resident on call would come running, eager to do her thing, and the laboring mom would be whisked straight up to a state-of-the-art birth suite with NICU doctors a short sprint away. But here in Oak Bluff, the OB doctor wasn't even in-house. And this young woman might be delivering her baby before she even hit the sliding glass doors.

There was no use regretting this, or Adam, or any of a number of bad decisions I'd made. It was time to get a grip. I had to get ready to do my job.

As the staff scurried around me, I took some deep breaths. *You've done this before, Ani. A bunch of times.* I wasn't alone. I *knew* I could do it. But I was the leader here. The *doctor.* The person who gave orders, who performed. And I was relatively new. I had to show the staff that I knew what I was doing.

At least until I got some backup.

BethAnn wheeled in a light and a warmer for the baby, which sort of looked, with its flat metal tray and bright warming light, like one of those food warming stations at a fancy wedding reception where someone might be preparing buttery delicious pasta in little pans or serving prime rib. *More cheese, some au jus?*

But I definitely wasn't at a wedding reception, about to be served a wonderful meal. My stomach growled in protest. The sugar jolt from that lone Oreo was long past.

I positioned my hands as if I were some famous quarterback standing behind my center, waiting for him to hike the ball. I checked the instruments. Cord clamp. Sutures. All the usual ER lifesaving equipment—adult and baby-sized—just in case.

Please, God, I prayed. *Help me. Help me to remember.*

And then that was it.

Everything hit at once.

Two EMTs wheeled in a gurney that held a woman—I'd be tempted to call her a girl—of slight build with a mass of long, dark hair damply stuck to her forehead. She was screaming with the pain of a contraction.

And I mean *screaming*.

The first EMT, Ted Logan, was the guy I went to prom with. As soon as I saw him, I began to breathe easier. He and his twin brother Irwin worked together, and they were known by the entire ER as the Dynamic Duo. Great guys, fun to work with, and they made their own wine, which made for great stories and occasional free bottles. But today, no time for small talk.

"Hey, Ani," he said, launching straight into his spiel. "Sixteen-year-old primip at term with contractions every three minutes. Water broke in the car fifteen minutes ago, and she's crowning. She gave her name as Jennie Jones, but she's got no ID to confirm." He dropped his voice. "That's probably not her real name. She started to say her name was Chris or something before she realized it. She says she's been to the free clinic a couple of times."

"She's going to go fast," Irwin, who was also a premed student, said.

Everyone bustled around, transferring the patient to the laboring bed, BethAnn helping her put her feet in the stirrups for delivery. "Someone's with her?" I asked. Someone this young couldn't possibly be alone at a time like this, right?

Irwin shook his head. "She was attempting to drive herself to the hospital when her water broke."

Alone, registered in my mind. Barely more than a child herself. Driving *herself* to the hospital in labor?

BethAnn did her vitals, placed a fetal heart rate monitor on her abdomen, and started to set up for an IV.

The baby's heart was strong and fast. I blew out a tiny breath of relief. Mom and baby were okay—so far so good.

I walked to the head of the bed. "Hi, Jennie. I'm Dr. Green," I said. "Do you want us to call anyone?"

She shook her head. Her eyes were big and brown and full of terror.

I rested my hand lightly on her forearm. "We're going to help you through this. I'll be here until the obstetrics doctor arriv—"

Another wail of pain, loud and raw, accompanied by writhing. Beth had stopped even considering trying to start an IV and was now holding Jennie's hand and coaching her through.

Ivy had taken down the bottom of the bed, preparing for delivery. One look and oh my god—there was the baby's head, covered with a mass of matted black hair, a wondrous and frightening sight. There was no turning back now. And there was no chance that the OB doc was going to get here in time.

More screams, terrifying ones. Words of comfort from Beth-Ann. Internal screams from me too, but outwardly, just pursed lips and lots of deep breathing.

"Jennie," I said. At first, she didn't look. I had to say it one more time before she faced me.

Sixteen years old, alone, no ID...definitely a fake name.

"The baby is almost here," I said in what I hoped was a calm voice. "On the next contraction, breathe like this. Shallow. Pants. I'll tell you when to push, okay?"

She nodded.

"Okay, girlfriend, you can do this," BethAnn said.

I gave her a reassuring smile. "You're doing great."

"It hurts, it hurts," the girl cried. And then the final contraction was upon her. She tried to breathe shallowly, but it was impossible to stop the inevitable tidal wave of force about to propel this baby into the world.

I barely had time to put on gloves and get into position when the baby's entire head delivered, loads of jet black, hair, a bit matted and not camera-ready yet, but so far so good. I made the football sign Adam had made half in jest, spreading my fingers wide, supporting the head as the shoulders cleared the mom's body and the rest of the baby propelled out into life.

The baby rotated to face up on the way out. After a quick check—"It's a girl," I said, my voice quivering. Because...it was a sweet baby girl. A miracle. A brand new...person. Her eyes were shut, little fists clenched tight to her chest. She was a rump-roast size, perfectly formed, a mass of black hair, rosebud lips. A beautiful thing. Reddish-purple, coated with some slippery stuff—hey, not an Insta moment...yet.

I curled my hand around her shoulder, the other under her neck and basically just caught her as she came up and out, keeping my grasp firm.

Like riding a bike. I'd remembered how to do it. Yay, me.

As BethAnn suctioned her nose with a bulb syringe, she took her first breath and exhaled with a zesty cry.

Another yay. *Thanks, God.*

The tiny little thing gave another big wail. And then another, each gasp making her pink up as her lungs filled with air and her heart carried the oxygenated blood through her body for the first time.

Welcome to life, sweetheart.

"Hello, little one," I said to the determined little bundle. I peeked my head around the drape. "You have a baby daughter. And she's just beautiful."

That was when I saw that I wasn't alone. Adam was standing beside me, gloved and gowned, ready to assist. He'd come in quietly; I had no idea when. I caught his eye, but I had no idea what he was thinking, as usual. Was he checking on me, making sure I was competent, or had he come for support? I hoped the latter.

My heart was racing a little, but it was from all the adrenaline, *not* because of his nearness.

"Nice job, Dr. Green," he said. The lines around his eyes crinkled, and his lips turned up in a smile.

I smiled back, knowing that he hadn't come in to check on my skills. He'd been there in case I'd needed him. Exactly like he was in Turks and Caicos.

That made my heart squeeze a little.

"You need anything?" he asked.

I shook my head. "I'm good." *Yes*, I wanted to say. *I just really want that guy I met last summer. Can you please bring him back?*

The baby was really getting the hang of crying now, each intake of breath pinking her up to a wonderful, living color. BethAnn cut and clamped the cord, wrapped her quickly in a blanket, then held her up.

For one brief second, I looked into the baby's eyes. Blinking, blinded by our lights, confused, helpless. And so beautiful.

I accepted the bundle and brought her to the head of the bed. "Here she is," I said, on the verge of tears. "She's perfect."

Jennie was silently crying, no doubt overwhelmed. She looked up at me, tears streaming down her cheeks. "She's all right?"

"Wonderful," I confirmed. Even her little head was perfectly shaped—the delivery was so quick, there wasn't even any flattening of her skull bones through the birth canal.

We only had a moment; the nurses were ready at the warming table to examine the baby, clean her up, and do her APGAR scores.

Jennie's gaze flickered from me to the baby and back. She was still crying. "Can I hold her?"

BethAnn gave me a nod. I handed her over.

Jennie touched the baby's cheek with her hand. Caressed her. Kissed her on the head. Then she lifted the baby up and handed her to me. "I'm not keeping her." She closed her eyes and turned her head away. "I'm giving her to you."

Wait-what?

I resisted. "You can hold her," I said, somewhat stupidly. "Would you like to?" *Please, please hold your little baby. Please keep her. Please...anything.* I wasn't thinking any further than this tiny innocent little newborn not having someone to coo and cradle her, shelter her, give her a future....

My eyes filled with tears. This girl was sixteen. Alone. So much was going on that I had no idea about.

Jennie kept her head turned away. "Please take her. I'm giving you my baby. I can do that, right? You take care of her."

I held onto the baby tighter, clutched her to me. Who would show her that she was loved, protect her from the realities of a world that was harsh under the very best of circumstances? My stomach churned.

I can do that, right? She was handing over her baby to a hospital employee, namely me. She'd verbally expressed her desire to give the baby up. She was activating the Safe Haven Law, which allowed a parent to legally relinquish a newborn without fear of prosecution. Typically, a baby could be brought to a fire station or hospital and handed to an employee—any employee. You could do it anonymously, without question.

"Is there—is there anyone you want us to call?" I asked, wanting to give her every chance. To what? To change her mind?

I knew nothing about her, about her situation. I didn't know what was right or wrong for her. I was only trying to keep all the options open.

She shook her head, her jaw set.

I touched her arm. BethAnn took the baby from me, and the nurses began to wipe her down under the warmer and take her vital signs. "It's okay," I said, squeezing the girl's arm. "You did an amazing job, you know that? You got yourself here to a safe place and you gave birth to a beautiful baby, and no matter what happens, you're giving her a good start. A great start."

Jennie turned halfway toward me. She was still crying. "I want her to have a chance."

"She'll have more than a chance," I said. What was I saying? How did I know that? *Be careful, Ani.* Sometimes my emotions led me to say things in the moment. I reminded myself not to make promises I couldn't keep.

"Promise me." She grasped my arm hard. "...that she'll go to someone good. Someone who can give her everything. *Promise.*"

"Is Jennie your real name?"

She said nothing.

"I—I just wanted to call you by your name."

"Crystal," she whispered. "It's Crystal."

"I promise, Crystal," I said with determination. "I promise I'll do everything in my power to see that she's taken care of."

I asked if I could ask her some quick health questions about her and her family, so that the baby would have some family medical history. I ran down the list quickly. Nothing stood out.

As soon as we'd done that, the door opened, and a woman of slight build burst in. "Hello, hello, Jennie, I'm Dr. Parik, the obstetrician. I'm going to be taking over now. We'll get you all finished here and to your room, okay?"

Crystal gave a weak nod. I squeezed her hand. "Hi, Dr. Parik," I said. Then to Crystal, "You're in great hands."

With a nod to my colleague, who was already bustling around, preparing to deliver the placenta and finish things up, I de-gloved and left the room, completely shaken.

Outside the room, I fumbled with the strings on my gown. I was physically shaking. Crying too, but trying to hide it.

Suddenly I felt someone quickly untying me, grasping my elbow, and gently tugging me down the hall. I felt strong hands on my shoulders, reassuring, urging me forward.

"We need to call the social worker on call," I said.

"Already done," Adam said. I'd lost track of him—he must have been waiting for me.

"How did your patient do?" I asked as I stopped to wash my hands, took a quick swipe at my eyes, and tried to pretend this was just another day in the life. There were inevitably patients waiting to be seen, and regardless of how emotional I felt, I had to carry on.

"Three hundred joules cured him from his v-fib, and he's upstairs in the unit."

"Oh, that's a relief," I said, a little absently. I was still shell-shocked and jittery from all the adrenaline coursing through my blood.

"You did a fine job in there," he said softly.

I nodded, appreciating that he knew it.

"That teenager did her research," I said. "If you hand over your baby to a health care worker and say you're giving it up, that's legally binding."

He touched my arm. There was a flash of sympathy in his eyes. But then he suddenly seemed to realize that he was out of character because he dropped his hand, cleared his throat, and stepped back. "This isn't a Hallmark movie. The world is a harsh place—for everyone. There's only so much we can do."

Dr. Grumpenstein was *ba-ack*. A pity, because I'd caught a glimmer of something wonderful beneath that fatalist façade.

If that mansplaining spiel was his version of sympathy, I couldn't take it. "No," I said, pulling my arm away, frustration overwhelming me. "I can't accept that. We can always do more." Then I pulled my arm away and went to keep doing my job.

Chapter Six

Ani

The next morning, a Saturday, I was awakened from a deep slumber by a knock on the door. More like *many* knocks, a haven of angry woodpeckers, rat-a-tatting me awake. I opened my eyes to a profusion of bright sunlight streaming through the family room of the house where I was dog-sitting. And speaking of that…I was soon accosted by a giant reddish-brown labradoodle who jumped on the couch and began walking all over me with his big paws like an ashiatsu massage, and then proceeded to lick me to death.

"Okay, okay, Arnold." I couldn't help laughing at his over-the-top way of greeting me. I sat up on the couch, threw off the crocheted afghan that I'd used as a blanket all night, and stumbled toward the door in my bare feet.

The McClellans' house was huge and beautiful and full of an amount of bright morning light that told me I'd waaay overslept. As I wound my way through the magazine-worthy kitchen and hall to the front door, I raked a hand through my hair, straightened my flannel PJ pants and Packers sweatshirt, and opened the door to my two best friends, Mia and Samantha. Arnold promptly shimmied straight between my feet and shot straight out the door.

All this before coffee.

"That dog is an escape artist," Sam reminded me with a warning voice.

"He's just misunderstood," I replied, to which she rolled her eyes. It was a drizzly morning, damp and cool, but with tons of birdies chirping loudly. Protesting the rainy Saturday, maybe. Or simply happy that it was finally spring.

The McClellans were off in Florida celebrating the arrival of their newest grandson. Mrs. M had recently recovered from back surgery but was still nervous about walking such a big dog, and Mr. M was a bit frail, so Arnold hadn't been getting scheduled walks. I knew that his breakouts had a lot to do with that and tried my best to give him the workout he craved, but I'd worked a twelve-hour shift yesterday.

I usually took him for a good stroll each morning and then let him frolic free in their vast yard—with supervision, of course—for a little while each day. So far, during the week I'd been here, he'd never taken advantage and always came when I called him.

I might possibly have ascribed too much moral conscience to him, but hey, I tended to believe the best in people...and animals.

"Do you need to get him?" my friend, Mia, the responsible worrywart, asked. She hiked a thumb over her shoulder at the dog, who was gleefully bounding about, nose to the ground, following some irresistible scent trail.

"I'll give him a minute." I ushered them in as Arnold happily trolled the perimeter of the big yard.

"When do the McClellans get back?" Sam asked, studying Mr. M's hole-in-one golf ball, which lived encased in a giant resin block on the coffee table.

"One more week," I said. "Perfect timing for my house to be done."

Tyler and I had bought a sweet little Cape Cod across the street —not on the golf course, like the McClellans' was. It was basically the tiniest house in a great neighborhood, and Tyler had seen value in that even if he'd thought it was too cutesy and old. I'd loved it from the second I'd seen its big old tree with sprawling branches and the charming transomed front door. The catch was that it was dated and needed a ton of work, most of which I couldn't afford—yet.

But hey, I'd somehow managed to buy Tyler out. And to wipe all thoughts of him out of my mind, I'd had every room painted something other than white, Tyler's favorite color. Which really explains everything about the two of us.

We'd managed to negotiate and sign papers regarding the house. We'd also taken care of all the leftover wedding bills. I'd given him back his ring. But we hadn't really talked. It was more and more clear to me that I'd hurt him deeply, even though I was certain I'd made the right decision not marrying him. And I'd surely embarrassed him by calling off our wedding so publicly. I'd left him voicemails, trying to apologize, but he never called me back. I hated that I'd hurt him in such a public way and desperately wanted to make peace.

"How's it looking?" Sam, my practical, no-nonsense friend, asked.

Oh, the house. "Nice," I said. A guy I dated from high school ran a remodeling company and had given me a great deal on repainting the kitchen cabinets (okay, I did choose white for those), and white quartz countertops to replace the ancient red Formica. And that's when my money ran out.

"I knew this was a bad idea, inviting us over the morning after your ER shift," Mia said, fluffing my bed head, which had expanded overnight, my hair no doubt curling in every direction. "What time did you finish?"

"After one." By the time I finally got home, I was still pretty wired. I'd watched *Gilmore Girls* for a while. More like a few hours. I kept thinking about that baby and that young mom, until I finally fell asleep on the sofa around three.

Then something weird happened—at around five, I'd woken up to what I thought was a baby crying. I'd sat bolt upright, but the entire house was dead silent, except for my buddy Arnold, wedged happily in between me and the couch back, snoring softly. Actually, I was halfway off the couch because he was a total couch hog, but hey, companionship came with a price, I guessed.

I glanced again out the window. Arnold was rolling over and over in the grass, which was soaking wet. *Great.*

"I'm sorry to oversleep, but I'm so glad you came." My two best friends were here to help me with the fun task of making bacon-wrapped scallops for my parents' fancy party tonight. Mia was in her first year of pediatric hematology/oncology fellowship, and Sam was a pediatric anesthesiologist, who, like me, was enjoying her first year out of residency and in a real job. Our friendship was forged during our residencies at Children's Milwaukee—we'd come to rely on each other at work—and also in our personal lives.

Both Mia and Sam worked in Milwaukee, but Sam and her boyfriend Caleb, an orthopedic surgeon, spent every Friday doing clinics at Oak Bluff. Mia's husband Brax spent his Fridays in my practice helping out with the overflow. My ambivalence about staying alone in Oak Bluff after I called off my wedding was tempered by knowing that my dear friends were nearby for at least part of the week. But they'd both found the loves of their lives. As for me—well, there weren't exactly a lot of potential suitors in our tiny town—so it was a good thing I'd sworn off men, possibly for good.

I led my friends into the kitchen and then excused myself to get cleaned up. When I returned, Sam had already started the oven and pulled cookie sheets out for the bacon, and Mia had coffee going. A quick peek outside showed that Arnold was still canvassing the wooded section of the yard for squirrel or chipmunk intruders, no doubt.

I sat down and poured myself a coffee, thanking Mia for knowing my need for caffeine without asking. I guess I'd zoned out, because I was startled to attention when Sam called my name. "You okay?"

"Sorry. Tough night."

"You shouldn't be doing this after working so late," Mia said.

"And your mom is having the food catered, so I'm not sure why you offered," Sam said. "I thought you weren't going to do things just to please your parents."

I got up, grabbed a box of toothpicks, and threw a bunch into a bowl of water to soak. That way, they wouldn't burn in the oven. "I know, I know. I just still feel like a disappointment after all the ruin of the wedding."

"Not marrying Tyler was a godsend," Mia said. "I'm not sure why you feel that you have to apologize for that."

No, I would never apologize for calling that wedding off. Tyler, a cardiologist, was brilliant and dedicated. I'd fallen in love with his logic and his organizational skills, both of which I fell short on. The trouble was that he was also self-centered and lacking in compassion, traits that I continually made excuses for. After the wedding disaster, he'd left Wisconsin for New York and never looked back. I was relieved that he was many states away.

I gave a dismissive wave. "Oh, you know, the expense. It was...a lot." This year was my first year out of residency, and the first time since my nursing career that I made a salary where I didn't have to live paycheck to paycheck. Tyler had been working as a cardiologist for several years. We'd insisted on paying a chunk of the reception money, but my parents had covered the majority of the expenses to give us a really nice wedding. They'd saved for it for years, and I was grateful for it.

I vowed to pay it all back. I didn't mention that the real source of my guilt was the fact that I'd waited until the eleventh hour to call it all off. It would have saved heartache—on everyone's parts—and money—if I'd pulled the trigger earlier. Much earlier. Why had I ignored the signs?

Mia and Sam exchanged glances. We'd been through all this before—my pathological need to please my mother, who meant well but seemed essentially unpleasable. My parents were likely the only people on the planet who'd left retirement in Florida to move back to Wisconsin. Their reason? To be five minutes away from me, which, given our relationship, provided many extra opportunities for what I could only describe as pure torture. In the most loving way possible, of course.

I did not have an easy relationship with my mother, and I wasn't sure how to make it better. But with the close proximity, I guess I had a chance to figure it out. Starting with these bacon-wrapped scallops that we were all about to make for the party.

"My mom wants to introduce me to someone," I confessed. "She's excited about it. But I'm just—not ready yet. I told her that." But I had this awful feeling that she hadn't listened. And if he was going to be at this party tonight, it would only underscore our communication problems.

"Good for you for telling her," Mia said, rinsing the scallops while the bacon par-cooked in the oven for a few minutes. "It's the first step toward figuring out what you really want."

Sam, unlike Mia, minced no words. "That means not what Tyler wants. Not what your mom wants. And not what your partners want." She tapped the island emphatically. "What *Ani Green* wants."

"Right." Frankly, I had no idea exactly what I wanted. Peace of mind? To not be talked about by everyone in town because I'd canceled my wedding? To forgive myself for my past mistakes? To figure out why I made them in the first place? To settle in and belong somewhere, and be content with who I was? Yes, on all those. Especially the last.

"And in the meantime," Mia said, "do what you always do. Do what made you Resident of the Year."

"Work like a dog?" I cracked a smile. She was referring to an award I'd received during my final year of residency. I had great test scores on my boards and was also recognized as caring passionately for my patients. At least that was life-affirming.

"Exactly," Mia said. "Well, not exactly, about the working like a dog part. Give it your all like you always do, and things will work out."

"You've been through a lot, and you're just starting out again," Sam added. "Give the dust a chance to settle, be firm, and set limits."

"Yes, see where the dust settles." Mia made sprinkling motions with her hands. Or maybe she was doing itsy bitsy spider, I didn't know.

"Thanks for the pep talk," I said. My friends loved me regardless of whether I made terrible decisions or good ones. They believed even more than I did that I would ultimately figure everything out. I had hope because they'd each found their forever person. Maybe someday I would too—if I ever wanted to actually date again.

On the counter, Sam lined up more baking sheets. We were ready to wrap and roll as soon as the bacon came out of the oven. I opened the door for a quick dog check. Arnold was helping till the garden, except that he was creating a hole the size of a volcanic crater. Plus, his paws had gone from wet to flat-out muddy. As soon as I called his name, he froze and tossed me a guilty-as-charged look.

"No digging," I called, knowing he would go right back to business as soon as I closed the door.

While I gave him a minute, I grabbed some old towels from the laundry room to wipe him off. Then I scooped out the organic breakfast that Mrs. McClellan kept in a bag in the fridge. I was ready to call him in when Sam said, "We heard about the baby. Everyone's talking about it."

I nodded solemnly as I refilled Arnold's water. "The baby's mom is so young. She drove herself to the ER. Alone."

For the millionth time, I wished I could do something to help. Something *more*. But what? I understood not to get too caught up in the heartrending difficulties people experienced daily—everyone in the medical field that I knew cared deeply for all our patients' difficulties, but we also had to do our jobs. This somehow felt different, more heartrending because of the teen mom whose life was forever altered in ways I couldn't fathom and the innocent little baby who slept peacefully away, completely unaware that the entire course of her future hung precariously in the balance.

"She handed me the baby." I got a little shaky as I recounted what had happened. "And asked me to take care of her. She made me promise that the baby would go to a good family. It was a little shocking. I'm still unnerved about it. And how on earth did a sixteen-year-old know about Safe Haven?"

"Did you?" Sam narrowed her eyes. "Did you promise?"

"Of course I did!" I said. "I couldn't not. She was pleading with me." I rubbed my forehead, still upset about this young person having to face such stark reality, such hard decisions—all by herself.

"She was worried about her baby," I said, still upset. My friends stared at me. "The mom wanted her to go to someone who could give her everything." My voice cracked. "She asked me for one thing, and it wasn't even for herself." Which was pretty incredible for anyone, let alone a sixteen-year-old.

Mia grabbed my hand. "You did the right thing. You can oversee the social work consult and the Children's Services placement."

I nodded. Of course I would.

Mia took a swig of coffee and caught Sam's gaze. Something passed between them.

"What?" I asked. "What is it?" It wasn't like them to withhold info, but the fact that they knew something they were hesitating to share made my heart drop.

Mia sighed. "The mom left against medical advice."

I sat up fast and clumsily knocked my coffee, sloshing some over the top. "When?"

"In the middle of the night. Pulled out her IV and took off. Apparently, she registered with a fake name, so they don't even know who she is or where she's from."

"Not that it would matter," Sam pointed out. "She didn't do anything wrong."

But she'd told me her name. *Crystal.* "No. She did everything right. She got herself to the hospital, and she followed the correct procedure. I have so many questions. And I want to know that she's okay." But it was too late. She was apparently gone for good.

"Thank God she gave birth in the hospital," Mia said. "Sometimes young women are afraid and risk their lives by giving birth alone someplace."

I still felt her intense grip on my arm. I felt the heavy weight of my promise.

Mia reached over and covered my hand reassuringly with hers. "I know you feel responsible, but the nursery will get social work involved and sort this all out." She pulled the bacon out of the oven and began slicing it in half while Sam drained the scallops and patted them dry with a paper towel.

I had a lump in my throat, so I just nodded. It was still so sharp in my mind, so heavy on my heart, how I'd held that tiny little bundle, looked down into those blinking dark blue eyes. All that potential, all that promise—what would happen to this innocent little baby who had no one to defend her?

"Otherwise, how was your night with Adam?" Mia asked. "He and Brax are old friends, did you know that? They went to med school in Philly together."

I jerked up my head, startled out of my thoughts by thinking of an entirely different night—definitely not the one she was asking about. I preferred the warm, moonlit, tropical one, because last night had been disastrous all around.

"Fine," I said. "I—if he'd chill a little, I'd like him better." I liked him a *whole* lot better when I thought he was normal. But maybe it was a good thing he was currently on my bad list. I thought of how difficult my life would become if he ever switched to my *good* one.

"You heard his story, right?" Mia asked.

"I know his wife died. But I don't know many details." I knew that he was heartbroken. That he was struggling to start his life again. But that still didn't excuse him for being such a grump, in my opinion.

Mia wrapped a scallop carefully with bacon and pinned it with a toothpick. I followed her lead and tried to do it like she had. But I was more focused on what she was about to say. "Adam's wife had a rare type of leukemia, and her stem cell transplant failed. So sad."

"Oh. Awful." Those few days in Turks, we hadn't discussed many details. "He's really driven about making the ER efficient. About people sticking to doing their job. It's like he's on a mission to stomp out all fun."

"That's not surprising," Mia said. "Brax said that he was devastated when she died. It really changed him."

My hands fumbled and the scallop tumbled out of the bacon and fell onto the floor. "It's kind of sad. When he isn't so on guard, he can be fun."

Mia frowned as she looked up from rolling. "How do you know that?"

For a second, I froze. I generally told my friends almost everything, but I hadn't been able to bring myself to tell them about what had happened before they'd arrived to be wonderful friends to me in Turks and Caicos. Maybe because sleeping with Adam had been so out of character for me. Maybe because I feared no one would believe me that I'd forged such an intense connection with someone I barely knew. Maybe I couldn't even explain it to myself.

I hadn't expected anything more from Adam. And I definitely hadn't expected to see him again in my hometown. So then why had his dismissal hurt so much?

Maybe I should come clean. I knew my friends wouldn't judge me—too much. I took a big breath. "Okay, you're not going to believe this, but—"

Mia turned from looking out the kitchen window. "Ani, did the dog ever come in?"

"Oh no. I forgot!" I jumped up, sprang to the window, and threw open the sash. Just kidding. I don't even know what a sash is.

Sure enough, no Arnold. Split. Vamos. Vanished.

Great. Another guy who couldn't be trusted.

Also, obsessing about Adam had lost me the dog. Nice.

I grabbed my windbreaker and ran into the drizzle, yelling "Arnold Palmer" at the top of my lungs.

<h1 style="text-align:center">Chapter Seven</h1>

Adam

"So what's happening with that baby everyone's talking about?" my friend Brax asked. Our pickups were parked side-by-side in my driveway, mine red, his black, and we were loading all the firewood we'd just cut up from a fallen tree in my yard.

Surrounded by woods but also sort of overtaken by them—that was my yard. And on this drizzly spring morning, it was a wild, untamed mess. I'd like to say that it had the potential for beauty to emerge—but I wasn't really feeling it.

I'd bought this dull gray ranch sight-unseen from Chicago because the realtor liked the price, because it was walking distance from my mom's, and because it didn't need any immediate work, other than the yard. And I *loved* yard work. The rest I didn't care much about. So yes, I bought a house based on the ability for me to whack an endless supply of weeds, dig up saplings growing where they shouldn't be, and chop down half-dead trees.

I felt sort of miserable. I'd handled things with Ani totally wrong—again. And I didn't think I could confide in anyone about this, even a good friend like Brax. The one-night stand, the way she'd suddenly shown up right in my ER—or the way I'd suddenly shown up in her hometown, if you want to look at it that way, and most of all, the bad way I'd handled everything.

"I don't have any updates yet," I said. "I only know that the mom took off in the middle of the night. And there's no precedent to go after her because she used Safe Haven. I mean, she's safe from prosecution but also not getting any kind of help or services."

"Safe Haven is when someone surrenders their baby, right?"

"She gave birth and then immediately handed the baby over to our new pediatrician."

"To Ani," Brax said.

Ani. Who'd never been far from my thoughts. I cleared my throat. "Yes. What do you know about her?" Brax was a pediatrician, and he subbed a day each week in the same practice Ani joined. I was eager to get some info—any info—about her.

"Mia's really good friends with her. We were all residents together, and I count myself as her friend too. We were all there when her wedding fell apart last summer."

Interesting. Also, if Ani had a connection with Brax's girlfriend, it was definitely *not* a good idea to get confessional about Turks and Caicos.

I avoided looking at Brax as I grabbed a log and tossed it into his truck.

I was used to keeping things close. And I wasn't the kiss-and-tell type. But I could've used a friend to talk to right then because life suddenly felt very complicated.

"Ani did a great job with the delivery," I said.

"She's a great doc," Brax said, "and a good person. She deserves better than that guy she almost married."

"What happened with that?" I winced. Bad question, totally inappropriate, none of my business. Yet I couldn't resist the ask.

Brax dusted off his bright yellow gloves and heaved a sigh. "It's complicated. Tyler is super smart and extremely organized but also kind of an asshole. I think she was attracted to his levelheadedness. But he like, has no emotions." Brax studied me carefully. "Do you care?"

Busted. "I-I was just wondering." I kept asking questions like a gossip. And stammering. Could I be more obvious?

I hefted a heavy piece of wood and pressed my lips together. Since Liv died, I'd struggled in many ways—I hadn't felt like going out with my friends. I became isolated. When I moved here, I vowed to do better, determined to push myself to keep up with my relationships. "If I tell you something, you have to promise to keep it private."

"Of course." To his credit, Brax wiped the surprise off his face, halted all activity, and stood there expectantly.

I had one last chance to keep this private. Aw, hell. I needed...a friend. So I plunged ahead. "I met someone. Last summer. In Turks and Caicos."

"Oh." He was smart enough not to ask further. But I didn't miss his raised brow, the little lilt in his voice. "Wow. Okay. You never said anything about that."

I shrugged, unsure of what to say next.

"Is this someone you would ever see again?" Brax asked.

"I never thought I would." I pinched my nose. That wasn't entirely true. "I mean, I looked up her name. I knew where she lived. Maybe I was hoping someday—but I swear, I came back here for my mom. I'm not some stalker—"

At that point, Brax pulled off his gloves and tossed them on the ground. "Wait a minute. Are you telling me—"

Stupid, stupid me. I'd started this avalanche. So I had to finish it. "It was Ani. She showed up in my ER last night. And I handled it all wrong."

"Wait, back up. Did you—did you *sleep* with her?" He raised his hands up traffic-cop style. "No, don't answer that. If you answer, I'll be keeping a secret from Mia, and that would be bad."

"Maybe. That might've happened. *Yes.*" I felt no relief.

He burst into laughter. I stabbed him with a glare. "Brax, I swear, if you say one word..."

He threw up his hands, still chuckling. "I won't, I won't. But... you like her. I mean, you obviously do, or we wouldn't be having this conversation."

"Yes, I like her. But I don't know what I want. And I hurt her feelings."

He parked himself on the woodpile and took off his ball cap. "Go on. I can't wait to hear this."

"Well, first she accused me of leaving my sense of humor in Turks and Caicos."

"You have a sense of humor?" He smiled a smirky smile that made me regret confessing my darkest secret. "Okay, okay, so let's be honest, you haven't exactly had a bounce in your step lately."

"Nor will I ever in the ER. I have to treat her professionally."

"And she told you off."

"In front of the staff. And then again in private. I-I didn't exactly acknowledge her as someone I knew."

"Wait—you acted like you didn't remember her?"

At this point, I was probably regretting my confession. "Because I was thrown. Was I supposed to say, 'Oh hi, everyone, meet my one-night stand. Great to see you again.' I got...confused."

Brax rubbed his neck, deep in thought. "I can't believe you slept with her." It sounded so loud when he said it. Aaand it was official. I *definitely* regretted telling him.

I shushed him and glanced around. No people, just two rows of houses, most of them tidy, except mine of course, and only a silly, curly-haired dog lollygagging down the street, his tongue hanging sideways in a semi-comical fashion. As I squinted, I saw that it was my neighbors' dog, Arnold.

"Anyway, she's staff," I continued. "When she's in my ER, I'm in charge. I can't afford a distraction like her."

He pounded me on the back. "Trust me, Adam, you *need* a distraction like this."

I scowled. Now that I told him, I was for sure gonna have to kill him.

He must have sensed my distress because he changed his tone. "I'm going to be completely honest. People have a certain sympathy for you, but it's not going to last forever. You can be...a killjoy." He let that sink in. "And that's the polite version of what I really want to say."

"I'm not there to be anyone's friend. I have to set rules. I have to make sure my staff is ready for anything that walks through that door."

He rested his arm on my shoulder. That made me a little emotional. "You're a great doctor, Adam. But having a branch up your ass isn't going to save everyone who walks through the door. You know that. You're punishing yourself for something that had nothing to do with you."

I looked into the distance, at the bright green grass of the golf course peeking through the houses across the street.

He was right, I couldn't save Liv. But looking back, there were tiny signs, tiny symptoms. We might have caught it quicker. Got her evaluated sooner. Then maybe her bone marrow would have taken. I vowed on her grave that I would make certain that nothing like that ever happened to anyone else on my watch. That way her death might have some meaning because otherwise, it didn't at all. Not one effing bit.

The silly labradog was now bounding down the street, on a mission, heading straight toward us, loping a little sideways with his awkward long-legged gait. He ran up to me and started running circles and jumping, excited to see me.

I stooped to give him an aggressively playful rub down. "Arnie, buddy, what on earth are you doing here?"

He answered by flopping on his back right on my lawn and wagging his tail for more.

"Who's your friend?" Brax asked.

"He lives around the corner." I gestured in the general direction.

"Ever since Mrs. McClellan broke her hip last winter, she and her husband haven't been walking him regularly. He hates being cooped up. I take him for a run with me when I can."

"Arnie! Arnold! Arnold *Palmer* McClellan *the Third*!"

Some golfers on the 9th hole looked over as a woman in a raincoat, red plaid flannel pants, and flip-flops came running toward us.

Brax broke out in a huge, smug grin. "Don't look now, but here comes your one-night stand."

I rolled my eyes. "This is why I don't talk to anyone about my problems."

He snorted. "If you have a problem deciding about whether or not you should go out with her again, then you need more than a friend to talk to." He paused. "But just to reinforce what you already know, she's been hurt badly. She deserves someone who's going to be there for her. You have to decide if you can be."

Oh. His friendly ribbing had taken a turn. I respected that he was looking out for Ani in a protective way. But his warning only underscored the fears that I already had about myself.

Ani seemed to appear magically before us, like I'd conjured her from my thoughts, looking disheveled but adorable. She was smiling her usual beautiful smile—until she saw me, that is.

"Hi, Brax," she said, a little out of breath. "Adam." I got a much less enthusiastic greeting. I got Princess Leia talking to R2-D2 about the Death Star—deadpan, mortally dangerous.

Her curls were everywhere. She had no makeup on. Her eyes were a pure clear blue—stunning. I had a sudden flashback of her in bed, hair mussed, nuzzling my neck. I pulled off my own ball cap and swiped my forehead with my sleeve. Was it getting warm out here?

How did this woman have the power to make me stupid? And

I wasn't the only one gaga over her. The dog licked her face when she bent to pet him, tail going a million miles a minute.

Wait a minute...what was the connection between her and my pal Arnie?

"Thanks for grabbing him," she said.

I slowly rose from petting the dog. She was a full foot shorter than me. A petite ball of fire. "No problem."

Brax glanced from Ani to me as we stared at each other awkwardly. "I—um—yeah, hey, thanks for the wood, Adam. I'll come back for the rest of it after I pick Mia up, okay? See ya, Ani."

He got into his truck and left, even though we still had a lot of wood left to load. I respected that he gave me some space. But I also hoped that when he came back, he would bring lunch.

"Well," Ani said, "I'd better get back."

I frowned. "Get back to where?"

She nodded in the direction she came from. "I'm dog sitting until the end of the week. The McClellans are visiting their new grandchild in Georgia." She looked around at my wild-looking landscape, my nondescript brick ranch. "This is your place?"

"I bought it for a project," I said. "I just moved in."

"Tyler and I bought a house across the street from the McClellans. I loved it; he hated it. So I bought him out and decided to repaint the whole inside. That's why I'm dog sitting."

I nodded. I understood trying to make a place your own, only I hadn't gotten there yet. Just leaving my former house in Chicago had taken a lot. All the memories. Knowing I was leaving forever. It had felt like saying goodbye to Liv all over again.

"Hang on a second." I jogged into my garage and returned with an old dog leash a friend had left once and snapped it onto Arnie's collar.

"Thanks. I ran out so fast I forgot his leash." Ani took the loop end from me, our fingers bumping. Her hands were soft but cold. She'd also clearly run out of the house without dressing properly, plus it was drizzling. "I'll make sure you get this back."

"I don't have a dog anymore, so keep it." As she turned away, I realized that this was it. I would lose my opportunity unless I spoke up. "Listen, about last night—" She turned back halfway. I only had a moment, and I had no idea what I was going to say, but I gave it my best shot. "I did a lot of things wrong. I-I knew you'd be working, but when I saw you, I was thrown. And—I didn't want my staff to see that we have a personal relationship."

"Do we *have* a personal relationship?" she asked, steel in her voice.

I searched for the words to let her know how much my time with her had meant to me. How I still thought of her. But I didn't know how I could put any of that into words and still be professional. Or maybe the real truth was that I was afraid to take that leap. The result was that I was completely tongue-tied.

When she saw that I wasn't going to say anymore, she said, "That was a strange time." She paused. "For both of us." She took a breath. "I think it's better if we don't discuss it. That way we can maintain a working relationship." She flicked her clear blue gaze up at me. "That's what you want, right?"

Oh. That *was* what I wanted, right? "Yes, of course."

"After all, you're in charge." She gave me a tight smile. "See you in the ER." Then she and Arnie took off, the dog casting me a single glance that seemed to say, *What a loser.*

I'd gotten what I wanted. Our time together last summer had been effectively erased.

Order was restored. No one would know about the night I made an impulsive, desperate choice. My reputation was intact, my ER orderly.

Then why did I feel so bad?

~

Ani

· · ·

"Hey, Mom," I said that evening as I entered my parents' kitchen with my somewhat fishy-smelling trays and set them on the expansive island. "Do you have the oven ready?"

My mother lit up with a smile, like she was genuinely happy to see me. She gave me a big hug, which felt nice. "Thank you, sweetie. Oh, those look wonderful!" She turned to one of the two women dressed in black and white who were setting out champagne flutes on gold trays. "Terry, look what Ani brought." She examined each scallop thoroughly. "If you see some loosely wrapped ones, just pin them a little tighter before you put them into the oven, okay?"

There was the mom I knew. She was really good at finding flaws. She hated anything less than perfect.

That was why I drove her crazy. I was inherently flawed. Divorced and with my recent marriage debacle, I was the ultimate flawed daughter. The daughter she was stuck with.

She turned her eagle eyes to me. "You look lovely."

Ah, we agreed on something. I really did like my silver sparkly dress with red heels and matching lipstick. "Thank you. You look nice too."

She was dressed in a simple black sheath dress with a silver neck wrap. Cute. I did not inherit her flair for style either, but at least I'd made an effort tonight.

"There's someone here we want you to meet."

Oh no. No, no. She'd promised—no fix-ups. "Dad's golf buddy who wants to have an outpatient center named after him?" I asked hopefully.

"Yes, the Stevenses are here, but so is their son. He's a doctor. A hepatologist, in fact."

My stomach dropped as I suddenly understood that she really had plowed ahead with the plan. "Mom, you promised."

My mom patted my back. "It was an opportunity I couldn't pass up. We want you to meet someone nice. Someone solid. Someone..."

"Who can handle me?"

That dropped like a bomb. She stepped back and frowned. "You said that, not me." She took a breath. "Look, Ani, we want you to be happy. Find a stable relationship. Settle down. You've been so sad lately."

"I can find my own stable relationship, okay?" I couldn't help being defensive.

"Can you, though?"

Ouch. This was the problem. My mother was always poking my sorest spots. Always trying to fix me. Not believing I could fix myself. For the thousandth time, I asked myself why my parents moved back here from sunny, warm Florida. *Specifically to torment me* did not sound like a fun enough reason, but for my mother, maybe this was her fun?

I bit back more comments, because what was I supposed to do, refuse to join the party? I didn't want to fight. And I was really good at holding in my pent-up feelings.

She walked over and held me by the shoulders. "With the right person, one chance meeting is all it takes."

I could only think about the airplane. How I'd never expected to meet anyone in the terrible state I'd been in. Adam had been so kind to me that day and afterward. He hadn't let me wallow in sadness. No matter how annoying he was now, he'd saved me at my lowest low.

That made me think about what he'd said this afternoon. *I did a lot of things wrong. I was thrown.*

But he clearly didn't want a friendship, let alone anything more. Did he?

"I'll meet him," I said, "but I don't feel ready to meet anyone yet. And I'm still learning the ropes at my job." At least I'd managed to say something honest.

"You're an excellent doctor, honey," my dad, who had just entered the kitchen, said.

"Thanks, Dad."

We side-hugged as he examined my scallops, which were now on round silver platters. "Hmm. What are these things?"

"An appetizer Mia and Sam helped me make. I brought dipping sauce too."

"How nice of you, sweetheart. I can't wait to try one."

"Just take a teeny little peek," my mom said in an imploring tone, beckoning me to the kitchen doorway. She was *not* giving up.

"Oh, my God, he looks like Dad!" came out of my mouth.

My dad gave me a look.

"As far as the hair loss goes," I said quickly. "I mean, you're very nice-looking, Dad."

"Thank you, sweetheart."

"The gentleman with the hair loss is his *father*," my mom said. "Look to the right. His name is Ken."

Through the crack in the door, I could make out a younger man with hair. Actually, quite nice hair. Like, noticeably thick, wavy, well-cut hair—actually, his hair was...amazing. And he was tall and good-looking. But I was too upset to care. I felt ambushed. Against my wishes. Plus, he wasn't Adam.

I didn't mean to think that. I just...did.

"Look, it's only dinner," my mom said. "It will be fun to have someone your age to talk to. That's it." My mom looked desperate and tired. Like she couldn't rest unless I was happy.

I tried to understand that this was her strange but oddly sincere way of showing love.

She wasn't content to stop there. "Ani, you're thirty-three. You're a busy career woman. Your child-bearing years are ticking away. I just think it might be wise to accept some help once in a while from the people who love you."

So here's the thing about my mom. She's really bright. She's a go-getter, and she's got her hand in every single charity in the community.

She almost went to medical school—she was even accepted. But she married my dad instead. My dad, who built the local hospital and other regional medical centers, and got very wealthy doing it.

I am an only child. Which means all of that intellectual and emotional energy is often directed solely at me.

Fortunately, Terry came up to us and said it was time to eat. Which probably saved my self-control from breaking.

Dinner was served in the dining room, all the leaves placed to accommodate fifteen guests. I had to say that my mom set a beautiful table, full of fresh flowers and sparkly glassware. And the scallops were to die for.

The good part of the dinner was that I got to discuss the pediatric clinic, especially with Carl Langerman, who had a few million he wanted to spend on a great cause. I explained that many subspecialists traveled from Milwaukee to see children here and from the surrounding rural areas, and that adding on to the clinic was definitely on the administration's wish list. I hoped that would be like a whisper in his ear or the ear of any of these people who had an itch to donate.

The bad part was that Dr. Hair was a dick. "I'm newly divorced," he said right off the bat. "I have a one-year-old and a three-year-old. You're a pediatrician. I bet you're great with kids. Do you have a profile on Hinge?"

"Um, no." What a waste of a great head of hair, was what I was thinking as I took a gulp of wine. One glass was definitely not going to be enough to get me through this dinner.

"E-harmony? Bumble? CoffeeMeetsBagel?"

"No, I—Ken, I'm sorry, but I'm not dating right now."

He flipped back his hair. "Your mother said you might be a little reluctant, but that I could probably charm you into giving me a chance. Except sometimes I get a little nervous and my words don't come out right."

I wanted to say that yes, there were better words to use than sounding like a man desperate for a woman to watch his children.

Forget about Hinge. He should've spent his time checking out Nanny.com.

But his comment also made me think of my interaction that day with Adam. I'd been pretty hasty to jump in and start talking to fill the silence. What if he'd been trying to apologize? I'd come in hot and hadn't given him a chance.

We were able to be frighteningly honest with each other last summer, but that was under dire, anonymous circumstances. So, shouldn't it be easier to be honest with each other now? Or maybe not, since this was real life, and there was no airplane to jet us away to our real lives.

I pulled out my phone, hoping for a text from one of my girl-friends. An invite for a drink. Or a *Hey, call me back*. Anything to get me out of this conversation. Hoping for an excuse to leave this party entirely would be too much to hope for.

Nothing.

Guess I would have to make my own destiny.

"But, hey, who needs words when you're this attracted to someone, right?" Clueless Ken continued not impressing.

Why not make my own destiny? I still had Adam's number in my phone from the summer. Why not text him? I'd just started typing when my phone vibrated.

My heart gave a thump. A text from, of all people, *Adam*. I'd summoned him through mental telepathy.

You're a problem I don't know how to solve.

Words which, on their own, sounded not very promising. It made me think of pesky medical problems. Constipation. Diaper rash. School avoidance.

But his words were followed by, of all things, heart eyes emoji.

I broke out in a smile. Another heart eyes followed. Oh my gosh, two of them. Be still, my heart!

Ken mistook my enthusiasm for agreeing with his awful comment and leaned in closer.

I scooted my chair back and quickly typed a response. *I'm going to go cuddle that baby.*

"I'm so sorry, but I just got paged," I said to Ken.

Want to meet me there? I quickly typed.

"Wait—you just got paged?" Ken asked, loud enough that everyone heard.

"Is everything okay?" my mom asked from way down the table.

"There's an emergency," I said, and left it at that. I bit my lower lip, so I didn't keep trying to explain.

Because there was—I had to get away from Dr. Hair, STAT. And my mother as well, before I irreparably damaged our relationship. So I wasn't really lying, was I?

"This late at night?" my dad asked.

I smiled. "Oh, you know, medicine is never nine-to-five." I stood and placed my napkin definitively on the table, avoiding my mother's gaze. "Great to meet you, Mr. Langerman, everyone. Mom and Dad, thanks for a great dinner. Sorry to have to leave."

Chapter Eight

Adam

The fact was that I couldn't focus on anything.

I was still at the hospital at ten that night, when my shift had ended at seven.

I'd done so much administrative work that I actually felt caught up, which never happened.

I kept trying to compose the right text.

Yes, we have a relationship.

That wasn't good. That sounded...pervy.

Yes, we have a friendship. We might have a friendship. We want to have a friendship. We might want to have more than a friendship.

Oh, come on, Adam, I chided myself. Friendship was the very last thing on my mind. Ani was beautiful, fun, charismatic, and interesting. If I saw her across the room in a tropical location and our eyes met, I'd be completely drawn to her physically.

Oh, I'd done that already.

But now I was also drawn to her mentally.

Maybe I always had been. Which might be a terrifying revelation considering the state she was in when I first met her.

One look at you and I lose all my words.

I definitely wasn't sending that one.

What I should have said but never would: *You scare the shit out of me. You are a problem that I do not know how to solve.*

I erased the first sentence and kept the second. And then I pushed send before I lost my nerve. And because I was an ER doc, not a writer, I stopped critiquing my prose and gave myself points for being as honest as I knew how to be.

And then I spent the next ten minutes trying to figure out how to un-send a text, but it was too late. Note to self: Learn the nuclear option first.

What had I done?

No three moving dots in sight. No answer at all.

I paced my office. Then I headed down the long corridor away from my staff because if they saw me, I had one hundred percent certainty of being pulled into...something.

Suddenly, a text popped up. *I'm going to go cuddle that baby.* And then, *Want to join me?*

Yes! I fist-pumped and texted a thumbs-up, lest I get too exuberant and drive her away with too many emojis. I forced myself to sit and send a few emails, so I didn't look too eager. Finally, I closed up my office, walked down the long corridor, got in the elevator, and punched the fifth-floor button.

It was nearly midnight as I walked down the dim hallway of the postpartum ward. It was strangely silent—not a peep out of any of the newborns, many of whom roomed in with their moms.

I turned a corner to the nursery. "Hey, Dale," I said to the charge nurse, who was sitting at the desk with his feet up, reading a dark fantasy novel.

Dale happened to be six-foot-five, with little gold hoop earrings, a ponytail, and lots of tattoos. He looked more like a biker dude than a nurse in charge of newborns—but I happened to know that his heart was a giant bowl of melted ice cream. On seeing me, he lowered his feet and set down his book. "It must be ER night in the nursery. Dr. Green just came to love up the baby up a little. You come back for another turn too?"

I hoped he hadn't told Ani I'd already been by twice today. Only to make sure things were getting done and to look in on the baby, whom they were calling "Baby Smith," an alias, of course, which made me feel sad. "I'm here this time to talk to Dr. Green."

And I'd better not screw things up again.

He hiked a thumb behind his head. "We've had staff from every floor coming down. Poor little thing." He shook his head, and I could swear he was getting teary. So I patted him on the back. Which was a little awkward.

But, it turned out, appreciated. "Thanks, Doc." Dale wiped his eyes under his glasses. "It's so unfair to get such a crappy start in the world, isn't it?" He sighed. "You can go on back."

I was thinking that I'd rather go into a pit of snakes than in a room with a handful of zesty newborns—and Ani Green, but just then, she looked up and saw me in the doorway.

She was sitting in a white wooden rocker, holding the baby. Her bright smile, her wave, the way she lit up—well, that same reaction overtook me that always did when I was near her—a sudden flush, a pounding of my heart, the strike of a match when our gazes met. As if I usually lived in black and white, but when she was near, I saw color.

I, who had responded to countless emergencies by acting quickly, froze. And then she gestured for me to come on in. And suddenly everything felt better. Except for my too-honest text.

Ani wore red lipstick. And a sparkly dress. Her curls were more contained but never fully, thank God. She looked incredible.

I couldn't look away.

I finally had to as Dale handed me a pale-yellow hospital gown, holding it open for me to slide my arms into. "When you go in, be sure to talk quietly. All the little peeps are asleep, and I want to get through the next chapter before any of them wake up. Once one wakes up, it's dominoes—a real war zone in there."

"Thanks, Dale." I walked into the nursery, where the lights were pleasantly dimmed. A half-dozen bassinets were lined up, each containing a little sausage-shaped bundle swaddled in white flannel and wearing a blue or pink cap. It was a baby dorm, and everyone was tucked in for the night.

It was a happy place, but unsettling for me to be here. Liv had loved babies. We'd both wanted one so desperately. I tried to tell myself that it was a good thing that we weren't able to have one, because I couldn't imagine how difficult it would have been for a child to lose her too.

I tried to focus on the positive vibe of the nursery and, of course, seeing Ani. She was all dressed up, with dangly silver earrings with pearls on the ends that matched her sparkly dress. A pair of red heels sat kicked off near her chair. And wow, those legs. No doubt about it. She was a knockout. My attraction to her was never the problem.

Or rather, maybe that was the whole problem.

It had been a long time since I'd noticed a woman like that— ten months, precisely.

As I took a seat beside her in another rocker, Ani gave me a quick nod of acknowledgment then continued beaming at the baby, fast asleep in her arms, her mouth a perfect little O.

"Angel kissed."

"What did you say?" I realized I was staring at Ani, not the baby, so I quickly changed my focus to the bundle in her arms.

She gestured with her head toward the baby. "She's angel kissed."

I had no idea what she was talking about. The baby was a tiny little thing with a shock of dark hair and tiny, elegant fingers splayed out on the blanket as she slept.

I had to look away. I had a hard time dwelling on such sweetness. It reminded me of an innocent time, of the person that I no longer was.

"See her eyelids?" Ani circled her index finger over the baby's face. Some mildly red marks were embossed over the baby's eyelids. "They're simple nevi that fade with time. But we call them angel kisses."

"You pediatricians." I shook my head. "Are you here to examine her?"

She laughed. "I kept thinking about her. So I stopped by." As she lowered her head to watch the baby sleep, I noticed that she had long, pretty eyelashes.

I tried to focus on something other than my growing desire, which felt overpowering. "Judging by the way you're dressed, there has to be more to that story."

"Let's just say that I'd rather be here than at my parents' fancy party and leave it at that. Did you want a turn to hold her too?" She moved to hand over the baby.

"No, I—" I was starting to sweat a little. "I'm fine watching you hold her."

"Good, more time for me. I want to hold her all night." Ani settled in, cradled the baby in her arms, still smiling.

She seemed really happy. It was so intriguing to me that of all things, she'd chosen to come here and do this, hold a little baby who had no one.

She kept throwing me curveballs.

"I hate that they call her Baby Smith." She pointed to the white card with a stork that was taped to her bassinet. "She deserves a wonderful, amazing name. Who will name her?"

"I don't know." The social worker? Children's Services? Ani was right. "Baby Smith" was generic yet ominous. A placeholder while her life was being decided by forces beyond her control.

For a moment, we sat in silence, listening to the backdrop of typical hospital sounds—phones ringing in the distance, Dale's big laugh, little noises from one of the babies stirring.

"You came to check on her earlier," she said, staring at the baby, taking in all her features. "Dale told me." She flicked her gaze to me. "You're not a complete grump."

I sat back and straightened up. "She was born under my watch. You're not the only one who feels responsible."

Ani frowned, lines of worry appearing between her eyes. "What do you think's going to happen next?"

"Well, the social worker will get the ball rolling. Hopefully, the end result will be that she'll get a great family."

"How long does that all take?"

It was a process. The baby had to be declared a ward of the state. A foster parent had to be found. Then adoption lists had to be consulted. "I don't know, but there's usually a wait list—I mean, newborns are in demand."

"What if she gets a dud family? Who will watch over her and make certain things work out?" I could see that Ani was emotional, *invested*. She seemed to wear all her emotions front and center. While I hid mine in bad texts.

I studied her carefully. "I have this feeling that you might generally think that it's on your shoulders to save the world."

"No, I just—I just have a more optimistic view of life than you do. I believe in trying to do what I can to make things better. Have you always been like this?"

"What? Practical?"

She rolled her eyes at me. "No. A stick in the mud."

The baby squirmed and got a wrinkly face and finally let out a giant burp. A strange sound for such a tiny little thing. Ani placed her deftly on her shoulder and patted her back. "See?" she said with a poignant look. "She agrees."

How was it that we went from talking about the baby to talking about me? "I have a lot of responsibilities. I have to be all business."

"Why is it that you feel like you can only do your job if you're a pill?" She flicked up her gaze. "You must know that they call you

Dr. Grumpenstein."

"Not until you called me that in the ER." I was startled again, on the inside, anyway. This visit was starting to chip away at my mental health.

"Telling people who never leave work on time because they care about their patients that they can't eat a slice of pizza behind the desk is just...wrong."

Now I was angry. Except my mad feelings were blunted by me having flashes of her lying next to me in bed, her softly rounded shoulders tanned against the bright white sheets. "I'm glad you have me all figured out."

"I don't have anything figured out. Especially not myself. Even you referred to me as a problem."

No—that wasn't it at all. I couldn't let her think that. "You're a problem *to me* because *I* don't know what to do with you."

Tiny creases appeared again in her forehead. "How so?"

I tried for a nonchalant shrug. "I've thought about you a lot. Sometimes I even wondered if you were real." I rubbed my neck. Then I gave up the pretense and looked straight at her. "That was the first completely honest thing I've said to you."

Her eyes grew wide. She flushed. She waved a hand dismissively. "We did something crazy. It was desperate times." But her voice cracked a little.

This time, I didn't run from the truth. "I'm not only talking about the sex part." My turn to blush. I looked around cautiously before I dropped my voice. As if the infants might get the gossip train rolling. "Well, that was unforgettable, but the truth is...I really like you. You're smart and honest and funny. I'm sorry I pretended that we hadn't met. I was discombobulated when I first saw you and I...I screwed up."

"I forgive you." She shifted the baby into her arms, who was back to being sound asleep. "Also, I'm going out on a limb here, but I really like you too. But remember, I don't have the best judgment with men."

I tried to pretend I wasn't suddenly very aware that something between us had shifted. I tried to make light of it. "We aren't at a tropical destination far away from our cares, our lives. We're here—where it matters."

"Right. We're *much* more sensible now." Was she kidding? Being sarcastic? A little while passed. "Unforgettable, huh?" she said, lifting a brow.

I gave a slow nod. "But the truth is, I'm still really...I can't be counted on for a relationship."

"I feel like that too. I'm okay with taking things one day at a time. Like, friends."

"Friends is great." Wait, no. What just happened? Somehow, our gazes locked. I felt that same inexorable pull, that same exact heat that I felt months ago—hell, a few minutes ago. I wanted to hold her hand. To touch her. And I really wanted to kiss her. So why on earth had I agreed? Friendship was the very last thing on my mind.

Across the nursery, one of the babies let out a long, loud wail. The bright lights flicked on, and Dale rambled in to tend his flock. He was followed by an older woman with shortish, nicely styled gray hair wearing a tweed skirt and jacket.

"Over there, Daria," Dale said, nodding toward us as he wheeled a baby out to join its mother.

"Thanks, dear." The woman patted him on the back and walked over to us.

"Are you the social worker?" Ani asked, an edge of concern in her voice. She sat up and held the baby a little closer, a little more protectively.

"I'm Daria," the woman said, extending her hand. "Yes, I'm a social worker, at least until Monday, when I officially retire. Nice to meet you, Dr. Green."

I glanced at my watch. "It's high time you showed up, Mom. It's after eleven."

"Busy day. And don't talk to me like that at work." She turned her bright green gaze on me.

Ani, eyes wide, looked from my mom to me and back again.

"Mom, this is Ani, our newest pediatrician in town and—a friend of mine." There, that time I made sure to try to do it right. "Ani, meet Daria Lowenstein. My mother."

~

Ani

I tried to process this information: that Dr. Grump had a mother who not only worked at the same hospital as he did, but who was also capable of throwing him shade.

Also, she looked like him, except she was shorter. Like, my height. I felt an instant camaraderie.

Why, oh why had I said the friend thing? He'd said he wasn't ready for a relationship, and I'd said we could take it slow, and then I had to go and add the friend thing. I guess I was afraid of trying again in general. Or maybe I was afraid of losing him. Even though he'd called me smart, honest, funny, and unforgettable. *I wondered if you were real.* Wow, I *loved* that.

Adam's mother nodded toward me. "Is she the woman from the vacation?"

I blinked, and my heart dropped straight into my stomach. The surprises just kept coming. And so many questions, starting with, What exactly had he told his mother? Also, I was a topic of discussion? And was that good or bad?

Before I got too carried away, I reminded myself that it could simply mean, *I met a woman clinging to the edge of sanity and I helped her back onto the cliff.*

Adam turned pinker than his mom's scarlet nail polish. He

cleared his throat. "Mom, Ani does shifts in the ER. *That's* how we know each other. *Professionally.*"

"You told your mother about me?" I blurted. Because...I couldn't believe it. And should I be afraid? I could only imagine what he'd said: "I met this woman when we were both miserable. I impulsively slept with her. And here she is!"

Adam was sending his mother stabbing glares. I stood there deriving a lot of pleasure from watching such an unflappable person be...well, very flappable.

He waved off the topic. "Only very briefly."

His mother said, "He said he met a woman on the plane who had just stopped her wedding, and he was worried about you."

"Mom." Adam gave his mother a lethal stare. "You've been talking to Brax, haven't you?"

"Don't blame him—he mentioned that Ani lives here now. And she's a doctor." She turned to me. "I know your mother."

"Is that right?" I hoped that was a good thing. "I'll have to tell her that we met. How long have you lived in Oak Bluff?"

"I moved here five years ago because I wanted to retire here. Such a quaint town. This is my final weekend of work. I've been a social worker for thirty-five years."

"Well, congratulations." I wondered how this homeless baby would complicate her very last weekend here. Then I turned to Adam, "Your mom seems very pleasant. Those genes must have skipped you, huh?"

He gave me a fake *haha*. "I think we agree it's great to have Ani on staff," he said in summary, like he was holding a staff meeting. "Now let's discuss this baby." He turned to his mom. "Ani delivered her. She was born twenty-four hours ago, at seven pounds, thirteen ounces. And she looks terrific. No complications."

Wait a minute. "Except for the worst complication of all," I said. "She has no home. Her mom is sixteen. She used a fake name. As soon as the baby was born, she legally handed her to me and took off for good several hours later."

"Did anyone ever find out her real name? Daria asked.

"No," I said. "Except she told me her first name. It's Crystal."

Daria made notes on an iPad. Then she set it down, crossed her arms, and looked from Adam to me. "You two are both young and single. Why are you both here at nearly midnight on a Saturday?"

"I could ask you the same question," Adam said. "But I already know the answer. You always work too hard."

Daria waved her son off. "Oh, I'm here for the same reason you are—I was worried. And I wanted to get things rolling before Monday."

"I just wanted to make sure someone was holding her," I said. Truthfully, I had the wild idea that I wanted this baby to know from the get-go that she was loved. Of course she was—the entire hospital was loving her. "Her mom trusted me, and I want to make sure that we're doing all we can for her."

Daria nodded. "It's my job to do everything in my power to find this baby a good home ASAP."

"Mom, tell us what happens next."

This was so weird. I was sitting next to the guy I'd slept with last summer while he talked to his mom, who also worked here. He clearly had a great relationship with her—easy and funny and honest. I found that all very intriguing. Not to mention that when Adam wasn't grumpy, he was sort of irresistibly attractive.

"A surrendered baby gets declared a ward of the state," Daria said. "So we contact Children's Services, and they file a motion with the court asking for temporary custody. They conduct an investigation, assume the medical care, and then find a foster family."

"Not an adoptive one?" I asked.

"Foster first. There's no shortage of people wanting to adopt a new baby. Often, people foster with the intent of adopting, and those folks get first priority."

"How do they pick a foster family?" I asked.

"Sometimes it can be relatives," Daria said, "but in this case, we don't have that. So the case worker will pick from the pool of foster parents. Oh, and the birth mother has thirty days to change her mind."

I stared at the infant tucked into my arm. I guess I got a little teary because Adam put his hand on my arm, which didn't go unnoticed by his mother.

It felt like rolling the dice, who she got as her parents. That seemed really scary. "How long does all that take?" I asked.

"We'll try to have her placed with a foster family within a week," Daria said. "It's the weekend, so as soon as Monday hits, we'll do everything we can to get the ball rolling."

"Yes, of course."

Daria moved to go. "I'm going to look through the baby's chart and start getting things ready. Is there anything we might need to know about the mom's health?"

"She was healthy," I said. "I got a brief family history—nothing really significant." I pulled out my phone and shared my list.

The baby was asleep in my arms, her hands on her face, fingers spread. She was so sweet, the picture of innocence. A fierce urge to protect her welled up inside of me. I wanted to be her shield. Her guardian angel. I wanted to vet everyone personally and find her the most spectacular parents anywhere so that she would feel no hardship, no pain. If only that were possible.

"I'd better go start the paperwork," Daria said. "I'll see you both on your way out."

"And I've got to do diaper duty," Dale said as he walked over to us with arms extended. "I'll take her, Dr. Green."

I suppose I hesitated, unconsciously unwilling to surrender the baby right away. I wasn't sure why I was taking this so personally.

"You want to hold her for a few more minutes?" Dale hiked a thumb over his shoulder. "I can start on the other end."

"Oh, I didn't mean to be a baby hog. Here you go."

I handed her over and accidentally met Adam's eyes.

He must have sensed the turmoil I thought I was hiding. "You can come back in the morning," he said quietly.

"No, it's not that." I cleared my throat.

He looked at me with kind eyes. It was a rare moment when he'd forgotten to put on his grumpy mask. "My mom knows all the case workers at Children's Services. She'll do everything possible to make certain that she gets a great family."

"I understand." He waited for me to get up, then gestured for me to go ahead of him out of the nursery.

We walked past Daria at the nursing station and walked halfway down the ward. It was very quiet, the blue floor lights illuminating the dark hall in a strange midnight way.

I was standing across from him, but I wasn't really seeing him. My brain was spinning with ideas that seemed far-fetched and improbable and yet seemed exactly right.

"I want her, Adam." I said practically at the same time that I thought it. It flew out of my mouth, low and soft, but not wavering.

He spun around. "What did you say?" He looked exactly like my dad did two minutes before my wedding when I said I couldn't marry Tyler.

I put my hand over my chest to still my pounding heart. "I want to foster the baby."

Chapter Nine

Adam

"No, you don't," were the first words out of my mouth as I grabbed Ani's elbow and steered her away from the nursery. We stood together in the middle of the ward, the ghostly blue floor lights shining off her sparkly dress. A dress that didn't fail to cling to any of her amazing curves, that was for sure.

Who was this woman, who'd come up with this life-changing idea as quickly as most people change a TV channel? Was she stable?

My words were obviously the wrong ones, because Ani cast me a death glare. "Yes. Yes, I do."

Unstable *and* stubborn. And I was as bound up in her as H2 and O were in water.

She was one of those scary people who saw a need and actually did something to make it better.

Either that, or she was a super-impulsive person who tended to make decisions that got her into trouble, like canceling her wedding at the last minute. But that seemed to be a really good decision from what I knew about Tucker. Trevor. Tanner. Whatever.

"You're feeling sorry for the baby, and that's understandable," I said in my calmest voice. "But you heard my mom—lots of people are waiting for babies. She'll go to a good home. Things will be okay."

Ani looked at once anguished and determined as she said, "Her mother handed her to *me.*" Then she looked up at me and frowned. "And you're mansplaining."

"I'm not mansplaining." To be honest, I didn't really know what that was. "Okay, I'm sorry if I am, but I'm trying to talk you out of an impulsive idea. One that could change your *entire life.*"

She shook her head so adamantly that her curls bounced a little. "Maybe my life needs to change. That baby needs a great life, and *I* can give that to her."

I swallowed. Because I saw the conviction in her face, heard it in her passionate tone. She was actually convincing me.

And something even worse. She was stunning, standing there in the weird light of that hallway. It wasn't just her beauty, which was considerable. It was how resolute she was. How unconvinced she was by my logic. She had her own logic, she was her own person, and it was...really hot.

It was as if, for the past few years, I'd been living in Jell-O. Thick, blurry, sluggish. Ani had clarity. She knew who she was. And she was going to fight for what she wanted.

I'd never seen anyone like her.

On the other hand, this was nuts.

I grabbed her by the arms. "Ani, I know you feel responsible. I'm sure it was very emotional, having a baby surrendered to you like that. But I feel like you're taking this way too—"

"Way too what?" Her voice held a warning.

"Seriously, okay?" I raked a hand through my hair and paced back and forth. "Hear me out. You're on your own. You'd be a single parent. Do you have any idea how much work a newborn is?" I counted the reasons out. "Plus, you have a job. Are you going to just spring this on your partners? You don't have any leave situation in place, and you don't have childcare set up. And—" I stopped dead. I'd said enough.

"And?" She crossed her arms, undeterred. "I mean, why hold back now? Just let it out and tell me what you really think."

"Maybe all this is a distraction from thinking about Byron."

"Who?" She might have said this a tad on the loud side.

"You know, your ex-fiancé."

Her eyes suddenly widened, and she looked around the hall, as if for a weapon. "Are you actually saying that I'm using the baby as a distraction from my failed wedding?" As she glared at me, a baby began to cry. Ani shook her head in utter disappointment and dropped her voice to a whisper. "His name is Tyler. And I can't believe you just said that!"

The wails were getting louder by the second. It always amazed me how such a tiny thing could have such a jarring, irritating cry. Worse than a ladder truck siren in traffic.

We walked down the hall and out the double doors near the elevators, where we could avoid being blamed and also continue our heated conversation. "You told me that you haven't settled in here," I said, "that you had some differences with your partners, that your parents were unexpectedly back. I mean, you've had a lot of upheaval in your life. Not to mention…us."

"Us? Her brows shot up. "What about us?"

That threw her, I could tell. Hell, it threw me too.

"I don't know about you, but I was shocked to see you. And that was only two days ago." It felt like years. Actually, this conversation—or was it an argument—felt like I'd known Ani for years.

It felt like no conversation I'd ever had before. Liv and I had had a very calm relationship. I'd definitely never had to try to talk her out of doing unlikely, improbable, wild things.

"Seeing me was shocking to you?"

She was looking at me differently now, curiously waiting,

tossing my curveball right back to me. She was asking me how I felt —about her, about *us*. "In an unexpected way," I said, stalling.

"In a good-shocking way or a bad-shocking way?" she pressed.

"Mostly good," I hedged. One look in her eyes and I knew I had to stop playing games. She deserved the truth. "I-I thought that I'd conjured you. That beautiful, confused almost-bride who had somehow ended up on that plane. I started out trying to help you, but it was you who ended up helping me. I felt sorry for you, but you were always going to be fine. And…" I squeezed my eyes shut. "You have conviction. You follow your heart. That's…impressive."

For once, she had no words. But I still had more to say. "You woke me up. You showed me that there was a way out of my quagmire of grief. I followed your light." I blew out a breath and sat down on an ugly blue vinyl bench between the elevators. "Except right now," I added, "I might be questioning your sanity."

She sat down next to me. "Maybe you should've been a lawyer instead of a doctor, counselor, the way you laid out that case. Also, you might be a little condescending, but you listened when I talked, that's for sure."

Fleetingly, I thought about all I'd just admitted. I felt raw and wrung out as I grabbed her by the shoulders, and searching her eyes, I said, "Of course I listened. And I hope you listen to me too. I'm not telling you what to do. I'm only trying to help you to think about how huge this decision would be."

"Anything is doable if you want it bad enough."

"Yes, but just because you can do something doesn't mean you should!"

Most people would be relieved not to have responsibility in a situation like this. Most of us would convince ourselves that everything would probably be okay. They'd be happy to pass the buck to someone—anyone—else. "Most people wouldn't ask for a burden like this," I said softly.

"She's a helpless little baby, not a burden." Ani sighed. "Look,

I can't explain how I feel." Her voice was full of conviction. "I just feel it. Deeply. I somehow feel that she's meant to be mine."

My worried expression must have given me away because she said, "You think I'm impulsive and do things on a whim. You think that maybe I'm someone who lets my emotions carry me away. But haven't you ever just *known* something? It seems impossible, it seems improbable, but it also seems like the rightest thing you've ever done. That's how I feel. Like I want to take my shot." She gave a little smile. And that's when I saw it—a look in her eyes —of complete calm and certainty.

Maybe I did think that she was overly driven by her emotions and also crazy to consider upending her life like this, but one thing was certain—she absolutely meant it. With every fiber of her being.

"Ani," I said. But she'd already taken off down the hall to find my mom, who was still sitting behind the nursing station.

"Ms. Lowenstein," she said, causing my mom to look up. "I wanted to talk with you about something."

"Of course." She looked up from the computer. "What is it?"

"What are the chances of me fostering the baby?"

I'd made it there just in time to see my mom level a surprised and skeptical look over her tortoiseshell readers. She said in a slow and careful tone, "A baby isn't a puppy or a novelty, my dear. We all have sympathy, but what this baby needs is a family. A *lifetime* commitment."

Oh, boy. My mom, despite her not-unkind tone, had *me* squirming, and I wasn't even the object of her reality check. Ani didn't squirm. She tilted up her head. Set her jaw. And said, respectfully but firmly, "How do I get considered to be her foster parent—with intent to adopt?"

I had to hand it to her; she wasn't intimidated by my mother's words, which Mom had not minced. Her resolve hadn't wavered.

My mom flicked her gaze at me, maybe to gauge the request. Or to wonder what on earth was my connection with this odd woman? I probably looked panicked. I *was* panicked, not so much for Ani, but for me. Maybe that was selfish, but I was only being honest. Starting something with Ani was one thing, but with a baby in the mix? I didn't have her impulsivity or her courage. I could barely handle myself.

"Have you fostered a baby before?" my mom asked in that same careful tone.

Oh no. Of course she hadn't. The process took months, unless you were a relative of the child needing placement and it was an emergency situation.

"No," Ani said doggedly. "But I'm willing to learn."

My mother took off her glasses and pinched her nose. Guess I knew where I got that habit from. "Becoming a foster parent takes a few months and involves home visits and inspections, a full health exam, examination of your financial records, and so on. So, unfortunately, if you aren't in the system—"

"Can she be fast-tracked?" I blurted. Because I must be insane too.

My mother leveled a gaze on me that said, *Are you really going there?* I could feel her worrying, just as she had about my loneliness, my isolation, my sadness—these years since Liv had been gone. Except that this seemed like the kind of worry a mother feels when she believes her son is thinking with other parts of his anatomy instead of his brain.

"That's usually the case for a family member when children need immediate placement because it's best to place them with someone they already know and love. In this case, even if we tried to fast-track you, our reasons are weak. The mother handed the baby over to you, but as a health care worker, *not* as the person she wanted to care for her baby. There's really no reason that you're a preferred choice."

"Yes, there is," Ani insisted. "I delivered her. I promised her mother I would look out for her."

"But she could have handed her over to any health care worker in the hospital. She had no special relationship with you. We need to find someone who can take the baby immediately. Every day that baby stays in the hospital without truly needing medical care is costly."

"I see. I understand." Ani paused. I could practically see her brain on fire, thinking, pondering, trying to figure this out. "Thank you," she said, then turned to me. "Thanks for meeting me here. I'll see you this week. I work in the ER Wednesday."

"Let me walk you out," I said.

"I'll be fine." Dale had gathered his coat and was on his way out too, and Ani hurriedly caught up with him.

As she walked down the hall, my mother and I had a staring contest. It felt like that time when I was thirteen and I'd decided that I was going to play guitar, stop doing my homework, and join a rock band.

She opened her mouth to speak, but suddenly Ani was back, leaning over the counter to talk to her again. "Look, Daria, one more thing before I go. I know you don't know me. But I—I believe in fate. For some reason, I was put there, in that moment, to deliver that baby into the world. And what I want might be unconventional and unorthodox, but I'm a great candidate for a lot of reasons."

She proceeded to enumerate them. Enthusiastically, I might add. "I have a great job. I have resources. I have enthusiasm. I work hard. I already know CPR and First Aid, don't drink— well, much—or do drugs. Unless you count caffeine. And yes, I'm single, but I understand what I'm getting into. I just—I just want to try. I want to present my case. I'm as worthy as anyone else."

"I will present your case," my mother said evenly. "That's all I can promise."

"Thank you." Ani turned to me. "Bye, Adam."

"Bye, Ani." I watched her walk down the hall and, this time, off the ward.

It felt like the silence after a hurricane blows through.

When I glanced at my mother, she was staring at me. "We have to talk."

~

"What on earth is going on between you two?" my mother demanded. "And I'm not just asking for fun."

As I pulled up a stool, sat down, and crossed my arms, I understood what she was asking. My mother had been a social worker for thirty-five years. She knew people. She had *influence.* "I'm not sure," I wavered.

She tossed up her hands. "I have no idea what that means." She wanted conviction, a yes or a no.

Mental snapshots ran through my mind, from last summer through now. I'd been coasting on the Ani train ever since, being pulled—mostly pleasantly, I had to admit—into whatever drama happened to be going on with her. But this—this was not a weeping-almost-bride-on-a-plane scenario. Or an attractive woman who needed a friend in a tropical island paradise. This involved a little *person.* This was life-altering.

This was something that only a crazy person or a saint would take on.

Gandhi. Mother Teresa. Malala.

I realized that even now that I'd been essentially a spectator. Noncommittal. I hadn't even asked myself the hard questions about how I really felt about Ani.

I didn't know her favorite food, her favorite color, or her favorite book.

But, I realized with a start, I knew her heart.

And I couldn't use my grief, my sadness, or my complete ineptitude at trying to move on with my life as an excuse not to get involved.

Ani was driven by some superpower that most humans didn't have. And I was in awe of it.

"You met this woman on a plane?" my mom asked.

I slowly nodded. "She'd just put a stop her wedding, and she somehow ended up on the plane alone for her honeymoon trip."

"Her parents are powerful donors," my mom said. "And I've heard people talk about that wedding. The expense. The catastrophe. Sounds like the parents didn't take the embarrassment well. But I won't judge them."

I barely heard her as I tapped a pen on the counter, trying to think. Who was powerful enough and might help Ani get credentialed or make an exception? As head of the ER, I had connections too. But not ones like the tiny but mighty woman in front of me.

"I see that doe-eyed expression," my mother said. "I know you want to help her. How badly?"

She was asking me—okay, forcing me—to take a stand. To beseech her to intervene on Ani's behalf.

I was doe-eyed?

"I mean, she was a wreck." I continued telling the story. I just wasn't sure how much I wanted to tell. "And all alone. I checked on her and made sure she ate and we—we spent some time together." And that was all I was going to say. Period.

My mom lifted a questioning brow but didn't ask anything more. "She's obviously sincere. But is she impulsive?"

"She's bighearted. Helen Rubenstein, the senior partner in her group, speaks very highly of her. Says she's well trained. Has great leadership qualities. The other night when she was working with me, she was nervous about delivering the baby by herself, but she did a great job." My mind wandered off. "She likes dogs. She brings medical journals and romance novels with her to work. She hates Bloody Marys. She—"

"Oh, Adam." My mom was shaking her head. "I don't need the dating-app version." She assessed me carefully. "You slept with her, didn't you?"

That was the thing about having a social worker mom. She never hesitated to talk to me openly about birth control, about sex.

About anything. I was certain the color of my face answered her question, so I moved on. "I've never met anyone who wasn't afraid to consider a huge, life-changing possibility like this. Most medical staff would simply be happy that *you* showed up to take the responsibility for this baby's future. You understand what I'm saying?"

She reached over and put her hand over mine so that I stopped tapping the pen. "I haven't seen you this invested in anything for a long time." She got a little teary, from relief or from worry, I wasn't sure.

"If you're asking me if we're romantically involved, I would say I'm one hundred percent not looking for a serious relationship. And I'm definitely not looking to be a sudden parent."

"If she gets the baby, what happens? Do you want to date her? Are you open to the possibility of dating someone with a newborn?"

I sat forward and tented my fingers together. "I'm not sure I can even bear being around a baby, to be honest. I'm just—not ready. Not for a baby. And not for a real relationship." I glanced up at my mom. "I've told her that—about the relationship."

She sighed. "Yet you think she should have the baby."

I knew what my mother was doing. She was weighing how important Ani was to me. Because my mother would do anything to help me start living my life again.

And that's what I was afraid of. Because, like Ani, my mother had superpowers too. She'd been a single mom raising me since after my dad took off when I was one. And much like Ani, she never hesitated to step in when there was a need.

"I know what you're thinking," I said. "It's too much. You're literally a day from retirement."

Now my mother crossed her arms. "Do you want her to have the baby, yes or no?"

My mom had fostered several babies when I was in college. But she'd said she'd never do it again because letting go tore out her heart.

"This isn't fair to you. I could help, but I couldn't handle being hands-on with the baby." I looked at my mother. "I'm being honest. There's got to be another way to do this."

"Well, I appreciate knowing your feelings," she said. "But what's the answer?"

Honestly, I hadn't made many choices about anything these past two years, except to take the Oak Bluff job and buy the only affordable house on the market.

She was still waiting for my answer. "Okay, fine. Yes, I want her to have the baby." Suddenly, something unfastened inside of me. I couldn't really describe it, except to say that it was like the feeling when you unloosen your shoes at the end of a long day. Put sweatpants on. Or the moment at night when your head hits the pillow, and you finally let go of the day. Ani would be a great mother for this baby. I knew it.

Strange, because I'd just created a boatload of complications for my mother, not to mention for myself. I vowed to help however I could.

"Then what are you still sitting there for?" My mother gave me an Are-you-sure-you're-smart-enough-to-be-a-doctor? look. "Go get her."

~

Ani

I was headed off the elevator and halfway down the glass-bridged corridor that connected the hospital to the parking deck when I heard footsteps behind me. I started and turned to find Adam running toward me. "I thought you were going to walk out with Dale," he said, a little out of breath.

"Because there's so much crime in Oak Bluff." I rolled my eyes and hit the big square button that opened the sliding glass doors to the parking deck.

Then I had a terrible thought—maybe he didn't follow me to be chivalrous. "Oh, my God, Adam. Did something happen to the baby?"

"No, no, nothing like that. My mother—my mom has an idea. You need to come back with me and talk with her."

"An idea? About the baby?" My emotions over the past hour had ping-ponged all over the place, from desperate to hopeful to completely hopeless. What he'd just said spiked them all the way back up again into the promising range. I seized his arm. Despite the chaos, I felt how hard it was, how corded the muscle. He was such a complicated man, but so good-hearted, even though he tended to hide it. Which complicated everything even more.

"What is it?" I asked. "What's the idea?"

He gripped my forearms. Again, I had the sense of cautiously restrained power.

Strong but gentle. Such a contrast from the Don't-eat-pizza-behind-the-desk Adam who ran the ER.

Who was this man who'd come running after me at midnight? Who didn't seem to think I was crazy to want that baby.

Well, at least not too crazy.

"I'll let her tell you everything. It's the nuclear option. She would foster the baby—if Children's Services agrees—until you could take over."

"Wait—your mother would *take the baby*?" I stared at him. She, a woman whom I barely knew, would take the baby until I potentially could?

"You'd have to negotiate the arrangements with her. I know you'll keep in mind that her retirement begins on Monday."

"Of course. But wh-why would she do that? She doesn't even know me." I was tearing up—again. "You did this. You convinced her." There was no other explanation.

"No, I didn't." He held up his hands. "Really. It wasn't me." He turned a little red, which told me everything. "Listen, this may or may not work. But it's your best shot."

He'd intervened for me, and he wasn't even taking credit. I started to flat-out cry. Right there on the bridge, I jumped straight into his arms and squeezed him tight.

I felt his hands slide around my waist. I felt him pull me in. I felt his muscle, and all of me remembered all of him. And it was all too much.

I pulled back and searched his face. He looked serious. And a little worried. It occurred to me that he'd been caught up in all of this. That I'd been thinking a lot about myself and what I wanted and not about anyone else. "Why did you do this?" I asked in a hoarse whisper. "We barely know each other."

"That doesn't matter. What matters is that you want to give this baby a life. So go for it."

"Adam, I can't thank you enough. I'll hire someone to help your mom watch the baby while I'm at work. I'll do the nights. I swear I'll do everything I can to make this easy on her."

"She's a lot like you, but I worry about her. Taking care of a baby is a lot—for both of you."

I took up his hand. "I understand." I paused. "All of this has been a lot. I just wanted to say that I don't expect—"

He cut me off. "I haven't done anything I didn't want to do."

"Please let me finish. I need you to know that I don't expect you to get involved with any of this. I'm not looking for love or a relationship or a sudden baby daddy or anything like that. But I- I'm so grateful for what you've done."

He smiled. "That's what friends do."

I realized right then, with a little bit of melancholy, that friendship was all he could give. All he was capable of giving. In this wild situation, that was a lot, I told myself. He'd given me the kindest, most generous gift of all—his belief in me. And that is what I would accept. And try not to want more.

# Chapter Ten

Ani

"I have a ten-month-old with a 104 fever and a runny nose," Penelope announced, approaching me as I left an exam room on Monday. "His fever is really high, and he's been sleeping a lot and not eating. I just can't tell if he's got an ear infection or not. Every time I try to look in there, he screams and his eardrums turn flaming red. Will you take a look?"

Helen, my other partner, who was sixty, glanced up from the central desk that was in the center of our office where she was charting. She shot me an ominous look. A Penelope-is-not-cutting-it look.

Oh heck. I wished Penelope would be more subtle about her requests for help. Because Helen's looks were getting darker and darker.

In response, I smiled pleasantly at her and at Pen. "Sure, of course."

I'd been going nonstop since 8:30. It was nearing lunchtime, and my stomach was in knots because I had to tell my partners that I was possibly going to be a mom before the week's end, as Children's Services would be determining the baby's fate—and my fate—sometime over the next several days. This news was going to upend our already rocky practice. Every minute felt like an hour. My stomach butterflies had butterflies.

I'd been suffering in this practice for ten months, trying to save Penelope's ass and placate Helen, who was a brilliant clinician, worked at half-effort because she could and because I worked doubly hard. Helen was completely *sink or swim*, had no compassion for Pen, and never helped her. So that fell on me too.

"Hey, you two," I said before I walked into the exam room with Pen, "I need to talk to you during lunch, okay?"

"What lunch?" Helen asked. "There's a nasty flu bug going around. We're double-booked all afternoon."

"It will only take a few minutes," I said in a level tone. "It's important."

We often worked through lunch. Or at least I did. I knew that Helen snuck into her office, closed the door, and ate regardless of what was going on. I knew this because I smelled the delicious lunches that she warmed up in the microwave each day.

She must have never played sports, partaken in student government, or joined any extracurricular club involving working with people because she earned zero stars from me on her team-playing skills.

I followed Pen into the exam room, bracing to find a lethargic toddler clinging to consciousness. Instead, a blond curly-haired little guy in a diaper was drooling and noisily crinkling up the exam table paper while his mother stood guard next to him. He looked up with giant blue eyes and shot us a giant, mostly toothless grin.

Oh, joy. I blew out a pent-up breath. Whatever little Henry had, it wasn't that bad.

"Well, hello," I said. "Aren't you handsome?" I turned to the tired-looking woman standing against the exam table. "I'm Ani Green, one of the doctors. Is it okay if I have a peek in Henry's ears? It gets challenging to tell what's going on when a child cries."

I went on to ask Henry's mom if he was tugging on his ears, rubbing them against his bed, crying when he lay down, or crying at night in general.

No, no, no, and no. Plus he'd been around his cousin, who probably had that flu bug going around.

I turned to Pen. "Were you able to tell if there's any bulging? Air fluid level? Poor movement of the eardrum?" These were the questions we asked med students and residents. I asked them now because I wanted to know what she'd seen so I could help her figure it out herself.

"It was bright red," she said, "and I couldn't get a good seal to puff some air in there."

I tackled Henry—gently of course—and did my job. It wasn't ever easy. Examining eardrums was pretty much a war zone. You had to be quick, confident, and have a good eye. I got coughed on a few times, but other than that, got out unscathed.

Pediatricians had Olympic-strength immunity, by the way. If I had a dime for the number of times I got sneezed, drooled, or snotted on, I'd be a bazillionaire.

"I feel pretty confident that his ears are normal," I said when I came up for air.

"Oh, that's terrific," Henry's mom said as I handed him to her.

Back in the hall, Pen said, "I hate to miss something with that high of a fever. Maybe I should treat him with an antibiotic anyway."

"Penelope." As I leveled my gaze on her, I could see that she was practically twitching with nerves. "Henry doesn't have an ear infection. He most likely has a virus."

"Are you sure?" Her expression was pained.

Ah, that was the golden question. As a doctor, if you couldn't live with uncertainty, you wouldn't last long. Funny, but they didn't teach you that in med school. For years you got nearly perfect grades in every single course you undertook because you learned the black-and-white answers, A, B, C, or D. Then you got confronted by a human person who often didn't play by the rules.

Humans almost never played by the rules. Especially men. That was why I sucked at relationships.

And Penelope didn't handle uncertainty well. She wanted yes and no answers. But I kept hoping that with coaching and encouragement, she'd turn the corner and become a great doctor.

"I'm ninety-nine percent sure," I said. "And you know why."

"Right." She didn't sound like she knew. But I knew she knew, because she'd aced every exam from every prestigious institution she'd attended with flying colors.

"Tell me why." I put my hands up, poised to count the reasons off on my fingers.

"Um, he looks good."

"Exactly!" Good answer. "He was smiling, he was drinking, he was playing. His exam was negative. He's probably going to be just fine."

In medicine, you played the odds. You weren't God, and you had to make tough choices, a million of them, every single day. Sometimes you had to be a cowboy, and other times you had to be a diligent professor.

"What if we missed an early otitis?" She wrung her hands. "I just—don't want anything to happen. Maybe I'll do a blood count to reassure myself that this is viral."

I examined her carefully. She was a clinical decision-making wreck.

Finally, I simply told her what to do. "Counsel the mom to use Tylenol, especially at night, and call if Henry gets worse. It's the best we can do."

She gave a grateful nod. "Okay. Yes, I see. Thank you, Ani."

She went to finish up with the family while I collapsed into a chair in our little conference room. I tugged at my blouse collar. I was sweating. I hadn't made any waves since I started here. I'd played by all the rules.

But I was about to instigate a tsunami.

Helen sat a few seats away eating a sandwich and studying a stack of brochures of warm and wonderful places, Turks and Caicos among them.

Oh. As my mind did so many times through the day, it turned to Adam.

He'd been so wonderful. He'd supported me and helped make my case.

My blind passion to rescue this baby had an unintended consequence. It was about to kill my relationship—maybe budding relationship?—with Adam. If it was budding, which was a bit unclear. But what normal man would want an insta-girlfriend with an insta-kid? Add a *grieving* man into that mix and you got...well, whatever you got, it wasn't a sudden big happy family. That was a no-brainer.

But that was what I wanted, right? I did not want a relationship.

I was undertaking this huge life-altering event—and I had no intention of asking a man to come along with me.

And this man couldn't.

And I definitely didn't need him to.

Even though he'd been there for me more than I ever expected.

I found myself thinking back to Turks and Caicos. Thinking about how he'd touched me. So gently, so carefully. So...magically. I was reliving that—a lot. But also wanting to do other things— like, hang out with him. Ask him things about himself. Touch his nice hair and feel his muscly muscles.

And then I thought of Dr. No-Pizza-Rule, and I wondered how both Adams could be wrapped up in that same gorgeous bod.

"I'm sorry, what did you say?" I asked. Why was I thinking

these thoughts when I was about T-minus-ten seconds away from upending all of our lives?

Helen swallowed and set down her sandwich. "I said, this thing with Penelope isn't getting any better."

"No, it's not," I admitted.

"You said you'd work with her, but she's using you like a crutch."

I hated those *You* sentences. Ascribing blame. Not saying *We*. As if this were my problem alone.

"I'm trying to make her think through the decision-making. Maybe that will help."

"She hasn't got the pediatrician gene," Helen said. "I'm thinking we might need to schedule a meeting. The writing is on the wall."

I froze. I couldn't allow this situation to get to that. I knew how much Penelope, as a single mom, needed this job. Plus, she was nice. She just needed confidence.

Unfortunately, confidence didn't come in a pill. Or a syringe. If it did, I'd booster her right up with one.

"Hey, what's up?" Penelope asked as she blew into the room and sat down, a little breathless. "I gave that mom my cell phone in case she needs to call me."

I bit back my words because if I said something, Helen would pounce. I decided to tell her privately later that if she valued any part of her life, then never, ever give a patient her private number. And that's not even counting the documentation and malpractice reasons.

I bit the insides of my cheeks until I tasted blood. *Please stop talking, Pen,* I wanted to say. I tried to signal this with my eyes but to no avail.

"I told her she can call me anytime."

"We're actually going to have a little talk about performance," Helen said.

"No," I said. Both of my partners stared at me. I'd never been this...*firm*...the entire time I'd worked here. "Something—something's come up. With me." I cleared my throat. "Something important."

Just then, Edith, our sweet, gray-haired, bespectacled office manager, knocked on the door, waving a good old-fashioned pink slip, the way we still received our phone messages. "Here you go, Dr. Green. A message. They said it's urgent." She handed it to me. It was from Children's Services, and it read, *Home inspection tomorrow. Case worker coming at 4. Be ready."*

My heart leapt and sank at the same time—basically weaving like a basketball inside my chest. Up because something was getting done! Children's Services was looking at my case, and a decision would follow.

And down because my house was...a disaster. And making it not a disaster by tomorrow would be...impossible.

"Oh, Dr. Green," Edith said, "we heard from Dale that you're working to adopt that little baby. How's that going?"

Did I say Edith was sweet? I meant that she was a devil in disguise.

"Adopt a baby?" Helen asked, her sandwich literally falling from her mouth. *Ew.*

Pen added, "The baby that was surrendered?"

I nodded. "If things work out, I'm going to be able to be a foster mom. With the potential to adopt. That's what I needed to discuss today—I have a plan for finding a replacement for myself for the next month or so." Which was all I could afford, since you had to be an adoptive mother to get real leave. "Would you like to hear it?"

"Oh, Ani," Penelope said. "That's amazing. Congratulations." She was so nice. I wished that I could figure out how to help her.

"You're a foster parent?" Helen asked with a frown.

"Daria Lowenstein is going to supervise me. She'll be the foster parent on record. And hopefully I'll get a chance to take over."

"We'll never find a locum now," Helen said. "If we're lucky, we can find people who are finishing their residencies and looking for a job. Everyone good is already hired by this time of year."

"I'll hire a headhunter," I said, although I needed someone *fast*.

"Someone inquired about a job," Helen said. "Edith, who was that guy who called the other day? He said he was headed out to LA in a few months but was looking to work in Oak Bluff until then."

"Dylan Baird," Edith confirmed, staring straight at me. She ran to her desk and returned with a few sheets of paper. "I've got his CV right here."

I closed my eyes. Edith had been around town long enough to know why.

"Ani, are you okay?" Pen asked, immediately picking up on something.

"I know Dylan," I hedged.

Pen practically jumped in her seat. "Is he a good doc? He's a warm body. Let's hire him!"

"Um, I'm not so sure—"

"Why not?" Pen flipped through the papers. "He's from a great program. He's got great recs."

Dylan had been my college sweetheart, the reason I'd applied to med school. He was a free spirit, very West-Coastian in his heart, very bohemian. "He's my ex," I said.

"Ex-boyfriend?" Helen asked. "Get over it."

"No, ex-*husband*," I said.

Penelope looked up. "Oh."

Helen sighed heavily. "Did he cheat on you? Lie? Steal?"

"No." But that didn't mean he wasn't irritating. And after ten years, I didn't want him back in my life, taking care of my patients, having to communicate with me.

"Then we need to call him for an interview," Helen said. "Any objections?"

"Helen is right," Pen seconded. "Can we call him?"

I couldn't believe it. It was a rare show of solidarity. But all that I could think of was that a case worker was coming tomorrow to vet me as a suitable parent and would soon find that I had no crib, no car seat, no...baby anything but also *no furniture* in my house. That made Dylan the least of my worries. "Okay, fine," I said, surrendering. "Call him."

Chapter Eleven

Adam

"Ani, you in there?" I asked as I peeked into the screen door of her house on Monday after work. I'd tried the McClellans first, then I'd jogged around the corner and down the street, dog leash in hand, to find all the windows open and figured she might be home. It was a beautiful spring evening, birds singing a riot, buds bursting out everywhere.

Ani's house was a sweet little Cape Cod, with gray stone and white trim, but the yard was overgrown, and the brick walkway was too.

I told myself not to look around. After all, I was only here to give the dog a good run like I usually did in the evenings.

I was here to do my duty. To Arnold. That was it, and I was sticking to that story. There was no answer, but the wood part of the door was wide open, so I tried again. "Ani! You in there? I thought maybe Arnie would like to come with me on my evening jog. Is he in there with you?"

"Um, yes. Yes, he is," she said, appearing briefly at the door. "Arnold!" she called. There was a pause. "I'll be right back."

"Aren't you going to invite me in?" I called through the screen as she went from room to room in search of the dog. I said it jokingly, but honestly, she was acting a little strange.

She ran back to the door, dog in tow. "We can come out to you," she said in an overly cheery voice. "Let me grab his leash."

She left again before I told her I already had one. So I stepped up and opened the door and let myself in.

The smell of fresh paint hit me immediately. I followed it through the empty living room into the kitchen. The old cabinets had been painted a fresh white. Blue and white Delft tiles were scattered amid white ones above the stovetop and in the tile back-splash around a big farm sink. I'd seen the same antique tiles lining the surround of a cozy little fireplace in the living room. The appliances were old but white, so they looked okay. "Cute place," I said, genuinely appreciating the wood floors, the detailed ceiling moldings.

As Ani clipped the leash to Arnie's collar, I glanced at her phone, which was sitting on the little peninsula. I couldn't help but notice it was open to the Pottery Barn website.

I cleared my throat. "Are you...ordering furniture?"

She started to hand me the leash until she saw the one in my hand. I set mine on the counter. "Well, I did order furniture—two months ago. But unfortunately, the delivery got delayed two weeks." She paused. Outwardly, she was calm, but I detected a slight twitch around her eyes. She was biting down on her lower lip. And she had a sense of nervous energy about her. "Have a nice jog."

"Okey dokey," I said in the cheeriest manner possible. As I took her leash, our fingers brushed the slightest bit. I noticed that hers were cold despite the pleasant evening. On the counter sat a lone granola bar wrapper. I was already wondering if she'd had dinner, yet I knew in my gut that she hadn't.

I forced myself to turn away.

This—whatever our relationship was—was not a carefree, no-strings-attached kind. It was loaded with more hidden grenades than a battlefield. Now more than ever, she needed calm, strength, and certainty. She needed anti-me. So I'd made a conscious decision to back away while she prepared for the baby.

"I'll be back in half an hour," I said, letting myself out the door.

"Okay, see ya." She turned immediately back to her phone.

When I got about twenty feet away, I slowed my steps, much to Arnie's chagrin. I thought I heard something.

It sounded like...a sob. I kept listening, but I didn't hear it again.

Arnold tugged. At first politely, then he yanked the chain hard. And shot me a look. *You promised.*

"Okay, buddy, okay." But my feet were already backtracking.

My head told me the logical truth. That there was a lot going on here.

What was it about this woman that made me defy logic?

I peeked in the window. Which I know was unfair, but there was Ani, sitting at the peninsula in the empty kitchen, rubbing her temples. "Can't I pay more for an expedited delivery?" she said into the phone. "I really need the furniture this week." She hung up the phone and lay her head down on the counter. And this time I confirmed that her sob was real.

I ran back to the screen door and called in, "Hey, Ani, I think Arnold needs a drink of water."

I let the dog into the house and dropped his leash, and I swear he shot me a pissed-off look. I ignored him and took a seat on a stool next to her. "What's going on?"

"Nothing for you to worry about, okay? Go. Shoo." She waved her hand at me.

I touched her arm and made her face me. "I know something's wrong."

"It's all good."

I nudged her elbow. "Come on. Out with it."

"You *definitely* do not want to be involved with this one."

My brain knew that. But my feet kept coming back for more. "I'm a great problem solver. Tell me."

"My first interview with Children's Services is tomorrow."

"Tomorrow?" I looked around at the empty house. I saw the problem.

"They're coming to check out my house, to make sure it's safe and ready. Only all my furniture has been delayed." She glanced at her phone. "I think if I leave now, I can make it to Bob's Furniture Emporium by eight. She started scrolling. "Let me see when they close."

"Have you tried moving the interview?"

She shook her head solemnly. "They want to get the baby out of the hospital ASAP. I literally can't say, 'I want this baby, but I'm unprepared, and I have nothing in my house.' No furniture. No baby things. *Nothing*." She wrung her hands. "My friends are coming this weekend to help me shop. And I think Children's Services might be okay with me saying it'll take a few days to collect the baby stuff. But how am I going to get furniture in here tomorrow by four?" She paused. "Maybe I could buy a few things from Facebook Marketplace and use your truck to pick them up?" She put her head in her hands. "What was I thinking? This is all too much."

"One more question. What about my mom's house?"

"We agreed that the baby would stay here. It's not fair to ask her to rearrange her entire house now."

"I get it." It was funny, but all my most dire warnings to not get involved dissolved into thin air when I saw her so upset. I was one second away from taking her into my arms, holding her, and telling her we'd somehow figure this out when we heard a tap on the door.

"Yoo-hoo, anyone home?" came a singsong voice.

Ani went pale. "Oh, not now," she whispered.

I turned to see a sharply dressed woman at the screen door. As soon as she let herself in, I immediately recognized the resemblance to Ani—blond hair, but straight and smartly styled, not curly like Ani's; the same pale blue eyes except she looked like she'd stepped out of a fashion catalog for wealthy older women; tidy, wrinkle-free ankle jeans with a crease; red flats, red nails, elegant makeup.

"Oh good, you're home from work," she said to Ani, her tone clipped. "I had a hospital board meeting, and everyone was talking about Dr. Green. Apparently, I'm the last person in town to know that my single daughter is about to adopt a baby."

Uh oh. This was trouble. Because this woman hadn't even acknowledged me yet.

I kept thinking of what my mom had said. *Parents were big donors. Embarrassed by the wedding fiasco.* And of course, they'd put a weeping wreck of an almost-bride on that plane. I had to admit, I wasn't pre-programmed to like Ani's mom.

"There's been a lot going on, Mom," Ani said. "Come in and I'll catch you up. And meet my friend, Adam."

There was that *friend* word again, which tended to never sit right with me. Ani's mom gave me a quick perusal. "Oh, hi, Dr. Lowenstein. I recognize you from your photo in the hospital newsletter a few weeks ago. Welcome to Oak Bluff." She extended her hand. "I'm Julia Green. I just got the auxiliary to sign off on new otoscopes for your ER."

I stood up and greeted her. "You're the president of the board, aren't you? Thank you very much for that. We really needed the update in technology." I smiled and reached out to shake her hand. She had a firm handshake. Okay, so maybe she wasn't a blond version of Maleficent after all. But I still wasn't completely sold.

"Adam's here to give Arnold a good workout," Ani said. I think to give me an escape route.

"Please, don't let us stop you," Ani's mom said to me. Then

she turned back to her daughter. "This is an enormous decision. And you've made it all by yourself?"

Ani stiffened. "Well, Mom, the last time I checked, I was a full adult."

"One who just might be prone to making impulsive decisions."

Okay, I'd been officially sidelined, but I was never good at taking the hint anyway. I cleared my throat and smiled at Ani, trying to send her support vibes across the few feet between us. "Ani and I were working together in the ER when a teenager arrived in active labor. Ani delivered the baby."

Julia lifted a perfect brow. "I heard that."

"She did a great job, too. But then the mother legally surrendered the baby. I think it's pretty incredible that Ani wants to foster her." I wasn't just blowing smoke. I did feel that way. Ani *was* incredible, although sometimes I felt that she didn't believe it herself. And maybe her mom didn't either.

Positioned as she was slightly behind her mom, Ani rolled her eyes to signal that I was really laying it on thick. I shrugged.

Ani's mom sighed. "Dr. Lowenstein—Adam—I can see that your head is in the clouds too. Neither of you has any idea what she's getting into. She's going to need a lot of help." I felt Ani prickle as her mother was now exclusively talking to me. "Hopefully, she'll find caring for a newborn for a few days will flush all this wild adoption thinking right out of her system."

"Mom," Ani said, waving her hands in front of her mom. "I'm right here."

Then a weird thing happened. Arnie walked straight over to Ani and sat down—right at her feet. A show of solidarity.

The dog was in love with her too.

Did I say *too*?

I respected and admired her. But not love. I didn't do love anymore. I rubbed my chest over my sternum. Because it felt a little strange.

Ani reached down and patted good old Arnold on the head, who had suddenly proven that he was a very useful dog, after all. "Mom, I have to pass a bunch of tests to get the baby. And one of them is tomorrow."

I did what I am known to do best—act. And turn on the charm, which I have to admit, I was pretty rusty at. I steered her mom away from the table and toward the little living room. "If anyone can make this work, Ani can. Because she's amazing. But you're absolutely right. She's going to need help. *Lots* of help."

I didn't have to look at Ani to feel the invisible daggers hitting my back.

"I *know* that my daughter is amazing," her mom said. "But she's also impervious to the amount of work some of her decisions entail."

"I understand how hard caring for a newborn is, Mom," Ani said. "I deal with new moms and babies every day. I feel really good about this."

Ani's mom cast a worried glance in my direction. Which I deflected because I wanted to make it clear that I was Ani's ally, not hers. "Maybe you can talk some sense into her," she said to me.

Ani, with her hands balled into fists, looked like she was about to murder someone, and I wasn't sure if it was going to be her mom or me. "Great idea," I said, "but we're going to need your help. Are you free right now?"

"Of course I'm free." She tossed up her hands. "That's why I came over here."

"Great." I punched some numbers into my phone. "Julia, would you mind ordering some dinner for us on my Italian Stallion app?" That was the best Italian in town, and they did carryout. "Ani, you can sit down and make a list of all the items you need for the baby. And I—I will take care of the furniture problem. And pick up our food."

Another incredulous look from Ani.

I shot her a frown. "Oh ye of little faith." I was great—make that *terrific*—at rolling in and taking care of things. Why would she not let me unleash my secret talent?

"Can we talk for a minute?" Ani got up and literally dragged me outside by my shirt. So predictable. Also, Arnie scrambled right after us. Apparently, he didn't want to be inside with Julia either. I managed to grab the end of his leash because all we needed right now was a lost dog to chase after again.

On second thought, he was getting awfully proprietary. Like he belonged to us or something. What would the McClellans say when they got home in a few days?

Ani reached down and pulled the granola bar wrapper out of his mouth, which he must have skimmed from the counter, and shoved it in her pocket.

"You—are mansplaining again," Ani said, out in the wild, unkempt yard. She was feisty, angry, waving her hands in gestures not unlike her mother's. "Jumping into action. Taking over." She poked my chest. "And *siding with my mother.*"

I couldn't help grinning. Because she was no longer on the verge of tears, a huge improvement. "I'm sorry, but that situation was getting a little toxic. Your mother wants to understand you. She wants to help."

"How, Dr. Psychologist, how do you translate *Oh, Ani, this is sooo much* into *I love you and I want to help you?*"

"A cry for help?" I got a glare for that. "Look, do you trust me?"

She folded her arms. "No." She paused. "Absolutely not."

"Oh, come on." I gave her my most charming look. "Let me take care of the furniture problem."

"No! First of all, it's *my* furniture problem. You can't just saunter in here with your big muscles and take over."

I crossed my arms. And flexed my big muscles. She *definitely* was noticing. "I'm a man of action. And I have a great idea. Just say yes."

"Tell me what it is."

"I can't. Because...it's a little nuclear."

She blinked. I held her by the shoulders. It was all I could do not to pull her into me and just hold her for a minute until she calmed down. Except that would have the opposite effect on me. I stepped back and said, "Give me an hour. I'll get back with you. Please."

"Why are you doing this?"

Yes, great question. Why was I here, involved, helping, when I knew that once that little baby came, I would not be able to stay?

But I had a secret weapon in my pocket, and I couldn't not use it. "Because you complimented my muscles," I said. "Now go... make some lists." I waved her off. "And send your mom on an errand. She wants to be useful. I can tell."

She opened her mouth to protest (also predictable), but I lightly held my finger over her lips. Which was a little forward and veered a little from the friend vibe. But I was on a fiery roll, I guess.

She blinked. And I...well, I froze, tangled up in her gaze, and realized that I was touching her lips. Her beautiful, soft, full lips. Heat rushed through me. I leaned forward without even thinking about it, needing to place my lips on hers.

The dog barked. I caught my breath. Tore my gaze away. Quickly dropped my hand.

I looked down to see him next to Ani, barking at me as if to say, *She's mine.* I know when someone's in competition for a woman. But in this case, maybe Arnie saved me from a big mistake.

Before Ani could utter a protest, I walked away, Arnie in tow. We'd missed our jog, but I felt certain that a ride in the car would pump him right up. Somewhat recovered, I called over my shoulder, "Be back soon." I winked at her as I pulled my pickup out of her drive. "Oh, and have fun with your mom."

Chapter Twelve

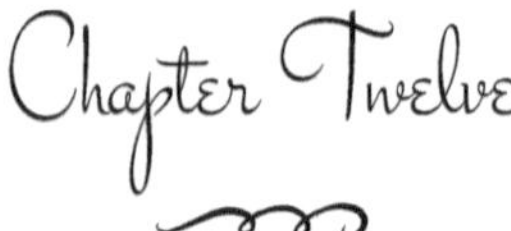

Ani

"Who is he, Ani?" my mom asked.

She was rummaging through my fridge. I slid in front of her and closed the door before she could examine the contents in full detail. "Adam? Just a friend. His...his wife died. And he moved here to be nearer to his mom."

"That's sad." She folded her arms. "Just a friend?"

"Just a friend," I confirmed. But my insides told me otherwise. My heart was pounding, and my lips were still tingling from his touch. *He'd touched me on the lips.* And it was full-on erotic. It had directed my mind away from the fact that I was losing it, upset with my mom, upset with Pottery Barn, and upset with myself for this predicament.

Adam was here, giving me his calm presence and his support. Again.

What did I do for him? I felt like he was always bailing me out, rescuing me.

Minutes earlier I'd been starving, but now it felt as if there was a roller coaster full of screaming riders with their hands high in the air, zipping around the circumference of my stomach.

"You're flushed," my mom said.

My hands flew to my cheeks. "I am not."

Her lips turned up in her I-know-you-better-than-you-know-yourself smile. "Okay, well, I know Daria is helping you." She opened the fridge again and pulled out a jar of pickles. "I wish you'd told me all of this." She placed it in the sink. "Instead of me having to find out at the hospital. You hate pickles."

"They're Mia's from when we made grilled cheese. I left you a voicemail," I said weakly. "You never called me back."

The pickles went down the disposer with a harsh grinding noise. "The voicemail said, 'Call me sometime,' not 'I'm adopting a baby and becoming a single mom.'"

"Okay, fine. I'm sorry, Mom. The truth is that I didn't know how to tell you."

She spun around. "Ani, I'm your mother. Why do you feel that you can't tell me?"

All this remorse I had over not handling my relationships well —I had to fix this, starting with my mom. I didn't know how to say things, important things that were difficult to say. This terrible flaw had led me to the altar with the wrong man, seconds away from a giant mistake.

I stood up straight. I'd made this scary decision, and now it was time to stick to my guns. "I know how this looks, especially after what happened with the wedding. But Mom, I've never felt so sure of anything. That tiny baby—so helpless." I closed my eyes, feeling the tug even now. "I just felt something. Something big. I—I can't explain it otherwise."

Oh geez. I looked into my mom's eyes, which were so much like my own. In them I saw something that she didn't usually show —vulnerability.

I capitalized on the moment by grabbing her hand. "Mom. It's been a hard year. I'm doing my best to start over and make up for the trouble—"

"You don't need to make up for any trouble," she said quietly, squeezing my hand. "I don't know why you keep saying that." She turned back into the fridge and pulled out a black banana, far past its prime, and pitched it into the trash.

I held my breath. There were reasons I kept apologizing, reasons I'd been afraid to bring up with my mom. And her sweeping everything away probably wasn't going to help us get to the bottom of them.

My mother surveyed me with her gaze, so familiar to me. Often critical, but sometimes wise. I wished that we could arrive at some kind of equilibrium. Finally, she spoke. "I would think that simply calming down after everything instead of starting a completely different adventure would be wiser."

Oh, my mother. She looked so great with a tan. Why on earth would she move back here to Wisconsin, to a place that had a four-month growing season?

That was the problem with us. We didn't scrape the bottom of the ugly emotion bowl. If I was a conflict-avoider, I'd learned from the best.

I tried to lay it out as truthfully as possible. "I can't explain this situation in any other way except that I know that this is right for me. I'm the one who is right for this baby. I want to be the one to love her and raise her and give her the best life ever."

I drew in a deep breath. "I want you to be a part of that, Mom. But you have to let me show you that this is right for me. I'm sorry I didn't tell you right away. It's been a whirlwind of a few days. It's an unusual situation, and there are no guarantees. A lot of people are waiting for babies. It may not even happen."

"Okay. All right. I believe you." She threw up her hands and hugged me tightly. When she was done, her eyes were watery. "I can see you're determined, and when you're determined, you can do anything you set your mind to."

She dug into the fridge once again, swiped at her eyes, and extracted my six-pack of hard seltzers, the final thing left, and examined them carefully. "Hmm. Are these any good? Because I'm taking them home."

She put them on the counter next to her purse. "We certainly don't want any liquor in your fridge for the visit tomorrow." She gathered the seltzers and her purse. "I'm going to do a quick store run. I think it will look better if you have some real food in there."

"Okay, thank you."

"You're welcome." She made a move toward the door and then stopped. "Also—I want to be involved with your life. I want to help. Let me, okay? I love you."

"I'm going to name her Rosalie," I said.

That stopped her in her tracks. The silence lasted so long I thought my mom didn't hear me.

"Oh, Ani," she finally said, breaking down crying. "Your grandma would be so honored."

Then I was crying and nodding, and we were hugging. I had a sudden impulse to grab back my seltzers, but I refrained and focused on giving this conversation one final shot. "Mom, I love you too. I can face this challenge. And—I'd like your help."

We stood there like that, together for a while. It wasn't bad. Actually, it was kind of nice.

"Hmm," she said a little later as she carried my seltzers out the door. "Seems like you might be facing two challenges. The baby and a very handsome and wildly concerned ER doctor."

Adam

"I literally must be desperate for food if I agreed to change out of my sweats and pull this feat together in three hours that I'm not even sure is possible," my sister Anita said.

I squeezed her shoulder as I pulled up in front of Ani's house. "I can't tell you how much this means to me. If anyone can do this, you can."

"You've been telling me that my entire pregnancy."

I had been telling her that. Among other things, like recommending that she tell her baby daddy, who was a doctor serving abroad in the army, that she was pregnant. But she'd flat-out refused, even though she had just six more weeks to go. She'd surely regret keeping that secret from him. But she was from a long line of stubborn Lowensteins, and there was no changing her mind.

"And you've done it, haven't you?" I said as I turned off my truck. "Your business is exploding."

Anita heaved a sigh. "Yada yada. We eat first, and then I work, all right?"

"Totally," I said with a grin, then ran around to help her out of the car.

I offered her a hand up. She reached forward, grabbed the carryout bag, and handed it to me. Then she took a big breath and heaved herself up, refusing my hand. "This woman must mean a lot to you if you're going through all this trouble to help her."

If she could be stubborn, so could I. "She's a neighbor and a colleague."

She scanned my face, reading me as only an older sister can. "Ri-ight."

"I like Ani a lot, but I'm not getting involved a relationship. Especially one where a baby is concerned."

She searched my face. "Just to be clear, you're going to love *my* small child, right?"

"That's different. Don't even ask that."

"I'm sure taking the step to love anyone again is scary. But a baby is just...a sweet innocent baby." She poked me in the chest, proving that siblings never lose their annoyance quotient. "I fully expect you to go full-blown uncle mode on me. In fact, I'm counting on it."

"I promise to be the best uncle ever." And I would, because I'd do anything for my sister. "There's nothing going on between us. Okay?"

"Okay, okay." She eyed me with the wisdom of someone who knew me inside and out. "You have a savior complex. You can't resist helping anyone you love. That's the story I'm personally going with."

I ignored that because she was my sister, and I could. I closed the truck door and led us to the house. I wish I could describe the look on Ani's face when she saw my very pregnant sister standing there in jeans and a flannel shirt, her long hair up in a bun-thingy, looking like a pregnant version of Joanna Gaines.

"Ani, this is—"

My sister barged forward and held out her hand. "Anita. I'm his big sister, I'm eight months pregnant, and I have dinner."

"Nice to meet you," Ani said, a giant smile on her face as she opened the door. "Let's eat."

My sister walked right in and started scoping out the place. That was the thing I loved about Anita—she didn't care who liked her, but nearly everyone did. "Did he tell you? I'm a house stager. I think I can get some furniture in here for you ASAP."

"ASAP as in, today?" Ani asked.

"If I can eat first, it's possible. And if we find some strapping guys to haul some couches." Anita did pack away two pieces of lasagna—"One for me, one for the baby," she'd said, but then she got right to work, walking around, taking photos, measuring things.

"Is your vibe 'Grandma of the '90s' or 'mid-century chic'?" she asked Ani. "I think I can handle a complete furniture set with either of those vibes."

"Hmmm," Ani answered thoughtfully. "What's Grandma of the 90s?"

"Checks, ducks, ruffles, mauve, that kind of thing."

"Aw, that's just like Grandma's house," Ani said to her mom.

"Ani likes traditional with a twist," Julia said. "Cottagey. No mauve. And definitely no ducks." She paused. "Did I get that right?"

Ani seemed surprised her mom had asked. "I loved Gram's house," Ani said to her mother with a sigh. "But okay. No ducks." But then she asked her mom, "Whatever happened to those duck cookie jars Grandma had?"

"If I know their whereabouts, I will never tell," her mother said.

"How do you feel about mid-century?" Anita asked.

"I hate that orange and purple stuff," I said before I realized that my opinion didn't count. After all, I wasn't going to be living here. I mean, that would be ridiculous, right?

"Ignore him," Anita said. "His aesthetic is dull gray. Inside and out." Then she shot me an evil grin.

I caught Ani's expression. Her eyes were smiling, if that makes sense. She was amused. Entertained. She liked my sister, I could tell. Most importantly, she was not currently stressing out. And that somehow made me very happy, savior complex or not.

"Okay, chicky, my job is done here. I'll do my best." Anita set down her clipboard. Do you trust me?"

"Yes," Ani said, but she was still looking at me. And her eyes were still doing that smiley thing that was doing something to me besides making me feel relieved. I felt this pull, this feeling like I could somehow read her mood, her emotions—and it was making me want to send everyone away and do a long, slow repeat of that last night in Turks and Caicos.

"I'm taking your truck," my bratty sister said to me. "Send the strapping guys to my warehouse as soon as you round them up."

I gave her a salute. Then I went to round up some friends with muscles.

~

Ani

It was almost midnight, and Adam was still unwrapping HomeGoods bags and mumbling things to himself like, "I'll have Arnie help me gather some sticks from the yard tomorrow. A fire would look cheery during the interview."

He was totally carried away while I sprawled, exhausted, on the new blue and white checked couch. (We'd gone with a modified grandma aesthetic after all.) But he just kept…staging. He was making a grouping in the corner of the dining room consisting of a tall vase with a feather thingy sticking out of the top. A short fat basket. Some strange wood carving that might be a monstera leaf and a banana, but I wasn't completely sure.

"This takes our relationship to a whole new level," I said.

He looked up, half-offended. "What do you mean?"

"I had no idea you were a frustrated decorator." I got up and poured each of us a glass of wine. Tomorrow was a workday, but I thought it might be fun to stop and celebrate our successes. "Come sit for a minute."

"Okay, I've almost got this." Ten minutes later he got up, dusted off his hands, and assessed his handiwork. He looked pleased. Then his gaze alit on the couch. "A few yellow pillows would perk that blue checked couch right up and give the room a cheerful ambiance."

I patted the seat beside me. "I think you're looking for reasons to go back to HomeGoods. You love it there, admit it." He headed to go fuss with the feathers again, I just knew. But as he passed me,

I tugged on his shirt, which pulled him backward, causing him to tumble down to the couch.

He landed next to me, the side of his body colliding pleasantly with mine. He was hard to my soft, long and lean and full of muscle, and it brought a simmering sense of yearning straight to the surface. I tried to focus by handing him a glass of wine and clinking our glasses. "It looks amazing."

Two blue and white checked couches with ruffles on the bottom, two really nice tan leather recliners (no ruffles), and an off-white coffee table with a little beat-up-on-purpose look. Anita even rounded up some peaceful-looking landscape prints for the walls. And Adam found an area rug with beige swirls that was really soft on the feet—thank you again, HomeGoods.

We sat staring at the dark fireplace, which wasn't lit, but I was imagining what it would be like if it were, and we were sitting here all cozy, enjoying our wine. I was weary and elated, frightened and happy, anticipating what was to come.

On top of it all, I had a deep sense of his presence next to me, which was making my heart speed up in a steady, quiet beat. His warmth and his simple clean scent flooded me.

The tiny, random noises of the house at night—the buzz of the icemaker filling up, a branch scraping softly against a window with the wind, an occasional faraway car driving down the street—all gave me the sense that it wouldn't be quiet this way much longer.

I closed my eyes and tried to hear baby cries, baby noises—but it all still seemed like an impossibility. This was the calm before the storm, and we both knew it.

"What are you thinking?" he said. He hadn't moved away. We were shoulder to shoulder, knee to knee, and I was having trouble thinking of anything.

I wanted to lean into him, slip my arm through his—i.e., cuddle. Maybe turn on the TV that I didn't have yet and watch something fun together. Or not watch anything at all and pull him down to me and kiss him silly.

I remembered every touch back in that tropical dream world, every frantic and every quiet one.

My heart was pounding. Not from everything that had happened in the past few hours, but because Adam was holding my hand. Right here, right now. Unexpected and expected both. And so, so nice.

I stared down at where they were joined—his grip comforting and certain, my hand smaller, paler, interwoven with his big one.

I went as hot and cold as a teenager on a first date. I got shaky. I felt blood rush into my face, and I could barely make out his words as he said, "You're going to do great tomorrow." He looked completely unaffected as he squeezed my hand and lifted up his glass. "To new beginnings."

I smiled. "To new beginnings." But my mind was already dissecting his word choice. Did he mean us too? Were *we* a new beginning?

"You're going to be a great mom, Ani." Such comforting words. They filled me with a confidence that I didn't quite have, because I could tell they were sincere. I knew that he believed in me.

I looked into his eyes, beautiful, brown, calm. "Thank you. I really needed to hear that right now."

He squeezed my hand again. "I believe in you. I always have." What would he do if I kissed him? Now, in this moment of calm before the storm? Would that be totally crazy, to start something now?

"I wonder why that is," I said, looking him straight in the eye. "People might think I'm flighty or impulsive. But not you. Why not?"

His mouth turned up in a half smile that made my stomach flip. "You're not afraid to do things. Actually do big things. I really admire that."

I held my breath, wondering if he'd lean in for a kiss. Because, oh, that was so what I wanted. It was all I could think of. I'd just about decided to do it myself, but when I glanced up at him again, something made me hesitate.

His look grew serious. He gave a small sigh. His brow furled in worry. He reached over for my other hand and sat there, holding both of them. I sat frozen, unable to move, afraid to breathe, wanting him so badly. I knew it was a crazy time, a crazy place, but I wanted him to tell me that he couldn't stop thinking about me, as I couldn't about him, and that he had to have me right now or else he'd die.

"Ani, I like you so much." I heard the "but" before he said it. "But I have to tell you right now, before the baby comes, that I'm a bad bet for a relationship. I just don't want to mislead you."

No relationship spun in my head. *Why not? Why the hell not?* I was half in love with him already. Didn't he feel the same way about me?

"Mislead me?" I managed.

"I love spending time with you, but I can't commit to anything. And when you add a baby into that mix—well, I feel like that would head us into disaster. I mean, we barely know each other. And being a staple in a child's life and then possibly leaving —well, that would be awful."

I wanted to object. I wanted to tell him to just take everything a day at a time. To keep going as we are now, which was the most wonderful thing I'd ever experienced.

But then I heard my own voice. *You're too much, Ani. Just too much.*

What normal man would begin a relationship with me? I was a bad bet, a wild card.

I couldn't argue with him. Not everyone was built like I was, doing crazy things, dreaming about life as though it would somehow all work out if you only had some faith. So I sat up straight and said, "You-you're absolutely right. It's complicated." I swallowed hard, trying to keep a lump down.

I felt like I'd lost something I never really had.

"This is for the best," he said.

I nodded, unable to speak. But I did not agree. I wanted to say, *You'll fall in love, just as I did. When you hold her, when you cradle her, you'll be under her spell.*

But I couldn't.

Finally, I said, "Thank you—for everything."

"Of course. Feel free to call me if you need anything."

I managed a nod. But I knew that I wouldn't call. I wanted him to come on his own, not because he had to. Not because I was a damsel in distress that he felt he had to save.

I thought about telling him that it was okay with me to keep things loose between us. No strings. I might have said it too, except it would have been so typical of me—to say anything to make things easier for him.

But it didn't feel right for me.

This time, my life wasn't just about me. It was about Rosalie and me now.

And I had feelings. Big feelings for him. It wasn't enough anymore to just fool around for fun. Or out of grief and desperation.

I wanted more.

This time I took up *his* hand. "You've done so much for the baby and me already. I appreciate everything."

Ah, but I was lying by omission. I *did* expect more. I wanted him to want me *and* the baby, as fairy-tale as that sounded. Sure, it was complicated, but I believed it wouldn't be if you really loved someone.

His grief or fear held him back, that was obvious to me. But I couldn't help wondering what would happen if he really could unleash all that love that he held so pent up inside.

Chapter Thirteen

Ani

"Here's your little girl," Dale said in the nursery a week later, holding up Rosalie and waiting for either Daria or me to make a move. Her tiny hand was waving in the air, and she was very alert and awake.

I was aching to take her right into my arms, afraid that this was all a dream and that I might awaken at the last second to find that none of it was real.

I glanced at Daria, knowing that she was in charge. She was Rosalie's official foster parent on all the paperwork, and I was on probation. So I deferred to her. But she already knew exactly what I wanted. Smiling, she gave a nod.

I smiled back in relief and held out my arms for my tiny little bundle of joy, tears flooding my eyes. "Hi, honey," I whispered. "We're busting you outta here. You're going home."

I wanted to think *daughter, my* daughter, but I was too terrified. What if the day came when I had to give her up? How would I?

Just love her, I thought. *It's happened so far. Have faith that it will keep happening.*

"Oh, she's so tiny," my mother said from my side. "And look at how bright-eyed she is. She's very intelligent, I can tell."

"You're so right, Julia," Daria agreed. "Very intelligent."

I was shaking, the mothers were oohing and aahing, and Dale was sniffling loudly, tears actively running down his face too.

Apparently, we were creating a spectacle. All of the nursery staff had gathered around, beaming. From the doorway came a loud *woo-hoo*! (much to Dale's chagrin) and clapping.

"Congrats, Ani!"

"Oh, she's so precious!"

"Time to go home, little one!"

I turned to see all my colleagues from the ER in a pileup at the door. They were all carrying brightly wrapped boxes and gift bags. Everyone was smiling and cheering, and that made me even more teary-eyed.

Dale promptly shooed them all the way out and said they had to wait until we left the nursery. Then he said fake-sternly as he swiped at his eyes, "Chaos, people! You're creating chaos. You all need to dress that little girl and head out of here."

As my mom, Daria, and I dressed Rosalie—I was determined never to call her "the baby" again—I realized I'd caught a quick glimpse of everyone—Cathy, Tom, Ivy, BethAnn, and Angie—but not the one person my heart was searching for.

That was just like me, wasn't it? Prone to fantasy, dreaming of the fairy tale. I warned myself not to diminish the momentous joy of this moment and chased away any stray thoughts of Adam as we finally brought the baby out into the hallway for everyone to ooh and aah over.

I held her for everyone to see. My mom had bought her this cute floral outfit with adorable ruffles on the butt and a pink head-band with a giant floppy bow. With her dark hair, tiny fingers, and rosebud mouth, she looked absolutely Annie Leibowitz ready.

Cathy presented us with a beautiful pastel seashell-stitch blanket with the softest yarn that she'd made between patients. "But don't tell Adam," she'd said in a whisper. Tom went in with Ivy, BethAnn, and Angie on a state-of-the-art car seat that had been delivered to the house yesterday, which I'd managed to install after much difficulty and a few tears, and not without wishing Adam was there to do it quicker. Angie also gave me the valuable gift of a month's supply of diapers.

There was nothing like a baby to spread pure joy. Especially one whose situation had seemed so sad. Everyone was happy and tearful and hugging, and my heart was full.

But where *was* Adam? Working, someone said. Part of me wondered if he simply hadn't cared to be part of this. I tried my best to understand. No matter how aggrieved you were, how was a baby not the best cure? But what did I know of true grief? I had to let all my thoughts of him go because I suddenly had someone in my life who would take all of my focus, starting right now. And that was more than enough.

It had to be.

~

Adam

"We're looking to rehome Arnold," Mrs. McClellan said when I stopped by her house to collect my jogging buddy for our daily constitutional. Late April had brought warmth and lots of sun, and it was a perfect day for a run.

"Rehome?" I repeated. My brain was a little fuzzy. It kept trying to remind me that according to my watch, Ani had probably just brought the baby home, and why wasn't I there?

No. It wasn't my place. Going over there meant that I was okay with being involved. That I could share in the love and the joy when I knew I was incapable of doing that. I couldn't bring myself to risk it.

That hadn't stopped me from wondering how things were going. Of course, the news was all over the hospital, and it brought well-wishes and baby presents from many departments. My staff was especially excited to pitch in to give Ani and the baby some really nice gifts. I hoped that Ani felt supported and loved.

Did her place look like a home? My creative side had really enjoyed zhushing it up. But it wasn't *my* home, and they weren't my family. My family was gone. My heart was dried up, and trying to pretend otherwise wasn't fair in the long run to Ani or to the baby.

So I'd hoped that my daily jog would get my mind off of everything, at least for a little while, but apparently not. Because now I was worried about Arnie too.

"Yes," Mrs. M said. "This big dog is too much for us. He keeps escaping, and he's impossible to walk. Now that we've decided to move near our grandkids, we think it's best to leave him here in Wisconsin. Know anyone who might be interested?"

I made the huge mistake of looking at good old Arn. He was sitting next to me, leaning against my leg, his red tennis ball between his legs. *Isn't it time for our run? Why aren't we leaving? I've been waiting all day for this.* His big brown eyes were so expressive, I could practically hear him saying exactly that. Telepathically, of course. *Break me out. Come on, you know you love me.*

Was it normal to think you could hear your dog speaking to you?

I didn't know about the love part, but I did know that he wasn't very objectionable, except for some bad breath once in a while. Plus, he was a great running buddy—focused and always pushing me to do more. My own doggie personal trainer.

But re-home him? Aw, no. My stomach churned with dread. I rubbed my neck as I thought about my life. I worked three twelve-hour shifts a week. Sometimes I left town when I had several days off in a row. Not the greatest schedule for a dog owner.

I quickly reminded myself yet again that I didn't get attached to animals either. But I *hated* to see Arnie down on his luck. "Um, what's your plan to find him another family?" I asked.

"We called One of a Kind Pets today." Oh, no. Looked like Arnie was headed straight to the local shelter. He was getting his bags packed as we spoke. The hourglass was about out of sand. I swallowed hard. "They told me that I could drop him off as early as tomorrow."

"Oh." My whole body froze with dread. Optimistically, I wanted to think he'd find a great family. But maybe he'd find a terrible family. Either way, it would be a scary, jarring experience for a guy who just wanted a decent daily jog around the golf course, a good meal or three a day, and a rub down or two.

Arnie's new fate sat heavily on my shoulders as we did our usual run.

He really was the perfect running partner. Endlessly positive, never giving up, and never giving me flak.

Until we got to Ani's street.

"We're not going down there now, boy," I said, panting a little as Arnie began to automatically veer to the right.

But Arnold was not having that. He tugged—hard—on the leash.

"Later, boy. Come on. This way." I pointed straight ahead— no detours.

That stubborn animal sat down right in the middle of the street. With a car approaching, I had to grab him by the collar and tug him out of the way.

"I'm not going over there today, Arn."

He cocked his head as if to ask, *Why the hell not? You know you want to.*

"It doesn't matter what I want. I-I have to cut it off somewhere. It will be better for everyone." I tugged on his leash and pointed down the street. "Let's run."

I guess hearing his favorite word, *run*, suddenly perked him up, and I was finally able to cajole him back to my street.

I let us into my kitchen. With Arnold lapping up a bowl of water, I looked around at the quiet house. I hadn't bothered to do any of the things I'd done to Ani's. No little touches. Basic furniture. The place was clean, but it was a little dark and a lot gray. But uncomplicated. Like my life. Or at least like my life was B.A., *Before Ani*. As Anita had called it, sterile.

Except for the gift bags on my countertop. I'd bought the most glittery, floridly pink ones I could find and the brightest green tissue paper to stuff into them.

I'd wanted the presents to shout *girl* all over them.

I grabbed my keys.

If I took Arnold, I wouldn't have to get that close to the baby. We'd be in and out.

Plus, I reasoned, Ani would be upset if she couldn't say goodbye to Arnold one last time.

Once again, his fate gave me a stab of heartburn, but I swallowed it down with a drink of water for both of us.

I'd be polite, pop in, wish Ani well, then go back to leading my calm, quiet life.

Which was exactly what I wanted, right?

Ani

"It uses AI to tell you if the baby's face or nose is covered, or if she coughs, cries, or rolls over," Penelope said, expounding on all the benefits of the state-of-the-art baby monitor she and Helen had bought me. "It tells you the baby's body temperature and her breathing and sleep analytics and you get to see her with night vision."

That sounded like something a Navy SEAL would take out on a recon mission, but what did I know?

"You can even take it with you when you go out, so you know what's happening with her when she's with another caregiver," Helen added.

I was madly in love with Rosalie, but even today, I knew that I didn't want to monitor her every move when I was out of this house.

I was grateful for everyone and for everything they'd done to welcome Rosalie, from the *It's a Girl!* banner they'd hung above my door to the many wonderful and sometimes high-techie gifts they'd brought me. Especially the one that dispensed a warm bottle of formula in any number of ounces you programmed in thirty seconds or less. I wondered if it would do that for my morning coffee.

But again I wondered, where was Adam? Surely, he'd come to welcome Rosalie home.

I was feeling overwhelmed. I loved everyone, but I wanted to be alone without all these kind well-wishers. At the same time, I dreaded being alone with the baby, because, yes, although I was a doctor and I knew a lot about newborns, I'd never cared for one twenty-four-seven. I had no idea what to expect.

Adam would understand. He'd probably say something funny. Or encouraging. Even his presence calmed me, and I missed it. I missed him, even as I had a sense of disbelief that I had these powerful feelings at all.

I thanked my partners profusely for the wonderful gift that seemed smarter than I was. Next to me, the baby was sound asleep in her bassinet next to the couch, her tiny mouth open, her face turned up.

"Dylan Baird called me again," Helen said, eyeing me carefully. "He wants to set up a time to talk with you, at your convenience, of course. He wanted to be respectful of your time with the baby."

"We liked him a lot," Pen said with enthusiasm. "He has great credentials."

Yes, he did, but still, I had an uneasy feeling. I couldn't imagine why Dylan would want to do locums here, in the middle of Wisconsin. He was all L.A.—sunshine, highlights in his blond hair, and surfing. He was the kind of person who needed an ocean within biking distance to catch a few waves before work each morning.

"I'm worried for your sake that we still don't have anyone lined up while you're on leave," Helen said in a blunt tone.

What she meant was, how many nights could I sustain being up with a newborn and working nonstop all day? That was the arrangement I'd made with Daria. She would be off the clock at five p.m. each day until I took leave. She would be involved daily in Rosalie's care until I was permitted to become the foster parent of record.

"Are you going to call him?" Helen prodded.

"Tomorrow for sure." The baby stirred, and I practically jumped, more than ready to step into action. But false alarm—she immediately fell back into a deep sleep.

Penelope put her hand on my arm. "Ani, call him. You're going to get exhausted fast, and he can start right away. He has fantastic references. We're okay with him if you are."

I had no doubt in my mind that Dylan was a great doctor. We'd developed a cordial, respectful—even warm—relationship over the years, with the mutual agreement that we'd both made a youthful mistake. Being cordial and seeing each other occasionally was fine. But this arrangement would bring him too close for comfort. A little feeling in my gut kept holding out for *anyone* but him.

Come on, locums people, check out this great opportunity. Where are you?

One of my elderly neighbor ladies stood in the dining room and pointed to Adam's decorating handiwork in the corner. "How cute is this?" she said, admiring the woven basket and the vases.

It reminded me yet again that I had so much stored up to tell him—how it took my mom and me a good ten minutes just to figure out the snaps on Rosalie's outfit, the wonderful kindness everyone had shown us, my surprise at learning that he'd somehow snuck over and cut the grass and edged around the beds before we'd brought Rosalie home.

"Looks like you've got a furry visitor running up your side-walk, Ani," Sam suddenly said, peeking out my front window. "And he's got a man in tow."

I bolted up from the couch, mumbled an *excuse me* to my partners, and opened the door. Arnold immediately pulled his leash free and ran in before Adam could stop him.

"Arnold!" I said, bending down to greet the dog, who gave me plenty of doggie kisses. "You came to see me, didn't you? I'm so glad!" I was saying that in my doggie voice to Arnie, but I knew whom I really meant.

I stood up to face Adam. "Hi," I said.

"Hey," he said back, our eyes meeting and holding longer than necessary. "Arnie couldn't stay away."

We stood there for a minute, both of us seeming to blame all our own feelings on the dog. At least, I hoped that was the case.

The dog, sniffing the air, bounded over to the bassinet. Adam ran after him in a panic. Arnold ran directly up to the bassinet, stuck his nose inside, and sniffed the baby delicately, starting with her head and ending with her butt. Practically perfectly behaved, except for the butt part.

"Arnie, meet Rosalie," I said, stroking his head. "Someone new for you to play with."

The dog was calm and seemed happy with that, but it was Adam whom I worried about. He simply stood there, staring hard at the baby. He appeared a little quiet, a little frozen.

Was he thinking of his wife? Their dreams, their life together? Perhaps, because he wasn't smiling like all the other people who had passed through. Plus, he stood back, not daring to completely approach.

Finally, he turned to me. "She's so sweet, Ani. I wish you all the best."

I got choked up because, to me, his words sounded final. Like a goodbye. "Thanks," I managed. "What did you bring us?" I pointed to the gift bag he was carrying. Anything to keep him here for just a few extra minutes.

He handed me the bag. "Open it."

I pulled out a tiny Packers beanie, green with a little top knot. I held it up and laughed. "Perfect!" Next was a baby blanket that said "Rosalie, Future Packers Fan," repeated all over in green and gold. He must have been concealing another, larger bag, which he brought out from behind his back. "For you," he said.

Puzzled, I stuck my hand into the bright green paper and pulled out a warm fleece Packers blanket. My eyes started watering, partly from his thoughtfulness to think of me too, and partly because he'd never sit next to me on that checked couch and wrap up with it as we watched a game together.

"I love it. Thank you." I saw the struggle on his face, so I knew that this was difficult for him. I reached over and kissed his cheek. "Thank you for coming. It means a lot to me."

He nodded. "Glad you like it." He paused. "How are you doing?"

I avoided a direct answer. "Everyone's been so wonderful." As I looked around the room, my neighbors, whom I barely knew, were sorting a big pile of baby clothes donated by Penelope and some of my colleagues. Sam and Mia were sitting on the couch, chatting with Penelope and Helen. My mom and Daria were sitting on foldout chairs on the tiny brick patio, deep in conversation.

"My dad's putting my old crib together in the baby's room." I met his eyes. I wanted so badly to tell him that I was happy but also terrified. I wanted to say that I'd been subconsciously waiting for him, and now that he was here, I somehow felt that I could breathe again.

He glanced around the room and out the back sliding doors where we could see our mothers drinking coffee and laughing. "It's a lot."

I nodded. "I sort of feel like I did before my first night of being on call. Restless, not knowing what to expect."

"Here's what to expect." He counted on his fingers. "Eating, pooping, sleeping. Eating, pooping, sleeping. Rinse and repeat. Easy peasy. You've got it."

"Thanks for the vote of confidence."

"You're going to be a great mom." He paused, looking a little conflicted. "I have to tell you something—about Arnold."

Oh. Arnold. Not the *I just couldn't stay away* that I was hoping for.

But then the doorbell rang again.

I opened the door to a tall, roguishly handsome man with longish light brown hair and a beard, wearing a Hawaiian shirt, Birkenstocks, and sunglasses on his head, who sauntered in carrying two giant picnic baskets. Dylan himself.

"Hey, lady, there you are." He walked right over to me and kissed me on the cheek. "I made you some power dinner. Where's the little lady?" He spotted the bassinet and asked permission with a lift of his brows.

"Sure, go on over," I said. Sticking out of his shirt pocket was a small leather-bound notebook that he still kept tucked there for when he was inspired to write spontaneous poetry verses. They were bad, but nevertheless, it was reassuring that he was still an original guy who'd remained true to himself.

Over the past decade, he'd tended to blow in and out of my life unpredictably, like a sudden storm that made a lot of wind and noise, stirred everything up, and left just as suddenly.

"Hi, Baby," he said in a higher-pitched voice, waving his fingers above the bassinet. "She's really precious," he said, straightening up. "Congratulations, Ani."

"Thanks," I said, noticing that Adam was watching all of this with lifted brows. Before I could make introductions, Dylan lifted up each basket that he'd brought. "I just took some homemade bread out of the oven. The rest is a burrata salad, grapes, and some chicken salad with nuts and a Greek yogurt dressing. Strength for the journey."

I gave him a side hug, reminded of how I almost didn't divorce him because he was such a great cook. "That was sweet. Nice to see you." He put his arm around me, and keeping it there, reached out a hand to Adam, who was still standing nearby. "Hey, I'm Dylan. Ani and I go way back."

"Way back?" Adam asked, his tone a tad suspicious as he shook hands with him.

"Dylan's an old friend," I said, taking a step away so that Dylan had to move his arm. "And my ex. And also a pediatrician." Might as well get it all out there, right? "Dylan, meet my friend, Adam Lowenstein. He's the director of the ER."

"Oh, hey, great to meet you," Dylan said. "Turns out I'm going to be in town for a while. I'd love to talk to you about a job."

"We're always interested in getting more primary care docs on staff. But all of them are also employed in the community."

"Well, I'd love to take over for Ani here for a few weeks, so what do you say? I'm in town, I'm available, and I'm here for my best girls."

Adam's brows shot up in surprise as the intimacy of that statement hit him. "If you take over for her, you'll do her assigned ER shifts."

This was just like Dylan. To present his case publicly. But to refer to the baby and me as *my best girls*? Way too much.

That was how he was—over the top. That was probably why I fell in love with him at such a young age—he believed anything was possible. He'd encouraged me to apply to medical school when I was working as a nurse, so at least I owed him for cheerleading me onward to follow my dreams.

"My practice is vetting candidates," I said in a neutral tone. "We should have a decision soon."

"I know I'm the only candidate," he said honestly. "I'd take good care of your patients. You know I would." He did a careless shrug. "I mean, I'm already vetted, right? You know me inside and out."

Oh no. I wished I didn't. I couldn't look at how Adam was taking this. "Well, my partners and I all need to agree. We'll have a decision by the end of the week."

I *had* to have a decision by then. Because I wasn't going to survive much longer going like I was. I had to do something quick.

"Inside and out, huh?" Adam bristled as Dylan moved on to meet my neighbors. If he'd had a sword, he'd have drawn it right then. And if I read his body language right, he didn't like this. Not one bit.

And that gave me a ridiculous surge of hope.

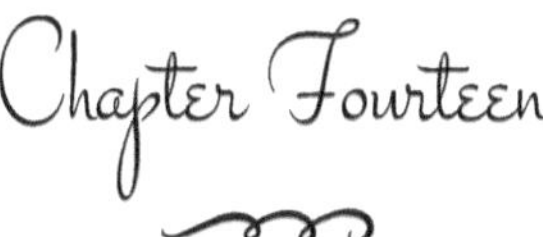

Chapter Fourteen

Adam

As soon as I walked into the ER on a Wednesday morning a little over week later, my phone buzzed with a call from my mom, who literally never called me at work.

"Hey, what's up?" I asked, answering immediately.

"Just making sure you're still alive," she said.

I frowned. "What's this about?"

"I'm just wondering if you're coming over here any time soon," she said in a where-have-you-been tone.

Silence on my end. *Over here* meant Ani's house, where she was spending her days. My brain was filled with a flurry of thoughts, the first of which was, why was my mom suddenly concerned about my relationship with Ani?

"It's complicated," I looked around to make sure none of my staff was listening.

"Well, you might want to consider uncomplicating it sometime soon, is all I'm saying."

I paused to think. "Is it too much? Caring for a baby all day? Do you need some help? I can help you find—"

"You don't need to help by proxy or whatever it is you're doing," she said, cutting me off. "Ani can hire someone to cut the grass. She doesn't need expensive coffee delivered by the UPS guy. Or brand-new placemats from Amazon. Or a fourth basket for that abominable dining room corner."

"Hey, don't criticize my decorating." I was mortally offended. "Exactly what does she need, Mother?"

"For you to get off the fence."

Ouch. I *did* get off the fence, I told myself. I *had* been honest with Ani about that. I'd decided on the safe course, one that would be better down the line for everyone. I checked my watch. I was meeting Dylan Baird to give him a tour of the ER, and I didn't want to be late.

Ani had finally pulled the trigger and hired him to take over for her, which meant he'd be taking her ER shifts as well. I personally hoped that his stay was temporary. I didn't care for the way he'd been so possessive of Ani, even though I knew I didn't have the right to care.

"I have one more minute, Mom, and then I've got to go."

"You're doing everything for Ani except being here. And *that's* what she needs." My mom's voice cracked a little.

Which concerned me. She never hesitated to tell me what she thought. But she did not typically call me to passionately stoke me into action. In other words, she didn't *interfere.* I wondered what piece of the story I was missing.

"I'm not capable of being there for anyone right now, Mom." There. She might as well know the truth. Life wasn't a fairy tale. But why did that sound so weak and...cowardly?

"How do you know unless you try?"

She was poking the bear. But I stayed firm. "I love you, Mom, but I have to respectfully tell you to please stay out of this."

"I love you too, Adam, but I have to respectfully tell you that

Ani needs more than Amazon deliveries right now. And that's all I'm saying. Have a nice day." And then she hung up.

From inside my desk drawer, Liv seemed to frown at me. Which scared me a little. I'd never imagined her disapproving of me before.

Liv would have admired Ani's gumption. Her courage. Her no-holds-barred way of embracing life.

You're afraid of living, she seemed to say. An imaginary eye roll from her. *You're an ER doctor. Be the badass that you are.*

I snapped the drawer shut. I didn't know which was worse, the fact that I was imagining my dead wife giving me dating advice or that my mother actually was. Either way, I didn't feel any better.

I walked out to the nursing station to find Dylan ensconced behind the nursing desk, casually leaning back in a chair with one ankle crossed on the other knee—I noticed he didn't have dress socks on under his khakis—and chatting up the staff. "I'm a huge proponent of baby massage. Baby yoga. Baby meditation. Calms the nervous system, reduces stress, and improves sleep. Does wonders for the whole family."

Baby meditation? Oh no. Was he one of those docs who threw traditional medicine out the window in favor of...other stuff? Crystals? Inner healing powers? Eye of newt and leg of frog?

"I mean, when there's nothing medically wrong, I like to do things to help parents handle stress." When he saw me coming, he rose and clapped me on the back. "Hey, Adam." He frowned and started to poke his thumbs aggressively between my shoulder blades. "Wow, you're tight back there." Whatever he was doing was a little weird but also felt kind of...good. Maybe I was more stressed than I'd thought. "You're holding in *a lot* of muscle tension. Have you ever had a massage?"

Maybe I really could use one right now because dealing with him was already starting to raise my blood pressure.

Cathy was blatantly crocheting. As I passed, she smiled and lifted up her work, not trying to hide it at all. It was a bright pink baby bootie. "Good morning, Dr. L. This is for Rosalie. I'm making a sweet fuchsia pink flower for it too."

"Oh." I stopped to admire her handiwork. And to marvel at how such a mini-sock could fit on a tiny human's foot. "That's really cute, Cathy." I mean, what else could I say? Everyone had stepped up in a big way for Ani and the baby. I decided to close my eyes to the defiance.

"So cute," Angie said as she grabbed a handful of caramel popcorn from a giant aluminum tin sitting on the desk. "How's the baby doing, Doc?"

"Settling in," I said, even though it was Friday, and I hadn't seen the baby all week.

"That little house is so cute," BethAnn said, thumbing through a Spafinder catalog. "Ani told us you snuck over there and did a bunch of yard work. It's really charming."

I nodded and smiled, letting everyone assume that I'd acquired an instant family.

"Too bad the air conditioner broke," Angie said, eyeing me carefully, as if she saw right through me. "Ani said she couldn't get a technician out there until tomorrow."

It had gotten unseasonably warm, unusual before May. I didn't have a chance to respond because just then, Dylan pulled a book out of his backpack. The title was *Sprouts, Workouts, and Other Power Moves for Your Best Life.*

"Do you rock climb?" he asked as I tried to move on with the rest of our tour.

"I'm a runner." We hadn't even left the main desk yet. And the staff seemed in no hurry to let us go.

"I rock climb," Tom said. He was bent over the counter, working on something with a tiny tool. At second glance, he appeared to be repairing his watch. *At work.*

"I do a little bit of everything," Dylan said. Of course he did. "Hang gliding, skydiving, scuba certification, hot-air balloon. Last winter, I climbed Kilimanjaro. The world is our oyster, dude. We have to spend every breath trying to draw in its full essence." To demonstrate, he sucked in a loud, deep breath.

"I love that!" BethAnn said.

Ivy cracked open her novel. "In that case, maybe I can get in another chapter before it gets busy."

They were all openly defying me. But I didn't have the heart to enforce today. Besides, I had other things on my mind. I knew a great technician for that air conditioner. I wondered if I could call in a favor and get him out there this morning, since the temp was supposed to reach the mid-eighties today.

"Come and see the acute side of the ER," I said to Dylan. He was a lingerer, I could tell. Wanting to keep chatting. I wondered if he took a long time with patients.

"Nice to meet you all," he finally said. "Cathy, I'm going to bring my mini-loom next time."

"Oh, exciting!" She waved him off. "I always wanted to learn to weave."

"Nice to meet you too." BethAnn looked up from whatever she was shopping for.

"My whole philosophy is seizing the moment," Dylan said as I walked him around the department, showing him all the state-of-the-art features like our new ultrasound machine and the rapid CT scan next door. "That's why I came here. I want to seize the moment with Ani."

I froze. "Does she know that?"

"Not yet." He checked out our urgent care clinic rooms. "But she will. In fact, I'm going to cook a gourmet dinner for her tonight and discuss things."

Fudge. My hunch was right. He *did* want her. "Discuss things?" I cleared my throat.

"We were so young when we married," he said, fiddling with the otoscope cord on the wall. "We didn't understand anything about life or ourselves. But she and I—we're both adventurers at heart, you know? She'll always be the one who got away, unless I do something about it. I've never met anyone like her. I mean, the way she fought for that baby—"

The way *we* fought for that baby, I wanted to say. But who was I to correct him? I'd jumped off the fence and right back into my small, confined, suffocating safety zone, leaving Ani territory free for a takeover.

But by him? I envisioned him in yoga pants, spreading his mat in Ani's tiny backyard, meditating with the baby while he simultaneously whipped up a five-star meal. *Ugh.*

I cleared my throat again. "Um, Dylan," I found myself saying in a dead calm voice. "Actually, I'm afraid tonight isn't going to work. I'm having dinner with Ani."

Ani

When I got home from work that night, I'd barely had time to say hi to Adam's mom and change into my shorts when Rosie started to cry.

"It's still a little warm in here," I said, flapping my hands to fan my face.

Daria was gathering her things. "It will get cooler in time. The repairman temporarily fixed the problem by adding more coolant, but he said you're eventually going to need a new unit."

Great. Another expense, and I'd just put myself on leave. Not good.

"She's starting to act a little fussy right around this time of day," Daria said.

We shared a look between us. "Are you thinking what I'm thinking?" I asked.

"Mmmhmm," Daria said. "The 'C' word." I closed my eyes and nodded, worried that the late afternoon crying spells might potentially be turning into the dreaded witching hours of colic. Rosie was nearly three weeks old now and had only just begun figuring out that nighttime is the time for sleeping, and day for being awake. But now this.

"You look terrible." Daria eyed me with concern. "You hire someone yet?"

I nodded. "Dylan starts tomorrow." I tried to make my tone cheery, but it was hard to fake. There'd been one further locums candidate to consider, but their references had been weak. At least with Dylan, I knew my patients would get good care. I only wished that I could shake the feeling that he was here for some other reason. And I hoped that reason wasn't me.

I could have gone further and told her that on the other hand, I definitely wanted Adam, whom I hadn't seen for over a week. I thought of him often, especially in the middle of the night when I was feeding and changing and repeating that for what felt like a million times. I didn't need his help, but I wished for his calming presence, his jokes, and his constant ideas to solve any problem.

I missed *him*.

Daria rested a hand on my arm and looked me over with a wise expression that she often wore. I felt like she could read straight through my forced cheer and straight into my brain. "At this point, it doesn't matter what you think of your ex," she said slowly and carefully. "You needed a warm body. It's a matter of survival. But you know that, right?"

I gave her a little smile. She'd summed this entire situation up perfectly in two words: *warm body*. And she'd been smart enough not to mention her son.

I gave her a little squeeze. "Thank you for caring. I get it." I let her out and then walked into Rosie's room to find her crying lustily at enough decibels to make me want to slap my hands over both ears.

"Baby, baby, it's okay," I crooned in my most calming voice, which didn't even cause a stutter in the loud and rhythmic *waah-*

waah-waahs that felt like a drum beat vibrating through my body. She was drawing her little legs up, clenching her fists tightly, and waving her arms.

For a tiny little thing, she had a lot of intense energy. I wished I could bottle a little of it for myself because the past few weeks had been a hurricane of excitement, stress, and now exhaustion.

How many times a week did I counsel parents on colic? I knew all the signs, symptoms, and theories of this mysterious malady that struck infants at around two to three weeks and kept going strong for up to three months. But I'd never experienced it in living color.

I picked her up and tried to follow my own advice. *Walk with her. Rock her. Put on soothing music or white noise. Swaddle her. Take her on a car ride.*

For the next hour after Daria left, I did everything on the list but the last one. Nothing worked. I was wishing that I could pull the batteries for a break. Press the off button. Change the channel. *Anything.*

My phone went off with a text. *Adam!* I immediately thought. Just a little message to make me smile. Maybe a repost from harried new parents on Instagram who'd managed to put a funny spin on the nightmares of babyhood. Something to let me know that he was out there thinking of me as I was of him.

But it was Dylan. *Hey,* the text read. *Pen and Helen got me acquainted with the office. Maybe we could have dinner tomorrow and I could fill you in on your patients.*

Great that he'd gone to the office. But I hardly needed updates after my first day off.

My phone pinged with another text. Dylan yet again. *P.S. Spoke to Daria earlier - If Baby R is colicky, I know some great techniques. Call me.*

"I won't call you," I said in an aggressive tone to the phone before I collapsed onto the couch with Rosie on my shoulder. That made her cry even more, so I somehow managed to haul both of us back up. This time I put her belly down in my arms and walked around, rocking her horizontally back and forth.

No luck with that either.

I was worn down, in a haze of sleep deprivation. I wasn't sure how long I could continue the demanding insanity of infant care without some kind of break.

I wanted to wail right along with her.

I didn't ever want to get to the point where I took my frustration out on the baby.

Even worse, with my tiredness and frustration, all my doubts came surging back. I couldn't do this alone. How could anyone? My knowledge about babies was all on paper, not based on real-life experience, which made me feel like I knew next to nothing. What had I been thinking?

I needed help. I needed bodies. I needed a fricking real maternity leave because I was a working single parent of a newborn and teetering on the edge. This arrangement with Dylan could last a few weeks at best, because it came with a loss of my income. I had remodeling bills, furniture bills, baby supplies bills, everything all at once. My temporary time off came at a great price.

I was stewing in worry and wondering if something else was wrong with Rosie when the doorbell rang.

Not now. Please, not now.

Had Dylan actually had the balls to march right on over here? If he had, I wasn't going to mince words. He needed to know that we had a business arrangement only.

"What is it?" I said in an impatient tone as I pulled open the door.

A blur of matted reddish-brown fur carrying a squeaky toy ran straight between my legs and flopped down in front of a couch, making himself right at home. Adam stood there looking anguished. Rattled. A little sheepish.

Because of me? Because of us?

I refused to be hopeful. I couldn't bear the disappointment of being wrong.

He looked after the dog, who had now jumped on a couch and circled three times before settling in with his special toy.

"Sorry about bringing Arnold."

"I love Arnold," I said tartly. Sort of petulantly, as if the corollary was *But I don't love you.*

I was happy to see him, but I suddenly realized...angry. But I couldn't tell if it was legit anger or if it was because I was nearing the end of my rope. If Santa Claus stood at my door, smiling and ho-ho-hoing right now, I'd probably snarl. "Sorry, I thought you were someone else," I said, apologizing for my gruff greeting. But I didn't offer to let him in. I wanted to hear what he was here for.

I refused to get my hopes up. I refused to feel the pull of attraction that always overtook me—just looking at his mussed hair, the concern on his face, the dark circles under his eyes. I couldn't help the warmth that started in my stomach and spread everywhere.

I wanted to throw myself in his arms and tell him how happy I was to see him. But where had he been? What was he thinking? How could he not want to be involved with this miraculous child? With *me*?

Or was I out of my mind, thinking that anyone sane would ever want to sign up and ride along on this wild ride I'd created for myself?

He was a savior, but I didn't need to be saved. I needed a friend.

And I wanted more. More than I was sure he could give.

"I want to help," he said.

Oh, he was here to bail me out. Because he felt sorry. Daria had probably called him on her way home, telling him how difficult things were.

I could barely hear him over the crying. "Thanks, but I'm fine," I said stubbornly. I started to close the door, but he did a quick move and stuck his big foot in the way.

I turned into the room and began bouncing the baby. He walked right in and shut the door behind him.

"Hear me out."

But the baby, maybe also picking up the strange vibes between us, was inconsolable. Daria told me before she left that she'd just fed her four ounces. Should I try more, even though that seemed like plenty? No amount of bouncing or patting on her back, singing, begging, or praying was making any headway. "We're going to have to continue this some other time. Please go."

I bit my lip because I was close to tears, but I didn't want to show it. I wanted him to go, but I also wanted him to stay.

I was angry at him, but angrier at myself. How could I have success unless I set myself up for success? I should have hired Dylan a week ago instead of burning myself out.

"Does she need to be checked out?" Adam asked.

I shrugged. "It's been happening all week at this time. Then, after about three hours, it ends, and she's fine."

"Classic colic." He paused. "Please let me help."

I opened my mouth to say that I didn't need his help. But no words came out. The truth was, I could barely see straight. Every cry felt like a little knife cut.

Adam looked worried.

I think he should have been worried, because I was too. I was overwhelmed and close to tears. But I couldn't ask him for help knowing he was just here to jump in and intervene like he'd done what seemed like so many times before.

He grabbed my arms, despite the wailing baby in them. His tone was gentle but insistent. "Ani, listen to me. I know you're angry with me. But hand me the baby."

Hand me the baby? I stared at him. He wanted the baby? I held my breath. Did that mean he was here for...us?

I forced myself to speak what was on my mind for Rosie's sake. Because I knew that

I could not continue like this, or I would lose it, which would be terrible for her. So I looked him right in the eye. "I don't want you to help me out of guilt."

"I'm not here out of guilt. I'm here because I think about you all the time. I miss you. Both of you. I miss being...here."

Did I hear him right? Did that mean that he could love this baby?

I couldn't focus with the crying. I couldn't focus on anything. I looked into his worried brown eyes. "If you want to help me right now, there is one thing you can do."

"Sure. Anything." He seemed sincere. "You name it."

Without any warning, I deposited the inconsolable baby into his arms. He froze, fumbled a little, and hung onto her. "Please take her and let me sleep for an hour."

He looked stunned. A little shocked. But hey, he'd offered, right? And he didn't turn away.

He stared at the tiny baby in his big arms, and I stared at him holding her in those big arms and held my breath. Rosie, startled by the sudden switch, stopped wailing for one second and then started right back.

I didn't wait to see what happened next. I ran down the hall to my bedroom, closed the door, and collapsed onto my bed.

Chapter Fifteen

Adam

At first, I was stunned. Terrified of the wailing, wiggling creature in my arms—even though I knew all about how babies worked, at least from treating them. But I didn't know squat about *caring* for them.

Let's be real. I didn't know much about caring for anybody.

"It's okay, Arn." The dog was pacing the hallway, worried about Ani no doubt, probably as upset as the rest of us by Rosie's screaming. "Everything's okay." I wasn't really sure if my weak attempt to calm him down was actually directed at him. It might have been more for my sake.

I only knew that I couldn't go on taking the easy way out, avoiding anything that might cause pain. Trying to control my ER, and every aspect of my life, to avoid being hurt.

Because if I kept on avoiding feeling anything, others would move in. With yoga mats and cooking skills, maybe.

One look at the purplish, screaming, toothless bundle in my

arms, and my armor cracked. Not a pretty sight to most, but to me she was, in all her earsplitting glory. A fierce surge of protectiveness came over me for both of the amazing females in my life. All the feelings I'd tried so hard to dam up came flooding through.

I, I thought fiercely, was the one who should be here. Not Dylan, not anyone else. Imperfect, closed off, grumpy me. I only hoped I could seize the moment to be the person they needed me to be.

"Hello," I said softly, my voice cracking as I backed myself slowly into the recliner. "Um, hi."

And then, a miracle. The baby suddenly hit the mute button. Her face was still a purply red, but she seemed thoughtful, like she was weighing her options. Like, further potential hours of crying weren't necessarily out of her wheelhouse if I made one wrong move.

I'd handled countless people on the brink of death, ones whose hearts had stopped, whose windpipes were blocked, whose lungs were full of fluid, who were hemorrhaging to death. I was given the gift of calm in dangerous, terrifying, life-threatening situations.

Yet this tiny, deceptively cute terror in pink footie jammies petrified me beyond words.

"I'm Adam."

She was a warm little bread loaf in my arms, smelling of baby shampoo and lotion, and her arms and hands seemed to move in slow motion as she extended her fingers, stuffing a bunch of them randomly into her mouth.

I stared at dark blue eyes, the dark mass of hair, the tiny little lips now making sucking noises.

For the past two years, I'd stayed away from Liv's and my friends as they'd begun having kids. I'd watched from afar as young couples strolled their children and held hands, balancing all kinds of diaper bags and strollers and paraphernalia while I kept my distance, at first a jealous watch.

And then I avoided it entirely. All of it. Everyone. I'd slammed the door on all my feelings. If I couldn't have Liv and the life she and I planned, I didn't want any of it.

"It's all good, baby. Everything's going to be just great."

Arnold looked up at me with soulful eyes. "I'm okay, you're okay, we're all okay," I chanted sing-song like a wild man, sneaking a hand down to rub his head. Do dogs roll their eyes? He was certainly wondering why I'd brought him here. I didn't have the heart to tell him that it was just him and me from now on, buds for life.

Rosie miraculously hadn't started crying again, but I was afraid to move a muscle.

I carefully reached for the TV remote. "Okay, Rosebud, what will it be? Arn? Basketball? Hockey? Definitely not the news. Then no one would calm down." I found us all a good basketball game and settled in.

I eyeballed the baby out of the corner of my eye. She was still sucking on her fingers and definitely not crying. Maybe she felt safe in a bigger set of arms, I didn't know. Maybe my deep voice was more soothing. Maybe I was a novelty. Maybe it was the squeak-squeak-squeak of expensive basketball shoes on the court. Or maybe her gut had somehow magically calmed down.

I figured that if I could only keep her quiet for an hour, Ani would get some rest. And when she got up, I was going to make sure that she got all the help she needed. That meant I was going to be here too, if she'd let me.

~

Ani

I woke on my own with the sinking feeling that I'd slept way too long. Longer than I had since I'd left my normal life behind, which seemed like a lifetime ago. I had another strange feeling too—being rested. Bright sunshine streamed through the window, indicating that it was actually after dawn, a novel sight.

Then it all came back to me. The helpless exhaustion, Adam at my door, me handing over the baby and heading for bed.

I covered my head with the pillow. Did I really do that? It felt desperate. And incompetent. And the baby—where was the baby?

Before I could catastrophize too much, I threw on my robe and ran to the family room, where I was stopped in my tracks by an amazing scene—Adam fast asleep in the recliner, the baby's bassinet at his side. Rosalie was sleeping on her back, swaddled carefully in her Packers blanket, her hands up near her head. Out like a light.

Adam wore scrub pants and a black Journey T-shirt, his bare feet sticking out over the footrest, his hair mussed, his muscled arms crossed over his nice chest. The Packers throw was askew across his long body. I would be lying if I said my gaze didn't linger on him in this messy, chaotic state—and it made my heart squeeze.

Scattered baby bottles, water glasses, and plates were everywhere. Along with the TV remote and Adam's eyeglasses, meaning he must have taken out his contacts. The floor and table lamps were all on, despite the strong morning sun flowing through the windows.

Arnie was fast asleep in a sunbeam. Passed out flat on his back with his big paws in the air, silly dog.

Adam had given me not an hour but an entire night of sleep, while sacrificing his own, a precious gift. And maybe—I hoped, I hoped—he'd done it for the baby as well.

I grabbed his phone and took photos of the two of them sleeping—well, okay, three, because I included Arnie too. I wanted to remember this forever. Had Adam rocked her to sleep? Had an intimate, one-on-one, middle-of-the-night conversation? Or had he held her at arm's length and done only what was necessary and no more? No, somehow, I knew he hadn't done that.

I tried to rein in the feeling that this was what I wanted, what I'd always wanted. This messy life right here in front of me.

I understood that I was a dreamer, sometimes a wild dreamer who got wrapped up in schemes, and most sane people did not follow along. But maybe he would. Maybe I wouldn't be too much for him.

And maybe we were just what he needed too.

As I was tucking the covers around the still sleeping baby, Adam stirred. "Hey," he said in a groggy tone.

"Hey," I said back.

"How are you feeling this morning?" he asked as he stretched his arms over his head. Which was also pretty hot.

"Better," I said, "thanks to you." I thought about what I needed to say. "I can't thank you enough." I paused. "It was unfair of me to do what I did." Which was basically dump the baby in his arms and flee.

He pushed the footrest of the recliner down and sat up. "I disagree. You reached a limit. You accepted some help before you reached the end of your rope."

I sat down on the arm of his chair. Our shoulders touched, but I didn't move away. Neither did he. "This situation was my fault," I said in a low voice. "I waited too long to make a decision on Dylan."

"Can I ask why?" He looked a little sheepish. Like the answer mattered. It occurred to me that he might be jealous. That might have made me laugh if my situation hadn't been so dire.

"He's a good clinician, so I wasn't worried about that. But we went our separate ways all that time ago for good reasons. I didn't want him back in my life." I was proud to say that I was restrained. I didn't say anything like, "You think *I'm* prone to wild schemes...." And I even left my suspicions that Dylan wanted something other than a temporary job out of our discussion.

"You didn't want him back in your life," he repeated, like he was digesting that. "Good," he said definitively. Then he changed the subject. "This is an exhausting job, Ani. I get it." His hair was sticking up on the right side. I reached over and smoothed it down.

He grabbed my hand and held it next to his cheek.

I melted.

I had so many questions. Did he start to fall in love with Rosie as I had, right from the start? Or was he ready to take off this morning and go back to the way we were?

"Can we talk?" he asked.

"Of course. Let me make some coffee—"

He took hold of my hand and tugged me to him. I sort of slid-fell into his lap. I'm not going to lie, it felt really nice there. I fit just right, and I had a bird's-eye view of that rugged stubble that I had to restrain myself from running my fingers over. While I imagined kissing his neck. And did other things. "The coffee can wait a minute," he said. "I have something I need to say."

"Sure." My heart was bounding in my chest. Somehow, I knew that this was going to be good. I could tell by the way he was looking at me. His eyes were like warm caramel drizzle. His beautiful lips were turned up in the slightest smile. And he put his arm on my back in a gentle, loving way that kicked up all the turmoil inside of me a few more notches.

"Ani, I didn't come here out of guilt." His voice was soft so as to not wake the baby, and a little gravelly from sleep. "I'm here because I can't stop thinking about you. I miss being with you, talking with you, hearing what you have to say. I love spending time with you."

A tear wound its way down my cheek. He wiped it away.

"I owe you an explanation. I never mentioned it. I thought it sounded...soft. Like an excuse. But now I realize I should have told you a long time ago that Liv and I tried for a long time to get pregnant. All she wanted was to be a mom. Every month when she found out it hadn't happened, she'd break down and cry. And then she got sick, so not only were we not going to create a life between us, but we also learned that she was going to lose hers." He paused, as if the sadness was still too raw to continue. "I would never want to be resentful, or sad, or take any of those emotions out on a baby. I'm still—figuring things out."

He rubbed his hand up and down my arm in a gentle way. "I'm sorry I stayed away. I'm sorry if I hurt you. I'm finally seeing a therapist who's helping me find my way. But you're my light at the end of the tunnel. You and Rosebud. I want to be with you both."

That was all I needed to hear. "Adam, I'm so glad you're here. I want to be with you too." I lowered my head and kissed him. At last.

His lips were warm and soft and wonderful, and as soon as we made contact, my breath caught from the sudden jolt of attraction between us. Warmth spread through me, and my heart started fluttering like a trapped bird in my chest before we even kissed. Our first kiss was light, tender, and brief. But then Adam gazed up at me and gave me a soft, *at-last* look that shone in his eyes, that I felt clear down to my toes. Then he reached up his hand, threaded it through my hair, and pulled me flush against him.

The next kiss was serious. Slow, lingering, lips parted. Less gentle, more feral. But tender too. He tasted wonderful and smelled a little bit like formula but, hey, that was just life. I curled my hands around his shoulders as he slowly began dragging a row of kisses down my neck. *Ah, heaven.*

I shuddered and made a noise from deep in my throat that made him smile against my skin as he wrapped his arms tighter around me and worked his way back to my mouth. I loved how powerful he was yet how gentle and tender too.

I thought back to the past summer, to that night in Turks and Caicos. How desperate we'd been, yet somehow how in sync, connected. I felt that same vibe between us—it was easy to be playful and fun and spontaneous and just...myself. But then, it had always been like that with him.

The dog stirred but kept sleeping. The baby sighed. A bird twittered outside the window. And then I heard nothing. I got lost in the heat and fire of his gaze and the depth of his kisses that became deeper, hungrier, and possessive. In that moment, I'd never wanted anything more than I wanted him.

Somehow, I managed to get up from the chair. I took his hand and tugged on it until he got up too and led him down the hall to the bedroom, making a quick ask of the sugar plum fairies to keep dancing in Rosie's head for just a little while longer.

"I guess Arnie's babysitting," Adam said with a chuckle as, halfway down the hall, he reached down and picked me up, slinging me over his shoulder, caveman style. I squealed a little, but quickly put my hands over my mouth.

"What's his rate?" I asked as we entered the bedroom.

"Free room and board for life," he said. I must have looked puzzled, because he added, "We can talk about that later."

It didn't really compute. He deposited me on the bed and helped me tug off my sweatshirt, which I tossed...somewhere. He peeled off his shirt with a fluid motion, joined me on the bed, and then began nuzzling my neck.

"Wait," I said while I could still think, "did you say *for life*?"

"Mmm hmm," is what I heard. Which did sound like an affirmative answer.

"But the McClellans are home," I said.

He stopped kissing me and rose up on an elbow. "Yeah, um, it's complicated. I had to make a game-day decision—basically between me or One of a Kind Pets."

"No! They wouldn't. You didn't." He turned a little red, and I couldn't resist capitalizing on that. "You're—you're a softie. A big, giant softie. It doesn't seem like you would be, but you are. Your heart is complete mush. Pudding. Applesauce. *Purée*."

He rolled over on top of me to shut me up. "I'd love to talk about this more, but we probably have, like, ten minutes before the crying starts again. Besides, I don't think now's a good time to talk about soft things."

I laughed, quietly, of course, as I slid my arms around his neck.

I had no nagging doubts, no feelings that I was swallowing down because they were too messy to bring up. I just loved him, silently praying that this wasn't all a dream, and that he could love me back just as much.

And then the world dissolved as he kissed me until nothing existed but the two of us together.

Chapter Sixteen

Ani

The next week, we took Rosie for her one-month pediatric appointment with Helen. Adam had the day off, so he came too. Right after we got her into her car seat, we smelled something nasty, which required a quick diaper and full-outfit change. I was afraid that we were going to be late. But Adam made getting her into and out of her car seat and lugging the diaper bag and the stroller look easy. By the time we finally got to the office, Rosie had passed out.

All the confusion and chaos of managing a newborn felt more manageable and not as big a deal with Adam nearby.

Entering my office felt a little weird. I already missed work, but I was also relieved not to be here, and grateful to have the time to focus only on Rosie, if that made sense. I saw no sign of Dylan, but Pen had let me know that my patients sent congratulations and were appreciative of Dylan's chill style.

"Helen had to run to see a patient in the hospital," Edith said from behind the front desk. "But Pen's got time to do Rosalie's exam. Sound okay?"

My heart fell. Helen was a great clinician, even if she was ornery. I was afraid Pen would raise a whole bunch of questions that would lead to a lot of worry and testing. Basically, I didn't exactly trust her to do a realistic assessment, even though I felt that Rosie was doing great.

Fifteen minutes later, we were settled in an exam room with a colorful flower garden painted on the walls. Penelope looked over Rosie's chart, and Adam cradled Rosie in his arms.

So far so good. Except it was strange for me not being in Pen's place.

"Her birth weight was seven pounds, thirteen ounces," Pen said. "Today, at one month old, she's eight pounds, ten ounces."

"Is she growing well?" Adam asked, sending an anxious glance from me to Pen. "Are we feeding her enough?"

"Her weight is excellent," Pen said with a smile. "And she's filling out nicely."

Adam wasn't reassured. "Sometimes she pulls her mouth away from the bottle, and I think she's done." He demonstrated the bottle motion with his hands. "But do you think I should offer her more?"

Pen's voice was calm and confident. "I think she's telling you she's done, and you're listening. So great job."

Adam pointed to the baby's face. "You don't think she's a little orange-y, do you?"

Pen craned her neck from her chair. "Not at all."

"Oh, that reminds me," Adam said, getting up. "Would you take a look at these little white things on her face?"

Pen walked over, even though it wasn't time for the exam yet. "Those pearly white bumps are called milia, and they're dead skin cells trapped under the skin. No treatment. They're a normal newborn thing."

I was a little startled to see Worrywart Adam, who'd obviously been saving his questions like a squirrel hoards acorns in its cheeks.

Pen started typing into our floating computer with a big arm. "How are her poops?"

Adam laughed. Pen lifted a brow. "Was that funny?"

Adam's laughter died. "It's just...are you serious? I mean, the questions you people ask."

"Well, *we people* want to make sure that babies are thriving," Pen explained. "Stools can provide clues to liver or bile duct issue, diarrhea, that kind of thing." As she prepared to type, she asked, "So how would you describe them? Corn on the cob, sausage, rabbit pellets, gravy, porridge, or chicken nuggets?"

He considered that carefully. "They look kind of pasty, kind of tan...like...peanut butter."

"Would you agree?" Pen glanced over at me.

I would agree that it was time to move on, except then Adam said, "I thought I might've heard a murmur the other day. Will you double-check me?"

"You've listened to her heart with your stethoscope?" I asked in an incredulous tone.

He gave a guilty shrug.

"Adam," Penelope said, redirecting. "Have you been spending time googling things?"

"What else is there to do at three in the morning?"

"My advice is to stay off the internet. You can always call the office with questions." Pen, probably having enough of Adam for the time being, addressed me. "How's her schedule?"

"Her days and nights are less mixed up," I said. "I think things are better now that I'm off. But the exhaustion is real."

Pen looked directly at me. "Are you two co-parenting?"

That stopped me in my tracks. Adam had stayed over every night since that night a week ago when I'd nearly lost it. I'd begged him numerous times to leave and get a good night's rest, but he never did.

I didn't want to box him in with something we hadn't discussed ourselves yet. "No," I swiftly said. I didn't want Adam to think—well, anything. Namely, that I was expecting him to parent Rosie.

"Yes," he said at the same time.

I felt my cheeks heat up, unclear if I'd heard correctly. I finally recovered enough to start to protest, to explain, when Pen cut me off.

"Excellent." She smiled at both of us. "Because I have suggestions."

"We'll take any suggestions," Adam said. "Anything to make these nights easier."

"Great. Decide what shift you want—8 pm to 2 a.m. or 2 a.m. to 8 a.m. The person not on duty gets earplugs and a bed far away from everywhere else. That way, you can potentially sleep five or six hours uninterrupted every night. That would help everyone in the household, including Rosie."

Adam considered that. Nodded his head, he mumbled, "Earplugs, great idea." Then he turned to me. "We could fix a cot up in the laundry room. That's far enough away that one of us might actually get some rest."

I pictured Arnold immediately finding my new bed and making himself at home—by sleeping right on top of me on a narrow cot.-That made me smile. But what really made me smile was that Adam was taking all of this to heart. He was...involved. Present. In our lives. That meant more than any amount of sleep.

Well, okay, maybe *not* more than sleep, which I craved more than food. But it meant a lot.

Pen did a thorough exam, narrating to us the entire time. I was really impressed with the way she handled everything. "The other thing is," Pen said, after she'd pronounced Rosie healthy, happy, and thriving, "we've found that physician parents tend to over-analyze everything. I mean, we know the worst, right? And emotions get clouded when it's your own kid. So no treating, okay? And call us. In this practice, you're just a mom and a dad."

After that wise advice sank in, we thanked her for everything. "I have one other recommendation for you," she said.

We both looked up. "You both need time together without the baby."

I immediately went into rational mode. "It's really hard because—"

"You two are smart," she said, cutting me off. Then she waved us away. "Just make it happen."

"Pen," I said as she was about to open the door. "Thank you. That was an amazing visit."

She smiled broadly. "You're welcome." After she left us to get the baby back together, I said to Adam, "She did a stellar job. She was informative, kind, patient, and thorough. She was more confident than I'd ever seen her."

Adam snapped up Rosie's onesie while I got her jacket ready. "I thought so too. Except I thought of a few more questions that I can email her through the chart."

I couldn't help smiling at his earnestness.

Pen was right, of course—about us needing time alone. I didn't think it was possible to fall in love in the middle of such chaos, but somehow, I'd done it. We were both riding the wave of emotion, of adrenaline, of banding together with all hands on deck with little time to spare. We hadn't talked about our relationship, about us, about the future. Terrifying stuff.

As soon as Adam left to pull up the car for us, Dylan appeared at the open door. "Hey," he said. "Can I ask you a question about a patient?"

"Sure. Of course."

"Do you mind if I switch Jimmy Oswald's asthma meds around a little bit?" He explained his plan, and I agreed.

I braced myself, for what, I wasn't exactly sure. To be hit on? To be given Zen advice? I didn't know.

"Penelope's really something," he said. He waved at Rosie, who flashed him a big smile.

"Yes, she is," I agreed.

"I mean, she really cares about her patients. She's an amazing teacher too."

This was interesting. "How's she doing otherwise?" I asked. "She sometimes has difficulty making the tough decisions."

"I'm helping her work through that," was all he said. "Listen, I —I'm all about honesty. I might have campaigned hard for this job because I've been thinking about you a lot lately."

Oh. I might've suspected it, but hearing it still threw me. I'd always thought of him as someone who lived in the moment, but got bored easily and then moved on to the next adventure. For awhile, I'd gotten swept up in that moment.

He gave a little shrug as he leaned against the exam table. "I guess I came back here because I've always thought of you as the one who got away."

Oh. That was surprising. And a little sad. But I was impressed by his honesty. "Dylan, I-I'm touched. Flattered. But—"

He mercifully interrupted me. Pushing off from the exam table, he said, "But you know what? I see that you're in love. And it looks great on you."

I swallowed hard, feeling a little guilty to be happy. But he'd called it—I really, truly was. I gave a little nod.

He pointed a finger at me. "I'm happy for you, Ani." I couldn't help but smile, because I could tell that he sincerely meant it.

"And I love this practice." *Uh oh.* That was a sudden switch of gears. "Pen and Helen told me that I could start incorporating baby massage classes." His face lit up. "Hey, you need a baby massage? I'd be happy to come over and teach you both how to do it."

He bent down to the baby's level. "You would love it, Baby R.

It would calm you right down." He stood up and paused for a beat, regarding me honestly. "Great to see you thriving, Ani."

"I'm not the one for you, Dylan," I said softly, reaching out to briefly touch his cheek. I tried to give him the same gift of honesty that he'd given me. "You know why? Because we'd lead each other in crazy tangents. Each of us needs a stability point, or else we'd wander from project to project, without something anchoring us home."

He seemed to agree. "I really respect you. You've got courage to do big things."

"So do you." I smiled. "You dreamed of med school. You changed my life."

We stood there hugging, Rosie fast asleep in her carrier on the floor.

"Can I ask you something that's been on my mind?" I got up the courage to ask.

"Of course."

"We married young, and we've both agreed in the past that we were the kind of people who might get easily swept away." I halted, unsure if I should continue. "Do you think...do you think that's a flaw of mine?"

I braced myself, because I knew he'd be honest. I had to hear the truth so that I wouldn't keep making the same mistakes.

He chuckled.

"What's so funny?" I asked with righteous outrage. "It took a lot for me to ask that!"

"Don't be so rough on yourself," he said with a big grin. "I mean, you didn't marry that Tyler guy, right? That's why we're here, to learn from our mistakes. Everybody makes them. You're one hell of an amazing woman, Ani Green."

"Well, you're an amazing guy," I said back. He deserved someone good and kind—but that someone was definitely not me. I felt oddly relieved as I picked up Rosie's carrier. I hope I'd learned from my past. I didn't want to start another relationship without asking the tough questions, having the tough conversations.

I kissed him on the cheek. "Thank you for that."

"I have that effect on people."

"Maybe we'll take you up on that baby massage," I said.

"You wouldn't be sorry," he said, then added, "I love you, Ani."

"I love you too." I gave him a hug. "Don't do anything bad to my patients, okay?" I paused. "Or to Pen," I added with a smile.

～

Adam

Ani and I had arrived home after work the next Friday, only to be immediately shooed out by both of our mothers. That was how we ended up having drinks on the grand patio of The Centurion, a grand old hotel downtown that overlooked Lake Bellevue.

The moms, as we called them, told us not to show our faces until checkout tomorrow. The reservation was made. They'd even packed us a bag. We'd been given the gift of eighteen precious hours of freedom.

I'm not going to lie. I wanted to spend every single one of them in bed with Ani. But I figured it would be polite to at least eat first.

"The sunset is spectacular," Ani said. I agreed. After all, this was the famous bluff with all the oaks, the famous view after which our beautiful little town was named. It came complete with beautiful Lake Eleanor, over which the sun was now setting in hues of fiery golds and pinks.

"Stunning," I said.

"You're staring at me," she said, frowning. "Why?"

"Because I have the best view."

She laughed and declared me full of it as I reached over and took her hands in mine. "What would you like to do with all this precious free time we have?" I certainly had a few suggestions if she didn't.

She smiled as she took a peek at her phone. "There's outdoor music tonight, kayaking, paddle boarding, biking...you call it." She scrolled through the hotel website. But then she swiped off the website and began to send a text.

"Is everything okay?" I asked, noticing her look of concern.

She glanced up briefly, then kept typing. "I can't remember if I told our moms where the prescription diaper rash medicine was. I picked it up from the pharmacy at lunchtime, and I think I put it on the counter near the fruit bowl."

"I think I remember seeing a white bag there."

"Okay, thanks." She set down the phone and gave me a weak smile. "I feel like I should have told them a million things. But anyway, while we're sitting here, I thought we could have a little discussion about things we haven't had the time to talk about yet."

Whoa. A discussion? Now? Couldn't we do that under the covers? Instead, I asked, "Such as?"

"Like, I don't know your favorite color. Your favorite drink. Your favorite book."

She looked genuinely worried about this gap in knowledge, so I said, "Blue, *Moby Dick*, milk."

She looked fake-shocked. "*Moby Dick*? Really? I'm not sure I can date you now."

Okay, she'd chosen to discuss books over my love of milk. That was okay, because I loved books too. "*Moby Dick* is all about the destructive power of obsession, the untamable power of nature, the conflict between humanity and nature, the limits of human knowledge...Shall I go on?"

She held up her hands. "I'm good," she said with a laugh.

"Can I guess yours?" I regarded her thoughtfully, tapping my fingers on the wrought iron patio table. "Your favorite color is that bright pink you always dress Rosie in. You love *Pride and Prejudice*, and as a girl, you used to stay up reading under the covers with a flashlight—and you could never limit yourself to one favorite book. And your favorite drink is...coffee."

Her eyes narrowed suspiciously. "How did you know all of that?"

"Your mom might have told me the covers thing," I confessed. Rather than look impressed or give me an eye roll or two, her gaze kept straying back to her phone.

"Ani," I said to get her to look up. "What are you worried about this time?"

"Do you think she's crying? You know that early evenings are her worst time. Do you think she notices that I'm gone? I forgot to take her laundry out of the dryer. What if she poops all over the place and there aren't any sleepers left?"

I reached across the table and covered her hand with mine. "All I know is that we survived, so our mothers could probably handle a baby for one evening."

"I'm sorry." She pulled away her hand. "I didn't think I'd be so stressed out. I was even wishing for that monitor app you can put on your phone so that you can actually see your baby from wherever you are."

A hard no. "If this is too much, we can leave after dinner." Her eyes teared up. "Hey, if you're that worried, we can leave right now." *But I would really hate that.*

"Do you mean that?" She swiped at her eyes.

"No, but I thought it sounded good." When she reached for a tissue from her purse, I got worried. "Wait—are you crying? If you're crying, let's just leave right now. Time away isn't worth it if you're stressed."

"It's not the worry." She shook her head as she blew her nose. "I'm thinking how kind you always are, even though I'm ruining our time away." She squeezed my hand hard. "I may not know your favorite food, but I know what's in your heart. And...you're wonderful."

"Pizza, hands down, for breakfast, lunch, and dinner," I said to distract her. "Now you know everything important about me. And you're not ruining anything." I paused. "Wonderful, huh? Undeserved. But you should also know that I think you're pretty wonderful too."

"Did Liv want you to date?" Ani asked without preamble. Wow, she was really getting everything off her mind, wasn't she? Did time off always do that to her? I sure hoped not.

I had to admit, her question threw me a little. But I remembered something that suddenly made me smile. "Actually, Liv told me once that I could never date anyone after she was gone. She even said that she was the only woman I was ever allowed to love."

Ani looked solemn. "I get it. I would never want to give you up either."

"Also undeserved but thank you. And if seeing how Dylan looks at you is any indication of my jealousy, I get it too." I sighed. "Liv said that partly in jest, but I understood what she was feeling. It was hard, you know? Knowing she was going to die." I shrugged and met Ani's gaze.

"Do you think Liv would like me?" She was still holding my hand in a vise grip.

"I know she would," I said softly. "She always admired people who weren't afraid to do big things. She was a teacher, and she did everything she could for her students." Since we were talking openly like this, I thought of something I wanted to ask her.

"Since we're telling all about ourselves, you never told me how you left things with Tyler? I've been wondering."

"We handled all the financial transactions from the wedding, but he won't speak to me about anything other than business." She lifted her shoulders in a sad shrug. "I feel that I need to apologize for the blindside, you know? At first, I felt justified, but now... Now I see the huge embarrassment calling off the wedding must have caused him." She folded her hands together. "I've called him, but he never picks up. I've left him a handful of voicemails."

"Maybe he just needs some time."

She nodded. "I'm not going to give up."

"It's good to put things to rest."

"Okay, well, I have one last thing."

"Hit me." I'd been hoping all this talking might be a form of foreplay, but now I wasn't so sure. But it was still nice. And I got the sense that maybe Ani hadn't done enough of it—talking, that is—with Tyler.

She took a big breath and continued. "My mom used to say I was too much. Sort of like, 'Oh, Ani. You're too much.' I know she mostly said it when I was a teenager, usually when I was creating some big scheme, but it stuck with me. It sometimes leaves me wondering if I'm too much for...anybody."

"You're not too much for me."

That got me the slightest smile, but maybe she didn't really believe me because she kept talking.

"People are raising their eyebrows at us. A friend of my mom's asked her about what we were doing in the grocery store. Apparently, we're the subject of gossip. How do you feel about that? I mean, we haven't really dated. Nothing is normal. We're both exhausted. Our 'arrangement' is unusual."

I leaned back in my chair and grinned. This was an easy one. So I spoke the words honestly. "You stop me in my tracks. You take my breath away. I admire everything about you. And now I see that you're a wonderful mother too. Every minute I'm with you, I thank my lucky stars for you. And I feel that way about Rosebud too."

That made her start to flat-out cry. Of course, the waitress chose that time to arrive to take our order. "I'll come back," she said, quickly backing away.

After she left, I handed Ani my napkin and said, "I want to remind you that this is supposed to be a fun evening." I'd figured that after all this high emotion, we'd probably end it by settling in bed watching Netflix. But that would be okay. At least we'd be together. She was still dabbing at her eyes. "Please don't cry."

She used the napkin to blow her nose and then met my gaze. "Adam, you're misunderstanding me. No one has ever said anything so wonderful to me."

Good. I wanted to tell her more wonderful things, preferably upstairs, but I wasn't sure if she wanted that. Out of the corner of my eye, I could see the waitress making her way back. "Are you hungry?"

She set down the napkin on her empty plate and said definitively, "I'm ready to go back to the room." She paused. "And eat from the minibar." She gave me a poignant look, and then glanced at her watch as she stood. "We'd better hurry. Sixteen hours and counting."

I'm sure I flashed her a giant, wicked smile. Could we spend the next sixteen hours in bed? I didn't know, but I was sure willing to try.

~

Ani

I don't remember taking the elevator. I do remember opening the door to a luxurious suite with a huge bed with lots of white puffy pillows and comforters and Adam immediately tackling me onto it. We landed together, laughing in the twilight, the warm spring breeze drifting in from a sliding door that led to a small balcony. I was trembling with anticipation. Then his lips were on mine, soft and warm and determined.

"Adam, I—"

"Yes?" His hair was mussed. Heat was in his eyes, all directed at me, which made my heart squeeze with pure joy. I reached up and pushed his hair back, ran my hand along his cheek, felt the roughness of his jaw. "Adam, I—I want you to know that I'm not always a chaos agent."

He threw his head back, bursting out laughing. "A what?"

I'd clearly thrown him. "A chaos agent. You know, someone who's always disruptive and unpredictable. This past year—"

His face held a bemused expression. But also a loving one. I mean, he hadn't said *I love you*, but it was in his eyes. I felt it in his touch as he gently slid my curls out of my eyes.

He took a moment to really look at me. Under his perusal, I felt like he was seeing the best of me, a version that he thought I was, but I wasn't quite sure I could live up to. Maybe that's why I'd said what I said.

"Honey," he said in his most roguish voice, "if you're a chaos agent, you are that in the best way. You shook me awake and got me living again. I've never met anyone like you. I wouldn't ever want you to change."

Then he kissed me, and I lost myself in the feel of his mouth, the heat of his body so close to mine. "By the way," he said as he lowered his head, "I'm not leaving this room until late checkout tomorrow. We'll DoorDash something if there's no room service."

"I'm only hungry for one thing," I said, and then covered my eyes and groaned. "That was so cliché."

"Honey, nothing about this night is going to be cliché."

He was fun and playful, and, oh, the man could kiss. And he tasted wonderful. He took his time, slow, gentle, thorough kisses that made me forget all about...well, everything. There was no baby monitor alerting us to every move, no sudden cry to rouse us out of a deep sleep, no dog snorting and dreaming of chasing small, helpless animals.

"I want to make love to you," he said, pressing kisses to my neck, trailing downward.

Oh, thrill. My head was spinning, my heart pounding. But mostly, I was filled with the feeling that This. Was. It. *He* was where my journey ended. I would never love anyone like this. I'd found the one person who truly got me. Who accepted me for who I was. Who liked me for *exactly* that reason.

As he returned to my mouth, I yielded to his lips, ran my hands through the thick silk of his hair, felt his muscles bunch and tense as I ran my hands along his back. I kissed his forehead, the ridge of his brow, the curve of his cheek, memorizing every bit of him.

We luxuriated in a time together that wasn't interrupted by... well, anything. Sort of like in Turks and Caicos, but a hundred times better.

As we both shattered to pieces, he was right there, kissing me, holding me, murmuring in my ear in soft tones how beautiful I was, how lucky he was to be here with me.

He took my hand and kissed it. Looked deeply into my eyes. Then he pulled me into his arms, and I settled next to him, my head on his chest, holding each other tight.

I love you was on the tip of my tongue. I was bursting to say it, but I restrained myself. I didn't want to say it first and then have him feel like he had to say it back.

He loves me, I thought. And he loves Rosie. He *would* say it, in his own time.

That was just like me, to always want everything, expecting everything all at once, wanting things tied up in a nice, perfect bow. I couldn't wait to tell him I loved him, yet I didn't feel like I was being impulsive any longer. I felt this with a certainty I'd never experienced before.

Adam was kinder and more wonderful than anyone I'd ever met, and I felt certain that he was my future. I was head over heels.

I just hoped that he was too.

Chapter Seventeen

Three months later

Adam

"How was your day today, Rosebud?" I asked Rosie, who was holding her cow rattle and sucking on the ears as I changed her diaper. I was expecting Ani, who had stopped by her office for a few hours, to arrive home any minute. It was the day of her final interview with Children's Services, and we were both anxious for it to be over. I kept telling her she had it in the bag, that she was a shoo-in, but neither of us was going to rest until the final documents about making her Rosie's official foster parent were stamped, signed, and filed.

"Mooo-ooo," I said with much expression, "That's what cows say. Mooooooo."

Rosie kicked her legs vigorously. "Oooooooh" she said.

Wow. Okay. Impressive. "You're an absolute genius," I said, taping the tabs on her diaper. "Brilliant."

I heard the door open and shut. Ani came flying in, depositing her book bag and purse and running over to the changing table, kissing me quickly on the cheek.

"Hey, Rosie-Posie, how was your day?" Rosie immediately abandoned the cow and beamed at Ani, displaying a giant smile that lit up her entire face. Actually, her entire body, as she excitedly kicked up a storm.

I totally got it. Ani had that effect on me too.

I picked Rosie up and got ready to hand her off. "She can moo like a cow," I announced proudly.

"What?" Ani asked Rosie. "You mooo-ed?"

The baby smiled a drooly smile and leaned toward Ani, who took her into her arms in that fluid movement mothers seem to effortlessly master. "You're perfect," Ani said to Rosie, kissing her on the head, "whether you are actually mooing or not."

"It was a *moo*, I swear."

"Almost-four-month-olds can imitate sounds," Dr. Ani said. "Like, she doesn't actually *know* that cows moo yet."

"I prefer to think that her language skills are very advanced. Today we'll review some farm animal flashcards just to make sure they took. Tomorrow we'll work on some algebra. I'll have her ready for med school applications by Christmas."

Ani gave me a look that might've meant *you're ridiculous*, but she broke into a big laugh.

Of course I chuckled right back. Our life was like that a lot. For the first time since Liv died, I went days without thinking of death, of endings, of tragedy. I was too busy living life.

Over Ani's shoulder, out the window, a black sedan pulled into the driveway. *Uh oh*. I was thinking of how to put a positive, lighthearted spin on the impending interview when Ani spotted the car too.

"Oh, I hope it's Charity again." I saw a flicker of worry pass across her face as she held out the baby to me, ran over to the kitchen sink, and began rubbing something on her blouse with a wet paper towel.

I prepped Rosie's bottle while Ani added soap and kept scrubbing. "Does my blouse look okay?" She inspected the tiny floral print. "When I was seeing patients this afternoon, a baby spit up on me."

"Very professional, no spit-up in sight," I said. "I'd definitely hire you."

"You're biased," she said. "I need to look competent. Today is the psychosocial evaluation. It determines my fitness not only to foster but also to ultimately adopt Rosie."

After assessing her grave expression, I decided to keep things light. "You are so competent." I shot her my most admiring grin. "And hot."

"You're sticking around, right?" she asked. "They'll be asking me household relationship questions today. Like, to make sure anyone involved in Rosie's life is safe."

"That's why I'm here." I squeezed her shoulder. "You got this."

She gave me a look that was half grateful, half worried, and then threw her arms around me in a giant hug. She didn't need say anything to let me know she was glad I was here.

She did have this. She was an amazing, wonderful mother in every way.

As I fed Rosie, I noticed a car in the driveway. A woman got out and began walking up the stone path, which I was proud to say was now very tidy and neat, thanks to my new rechargeable weed whacker. She wore a navy blazer outside, despite the July heat, a long skirt, and rubber-soled shoes, and her hair was tied up in a tight gray bun.

"It's Ms. Nelson," Ani said, her tone crestfallen.

I got the concern. The woman looked terrifying. "Does Ms. Nelson have a first name?" I asked. "Ursula? Narissa? Cruella?"

"Glad to see that you're up on your Disney villains." Ani

walked up behind me and rested her hand on my back as we peered out the window.

"She looks like someone you'd never call by their first name," I said to be funny.

"I know," Ani said in a somber tone.

I turned around and grabbed her hands. "You're going to nail this. You're an awesome mom." I kissed each of her hands in turn. I was hoping for a smile, but she immediately teared up instead. "I love her so much, Adam. I don't want to do anything to screw this up now."

"There's nothing to screw up. We have seven smoke alarms, four carbon monoxide detectors, and you can't even plug in the coffee pot without removing a child safety cover."

She laughed a little at that. "You know that's not what I'm worried about."

I knew she was worried about what she called her "imperfect relationship history." "No one's perfect," I said in my most reassuring voice. Then I kissed her on the nose. "But you come close."

I wanted to tell her not to look back. To keep moving forward. That had been the mantra for both of us these past few months. But I figured she didn't need me to spell it out. The doorbell rang, and I tapped her playfully on the butt as she ran to let Ms. Nelson in.

She looked back and smiled.

I shot her two-thumbs-up as I went to put the baby down for her nap. I knew that Ani would be great. This was a no-brainer. What could go wrong?

~

Ani

. . .

On the way to the door, I rehearsed my past mishaps, my past failed relationships, and tried to figure out the best way to explain Adam's presence in my life. I was blowing things out of proportion thinking the worst. No one had a perfect life, right?

Surely, I would gain points for being a responsible human and for working so diligently to make this happen. I truly believed that I was the one to be Rosalie's mother, and that belief gave me strength. What else really mattered?

Why, oh why couldn't I have gotten Ms. Charity this time instead of Ms. Nelson? As if in response to all my wild thoughts, Arnie bounded up from his bed and raced me to the door, skidding to a frantic stop right in front of it and letting out a loud bark. I sent him a warning look as in *Please be a good doggie*, and he answered by barking again in adolescent rebellion.

"Come in, Ms. Nelson," I said, waving her in. "May I get you some coffee, water, a Diet Coke?"

"I don't use caffeine or artificial sweeteners, but thank you," she said as I guided her to the couch. Arnold followed on her heels, and once she sat down, he sniffed her legs. She ignored him. Arnold, offput, growled.

He never growled. Like, *never*.

Ms. Nelson, looking offended and maybe even a little disgusted, said, "Does he bite?"

"Oh, no," I said. "Arnold is the sweetest dog."

He growled again.

"Ice water it is," Adam said, suddenly appearing after putting Rosie down and beelining for the kitchen.

"My teeth are sensitive, so no ice, please," she called after him.

"Adam, will you please get Arnold a treat while you're in there?" I called.

Mention of Arnold's favorite word usually sent him bolting into the kitchen to stand in front of the broom closet where we kept his dog cookies. But not this time. He remained parked in front of Ms. Nelson, standing guard and emitting an occasional low growl.

"Arnie, come here," I said, to see if I could get him over to me where I could give him a nice calming rubdown. However, Arnie wouldn't budge. The muscles around my mouth hurt from smiling already. Inside, I felt total dread vibes that I couldn't shake. Ms. Nelson hadn't even begun her questions, yet all signs indicated that she was uncompromising and inflexible.

What if I lost Rosalie? I couldn't bear it. She was everything to me. I loved her with all my heart. I would do anything to keep her.

Ms. Nelson ran a finger along the coffee table and examined it for dust. I'm certain she found plenty. Out of the corner of my eye, I spied a giant clump of dust bunnies clearly visible under the couch. There was an old bottle of Rosie's on the table too. Points off for bad housekeeping.

Strike two, strike one being our fierce dog. She was literally looking for flaws. This could not possibly go well. My blood pressure was skyrocketing, and I felt exactly like I did right before my last Peds board exam.

I scored in the 90th percentile on that, I reminded myself.

Maybe I *was* flawed. Maybe I'd made some mistakes. But I was the right person to raise Rosalie. *Me.* I would fight for that privilege with my last breath.

Adam cleared his throat as he sat down, placing two waters on the table, one apparently for me. As he introduced himself, he gave me a half-hidden thumbs-up. *You got this*, he mouthed.

That calmed me—a little. And reminded me that he was perfect. Wonderful. The best part of my life. How lucky I'd been to be a distressed, failed bride that day a year ago on the plane. I just worried that Ms. Nelson would ask me to define a relationship that we ourselves hadn't yet formally defined.

Ms. Nelson opened a fat navy binder full of all the minute details of my life—my financial history, my house loan, my 401K, my health history, the house safety inspection, the classes I'd taken online, and the passing scores of the exams I'd had to take. So far, so good.

She opened the binder to a page and neatly folded her hands over it. "As you know, today is the psychosocial evaluation. We'll be talking about your emotional health, relationships, and your motivations for fostering and adopting Rosalie."

Arnold objected by growling again. He hadn't moved an inch. It was like he was telling Ms. Nelson that if she made one false move, it was off with her head.

"Arnie, come here, *please*," I said in my most commanding voice. Our dog looked at me and turned his head to the side, as if to say, *I see your lips moving, but I can't really hear you.*

Teenager, indeed.

I sat rigidly in my chair. I wished I'd chosen a seat next to Adam, who was sitting on a couch. He was leaning forward, endlessly tapping his fingertips together, the only evidence of his underlying worry. As tempting as it was, I couldn't physically lean on him now. I had to stand on my own. I'd come this far. I prayed for the strength to see this through.

"We know you're a pediatrician, and that financially and health-wise, everything's worked out." Ms. Nelson flipped through the many pages. "But today we're going to concentrate on you personally. I'd like to talk about stability of relationships. I understand you've had a divorce in the past and a failed wedding last year. You decided that you wanted to adopt this baby quite suddenly, after the mother handed her to you. Had you been planning to adopt a child, Dr. Green?"

I took a breath and jumped in. "When I delivered Rosalie, I promised her mother she'd be in good hands. It was an extension of that sentiment that made me realize that I wanted to be the one to care for her."

"That's a highly unusual move. Plus you're single," she said. "That makes things more difficult, of course. We have to make certain you're aware of that."

"Single moms raise children successfully all the time," Adam pointed out.

Of course, they did. "My decision might have come about in an unusual way," I said, "but it was sincere. I felt an immediate connection to Rosalie—and to her mother's plight. I feel that I have what it takes to give her a great life—a good job, a home, and most of all, plenty of love."

"I see," she said in a deadpan tone. She scribbled something down, seemingly unmoved by my sincerity.

"As for adopting, no, I wasn't considering it as an option. But I've always wanted children." Maybe I should have said that I'd always wanted to adopt. Maybe I should have practiced becoming a better liar.

"Let's start with your first marriage." Ms. Nelson sat with pen poised. "Was that an impulsive decision too?"

She was baiting me, no doubt about it. But I stuck to stating the facts. "Dylan and I dated for several years in college." I omitted the fact that we'd eloped in Vegas.

"And you divorced because..."

"We were young. We wanted different things." Did this have anything to do with who I was now? I almost protested, but I didn't want to appear angry or emotional. I just wanted to get through these ghastly questions.

"And the man you almost married last year—Tyler Banks. What happened there?"

"These are very personal questions," Adam said. "I think the important thing there is that Ani avoided making a mistake. It's really irrelevant to fostering Rosalie."

"I'm simply looking for patterns of impulsivity and instability," Ms. Nelson said, turning her sights on Adam. "What is your relationship to Dr. Green and the baby, Dr. Lowenstein?"

"We're dating," Adam said simply.

"I see." She wrote that down. "For how long?"

"Since we met last summer." I knew immediately why he said

that—to make it seem longer than it was. We'd really only been dating for less than four months. But I had no doubt in my mind that Adam was my forever person. I couldn't imagine myself with anyone else, and I'd never wavered in that certainty.

"So you began dating right after the canceled wedding?" She looked above her glasses at Adam. "Were *you* the reason for the cancelled wedding, Dr. Lowenstein?"

"No!" I said a little excitedly. *Oh no.* I was messing this up, letting my nerves show. I immediately forced a calmer tone. "What he means is that we met last summer, and we became friends. And *then* we started dating."

I caught Adam's eye across the coffee table. There was no winning here, and I felt the doom sink like a rock tied to my feet.

"So you began dating amid the chaos of caring for a newborn?"

"We love the chaos." Adam calmly draped his arm across the couch. He seemed very relaxed—and truthful. I loved him for the effort. "I'm very committed to Ani and the baby."

"And what exactly is your role to the baby, Dr. Lowenstein?"

"I love Rosalie," he said. "I help care for her."

"Do you live here?"

"My house is a block away. Ani and I tag team watching Rosie around our schedules."

"I see. Well, it's one thing to foster," Ms. Nelson said, "but another entirely to adopt. And I must say, as a single woman with a demanding job, men who could potentially drift in and out of the baby's life, a series of impulsive decisions made on a whim…"

"Wait—there are no *men*," I said. "There's one man—Adam."

"…who is actively involved in her care, and whom you date, Dr Green. Who may or may not continue to be involved in the baby's life. It seems to me that there are a lot of transient relationships here. A failed relationship that nearly led to marriage, followed by an impulsive decision to adopt a baby that you were basically handed in the delivery room, followed by another relationship where you, Dr. Lowenstein, have become a primary caregiver in a very short time. Plus, both of you are physicians with demanding schedules."

My entire body went cold. I started to shake so uncontrollably that I had to sit on my hands to stop. Even worse, Arnold left his post and began pacing back and forth in front of the fireplace. And then let out an aggravated bark.

"You're looking at my life on paper, Ms. Nelson." I tried not to plead, but I had to make my case. "I have a great job, a caring family and friends, and a home. Loving relatives care for Rosalie when I'm at work, like many other people who work with children. Most importantly of all, I love this little baby with all my heart."

"Ani felt passionately about Rosalie from the beginning," Adam said. "She knew that she could make a difference. That's not impulsive—it's proactive. I'm committed to Ani and Rosalie," he said. "I love them both. While our relationship is new, I'm deeply committed. Ani is a great mother. I can vouch for her emotional stability."

Ms. Nelson kept writing, God only knew what. "Let's move on. May I ask, how do you two handle conflict?"

"We talk things out," I said. "Right, Adam?" That was a good answer to another hellish question, wasn't it?

"Absolutely," he said. But then I wondered, what conflict did we exactly have? We'd put everything else in our lives aside to care for Rosalie. We got to know each other in between bottles and diapers, exhaustion and sleep deprivation. How on earth was this a normal relationship?

Then I thought of how, with Tyler, I was constantly talking myself into believing that we were on the same page. If he didn't hug me often, I'd tell myself that I didn't need the assurance that he loved me. If he gave me a dirty look, I'd think that it was normal to sometimes be frustrated.

When he assumed I would do the dishes every night, and I told him we needed to switch off, he'd tell me how important his job was compared to mine, and he didn't have time for dishes. And then I'd blame his egocentricity on his stress.

No, my relationship with Tyler was not a normal one. But my relationship with Adam was. "Adam and I are on the same page most of the time."

"We want to be Rosalie's parents," Adam added. "We want to give her a great life. It's our intention to marry one day."

Aw. I loved hearing that, even if I wasn't sure if Adam was just trying to get us out of this mess.

"Your *intention* to marry?" Ms. Nelson wrote that down too. "It would be easier if you *were* married. The stability of marriage for children might be prioritized over a single-parent household."

This was a slow, painful death. Dread was slowly choking me like twining vines wrapping around my throat. I had to know the truth. "Ms. Nelson, are you going to recommend me to be Rosie's parent?"

She sniffed and kept her head in her notebook. "I have reservations."

Adam stood. "Anyone can see that the baby lights up when Ani enters the room. And Ani loves this baby more than anything in the world. I give you my word that she's an amazing mother."

I shot him my most grateful look.

Arnie stopped pacing and sat forlornly, now whimpering. This awful interview was stressing everyone out. I leaned over and clapped my hands lightly, and he finally came over and let me love him up.

"That may all be true, Dr. Lowenstein," Ms. Nelson said, finally looking up from her binder, "but there is evidence of a tendency toward impulsivity that might possibly be interpreted as uncommitted."

"There's no one more committed to this child, Ms. Nelson," he said in a firm tone.

I could tell his calm demeanor was finally cracking. "What would help my case?" I asked.

"Stability. Commitment. Marriage."

Adam's head suddenly jerked up. "I care very deeply for Ani."

This woman was practically doing bloodletting. Where were the leeches?

"That's a lovely sentiment, Dr. Lowenstein, but unfortunately, sentiments don't move judges."

"We want to give Rosalie a stable home and a great life, Ms. Nelson." He paused for a long time. "That's why we want you to know that we *are* getting married." He turned to me. "Tell her, Ani."

Chapter Eighteen

Adam

Ani blinked. She stared wide-eyed at me, in that way that someone looks at you when they don't comprehend a single word you've said. "You want to marry me?" Her voice was barely more than a whisper.

My stomach churned sickly. This was definitely *not* how I envisioned asking anyone to marry me. But I'd been backed against a wall, and I could not allow Ani to lose Rosie. I rubbed my neck, getting up the courage to look Ani in the eye. "Yes." My voice sounded deadly calm and serious—not excited or jubilant. I cleared my throat and tried for better. "I'm committed to both of you."

Ani suddenly began to cry. I mean, big, giant sobs. At first, I didn't understand what was going on until I saw that she really was overwhelmed. I got it—the possibility of losing the baby was overwhelming me too. She ran over and threw her arms around me, clinging on so tightly that I had trouble taking a breath. "I love you!"

My heart sank as she kept sobbing. She was not acting. I held her, but I couldn't think. My life had been a whirlwind these past few months. I'd become a completely different person because of her, for the better, but this...

So far, I'd been riding the wave of each day, showing up, learning, cruising along. But what I'd just done...this was a blind leap off a cliff the height of Everest, and I was free-falling without a safety net.

Help.

My heart was pounding so loudly and fast that I felt faint, and a trickle of sweat slowly snaked its way down my back. In the moment, I'd gone overboard. Went into savior mode. Said anything to get Ani what she wanted most, the ability to mother Rosalie, and Rosalie the chance to have the mother who loved her unconditionally. Which I knew with all my heart that both of them completely deserved.

But what did *I* want? From day one, I'd been swept up onto this wild rollercoaster ride that was Ani.. But I hadn't even said *I love you* yet. All throughout these extraordinary circumstances, I'd shown up for everything, day or night, and had loved every minute. But was I ready for marriage? *Now?*

My skin felt clammy, and my throat became so dry that it felt clogged with a bunch of straw.

Ani pulled back and searched my eyes. "You look a little pale. Are you okay?"

"Of course." I was aware that our friendly caseworker was witnessing all of this. I tried to talk myself down, think positively.

I'd just been getting my bearings. I'd come a long way, but I wasn't *ready*. But what choice did I have?

I'd sat there while Ms. Nelson was grilling Ani and googled statistics in our state that seemed to favor married couples over single people for adoptions. It was apparent that this woman was disapproving and hard-core, and I could tell that she wasn't thrilled with any of Ani's answers. It was almost like she'd wanted her—us—to trip up.

I turned to Ms. Nelson, who was still sitting there with a sour look on her face, no doubt because of our PDA. I kept my arm around Ani and said as confidently as I could muster, "Ms. Nelson, sometimes extraordinary circumstances require extraordinary measures. I adore this woman and this baby. Together, we are committed to giving her a great life." I paused. "Also, I want you to know I'm hiring a personal lawyer to look over all your agency's paperwork to make certain we're being fairly represented. We wouldn't want any mistruths or exaggerations now, would we?"

Ms. Nelson, possibly flustered by this new turn of events, quickly gathered all her paperwork and shut her big, horrible binder. "I believe we're done here. Congratulations on your engagement."

As soon as the door shut behind her, I backed up to the sofa and sat. I tried to take a couple of deep breaths without looking like I was doing that, which probably only made me seem weird. Ani was examining me now, in that assessing doctor way. And I feared that she was smelling a rat.

She sat down next to me and grabbed my wrist. "Your pulse is pounding. Your skin is that dull, yucky color of the walls in your house. Either you're having a heart attack, or you're scared out of your wits. Which is it?"

She knew me. Inside and out. Sometimes, that was the best thing. But now it was the worst.

I managed a smile. "That was...that was one tough interview." I tried not to reach up to wipe the sweat accumulating on my brow.

That seemed to pacify her. She nodded, sat down next to me, and took my hands in hers. They were warm and soft and fit so well, interwoven with mine. That calmed me a little. Reminded me of how great we were together.

"Adam, I was so frightened. I thought I'd lost Rosie."

"I would never let that happen." There. That sounded like me. Of that I was one hundred percent certain. If only I could feel that way about everything else.

Maybe Ani knew that what I'd done was to save the interview. Maybe I wouldn't even have to explain further.

She searched my eyes for a long time, as if reassuring herself that I'd been sincere. "I love you," she said again.

Okay, maybe she'd taken that proposal at face value. "Me too," I managed, holding her as she rested her head on my chest. I had to force myself to relax my muscles, to not appear as rigid as a piece of steel.

Ani lifted her head and gazed solemnly into my eyes. "Adam, I've never felt as comfortable with anyone as I am with you. I know that these past few months have been a whirlwind, but I know you're the one." She pressed her hands to her chest. "I know it with my whole heart. I can't thank you enough for what you've done."

Of course we made love. I kept telling myself that all this was for the best, that I would've never forgiven myself for not doing everything I could in that moment. But I was rattled. In bed afterward, Ani clung to my side while I held her in the most comforting way I could. Yet in the darkness, I stared up at the ceiling, wondering, *What the hell have I done?*

～

Ani

The next morning was Saturday, and I awakened to the smell of fresh coffee and also to a fresh panic attack. I'd slept terribly, having nightmares of a comically dressed Ms. Nelson with smeared red lipstick snatching Rosie away and cackling like the witch when she stole Toto and stuffed him into her bike basket. My nightmares had brought clarity, making me realize that I'd gotten desperate during that interview, willing to grasp at anything to get things back on track. But the straw I grasped at came at an enormous price—I knew that now. And I didn't know what to do.

The previous night, Adam was quiet and stiff and out of his usual jokes, the biggest indicator that something wasn't right. He'd seemed preoccupied during our lovemaking and soon rolled over and went straight to sleep, also troubling.

I grabbed a cup and said hi. He already had Rosie up and changed. She was sitting with him in the recliner, their favorite chair, chugging her morning bottle, her little hand rubbing back and forth over his as I kissed her on the head and took in her sweet baby smell.

She loved him. He loved her.

It all seemed perfect. But I knew in my heart that it wasn't.

I'd always been amazed that Adam seemed to sense when something was wrong with me without me saying a thing. Apparently, I could do the same, because I was definitely feeling major unsettling vibes radiating off of him in every direction, despite his extra calm demeanor and his tightly controlled smile.

"Hey, I—" *Are we okay? Can we talk?*

"Hey, watch this," he said at the same time, effectively cutting off my panicked train of thought. "Rosie learned a new trick."

"Okay, Rosebud." He set down her bottle, got up, and transferred her to a blanket he had spread out on the carpet. "Let's show Mommy what we learned."

Mommy.

Stab my heart. I actually clutched my chest. *Mother* was a privilege, an honor. One that I wasn't sure I would ever fully achieve. I looked at this big man sitting on the floor with this smiley baby, and I saw how fleeting life could be. How precious. How lucky. How fragile.

I loved him, plain and simple.

I cleared my throat. "Hey, I'm meeting Sam and Mia for coffee this morning," I said. I needed some clarity. I needed my friends to help talk me down from this crisis. I needed to get away from here and think.

He raised his brows. "Oh, okay. Well, watch this." Rosie was on her back, kicking up a storm as he held up her favorite cow rattle, the one with the gross ear from her sucking on it all the time. Of course, she immediately grabbed for it and brought it straight to her mouth.

But then Adam shook it, made it dance, voice-overed a few mooooos, and placed it down on the ground out of her reach. "Go get it, Rosebud."

"She can't," I said.

He shot me a mischievous grin. "Oh, yes, she can."

For a moment, everything seemed to return to that fun, light, easy way we had, where we marveled at every little thing.

Rosie lay there, kicking, smiling at Adam. He smiled back, then glanced in my direction, a crease of worry between his brows. "Before you go, I have to ask you something. What kind of engagement ring would you like?"

I sucked in a breath of surprise. And suddenly got choked up—with an aching sadness. I scolded myself—after all, Adam had sacrificed everything, himself, namely, to ensure that I got Rosie.

But he'd just asked me about an engagement ring in between making silly faces at the baby while I had one foot out the door as if he were asking *What kind of milk should I pick up at the store, almond or 1%?* Everything was really...off kilter.

"My grandma left me an old-fashioned cut diamond," I said. "I thought it might be nice to make a ring from that someday." I thought more about that and added, "But don't rush, okay? I-I think we should let all this settle a bit."

"Okay," he said in a wary, tired tone.

I didn't want to talk about rings. Which was strange, because I'd had a vision for the ring I wanted for a long time, which meant even more to me now that my grandmother was gone. And it was wonderful to be asked about what I wanted. Tyler had bought me a two-point-five carat marquise-cut diamond in a very modern setting without asking me beforehand what style I might want. It was so weighted down that it flopped constantly around my finger, even after I'd had it resized. In retrospect, that should have been an omen right there.

On the floor, Rosie got her core muscles moving as she planted her legs and started to rock her body.

Then suddenly, *flip,* she did it. Rolled over and grabbed her precious cow.

I captured the whole thing on video. "You're brilliant," I said. "So smart."

"Atta girl, Rosebud," Adam said. "You're a go-getter. Just like your mama." Rosie lay there sucking the cow ear and kicking her little legs, looking very pleased.

My eyes watered. Mostly because Adam was still supporting me *and* complimenting me, even though he was upset.

I couldn't bear it.

He glanced behind his shoulder at me just as I'd finished swiping at my eyes. "Hey, why don't I come with you?" he asked. "Then we can tell everyone about our engagement."

I stared at him. I wanted to tell him no. That nothing felt right, and how could we keep pretending like this?

But I couldn't sort out my feelings. Of course, I was terrified of losing Rosie, and I would do anything, anything in the world, to keep her. Was I also panicked because I was gun-shy, owing to my awful experience with Tyler? Was I unsure of what I felt for this man who'd put everything on the line for me, even if he wasn't ready to marry me?

No. I wasn't unsure of that. But everything else felt so...wrong.

Just then, Rosie had a total blowout diaper, necessitating a bath, an entire load of laundry, and all hands on deck. After that, she was hungry and tired, and Adam said he'd stay and put her to bed.

I thanked him and left out the door, relieved to get away somewhere where I could think.

~

Ani

It was bright and sunny by the time I joined my friends on the outside patio of *Bean There, Done That.* They were sitting under one of the bright red umbrellas on the patio that faced Main Street, among groups of people chatting and enjoying the warm summer day.

Ordinarily, I would have loved the free time on a lazy Saturday to sit and catch up with my friends. But I was too distressed, and that was impossible to hide.

"Are you okay?" Mia asked before I even sat down.

Sam placed a chai tea latte and a piece of banana bread in front of me, my favorites that they'd already secured for me. Except today they made my stomach churn, even as I thanked them for their trouble. "You look a little shell-shocked," Sam said. "Did something happen?"

"Nothing's wrong," I said quickly. "I mean, nothing *should* be wrong. But it feels like everything is." I suddenly burst into tears, which caught me by surprise. My friends immediately started handing me napkins, patting me on the back, coming to my rescue as we always did for one another amid all our life moments, good and bad. I loved my friends, but I hated falling apart in a public place.

As I tried to get a hold of myself, I couldn't help noticing a young couple about to sit down at a table in the corner of the patio. They were with a baby in a stroller and a little girl who looked to be around four years old. The guy parked the stroller and bent down to check on the baby while the woman pulled out a squeezy container of applesauce for the little girl and broke a large chocolate chip muffin in half for her. The couple was laughing and joking, obviously used to tag-teaming the kids.

I felt a stab of longing. For a family. A caring partner. For the simple joy of being outside in the sun with each other on a Saturday outing. Could that be Adam and I one day? Or was I just always looking for the fairy tale, ignoring the reality, like I'd done in the past?

"Ani, tell us what's wrong," Sam said.

I pulled myself together and told them my troubles. "My last interview with Children's Services yesterday went off the rails. It was the psychosocial one and the case worker was very disapproving about the fact that I'm divorced, that I called off my wedding, that I decided about fostering Rosie on a whim, and that Adam is basically living with me and helping care for the baby. It all made me look like I was impulsive, whimsical, and uncommitted."

"We all know that's not the case," Sam said firmly.

"You did something that no one I know would," Mia added. "You changed your life for that baby."

I shook my head. "I'm nothing special. My emotions drive me to do things, and sometimes that's a good thing, and other times it creates havoc in my life." I did understand this. But I also felt like my life on paper looked a lot sketchier than my real life. Getting rid of Tyler was the beginning of a life I'd become really happy about —until yesterday.

Across the way, I noticed that the little girl had on a sparkly pink tutu. Maybe she'd just come from dance class. Or maybe she was in a tutu-wearing stage like Taylor, who alternated between wearing five different *Frozen* gowns throughout each day.

The woman said something. The man placed his arm on hers and laughed. It was a tender, spontaneous moment that made me yearn for what they had—something easy and simple and authentic. I knew in my heart something like that couldn't be forced.

I felt Sam's hand nudging mine. "Tell us," she said.

I took a breath and plunged in. "Adam saw the interview falling apart, so he jumped in and said...said we were getting married." I covered my mouth with my hand, stifling a sob. Not exactly the way one wants to remember a proposal. Adam's was a defensive war cry, a savior move that had little to do with *us* and everything to do with keeping Rosie.

"Afterward, he looked like he'd suddenly contracted a GI bug. He'd made the ultimate sacrifice—for me. But that was just the thing—it was a sacrifice, not a celebration."

"Are you sure he wasn't just a little nervous?" Mia asked. "I mean, you're right, that wasn't the ideal proposal, but it's obvious that you two are great together."

"You two are meant for each other," Sam said over a sip of her mocha. "Everyone can tell."

"This is a tiny glitch," Mia said in her most reassuring tone. "You two will work it out."

Why were my friends not understanding? "It's not wonderful. It's not *real*. He did that so that I could get Rosie. He threw himself on the pyre for me!"

"Because he loves you," Sam said.

"We love Adam." Mia squeezed my arm. "I think you just need to have a discussion."

"Is this Nurse Ratched that bad?" Sam asked. "Are you sure she would go as far as not recommending you to keep Rosie? Because you can contest whatever she said. I'm sure all your recommendations are glowing. You're financially self-sufficient, you have a great job, and you've rearranged your entire life to become a foster parent. I mean, come on."

"She's pretty bad," I admitted. "But I'm afraid to rock the boat. I-I don't know what I would do if I lost Rosie." I looked down to see that I was wringing my hands. "I can't think straight about anything else."

That was what it all came down to. That not-even-twenty-pound rosy-cheeked bundle that I loved more than life itself. What wouldn't I do for her? But would I sacrifice Adam's happiness to keep her?

"Rosie takes priority, is what I say," Sam said. "You can't risk not getting her. Not after everything. I mean, you're her mom, period." She waved her hand impatiently. "Just do whatever it takes. You two were meant for each other anyway."

The little family was clearing their table, tossing away their trash. They walked off the patio and down the street, the mom pushing the stroller, the dad holding little tutu-girl's hand. A sweet family picture. A happy ending. It seemed so easy and uncomplicated.

I squeezed both their hands. "Thanks for all that. I need some time to think." I didn't feel calmer. And I didn't feel reassured, even though they'd said all the right things.

Chapter Nineteen

Adam

I usually fed Rosalie her last nightcap bottle in front of the TV while catching a game. But tonight, I sat in her dimly lit room rocking her, singing her some silly lullabies, and trying to think my way through the past day.

I would give my life for the tiny baby in my arms. Period. And I was pretty sure that I loved Ani. But marriage? A child? A lifetime commitment? That was...a lot.

Guilt and confusion hung heavily over me like an anvil about to fall. Ani was extraordinary. The baby was wonderful. What was my problem?

Liv had been gone for a long time, and the dull ache had finally dimmed. I was slowly understanding that love was possible again.

But what if tragedy unfolded again, the kind that I'd been so helpless to stop? Now I had two people to protect, to keep safe, and what if I couldn't? Life was random and out of control. I couldn't survive that kind of pain again.

I was startled by a faint rap on the doorframe. Ani stood there in her pink fluffy robe, her hair wet from the shower, looking fresh and adorable. She shuffled into the room with pink fuzzy slippers and sat down on the carpet in front of the rocker, crossing her legs.

"Thanks for grabbing her while I was in the shower."

Rosalie had passed out, her head lying on my arm, her arm tossed out with complete abandon. "Look at this," I whispered to Ani, marveling at Rosie's ability to fall asleep in the silliest positions.

Babies were so amusing. I tried to dwell on the lighter side because something in Ani's face looked absolutely grave.

It made me hold the baby a little tighter. Thoughts rose in my head, possibilities that this life was all a dream, one that could be taken away at any moment. Even with all my confused thoughts, I didn't want to lose Ani or Rosalie. I was facing a wall of pure fear that I had no idea how to climb over.

I set the baby in her crib, covered her up, and quietly turned on the monitor. We filed silently out of the room and closed the door.

"It's a nice night," Ani said. "How about we go outside?"

I followed her onto the tiny brick patio. Moonlight was streaming over the little yard in bright stripes, washing everything in a white-gray glow, hitting the overgrown but crazily-blooming rosebushes in a way that looked ethereal.

We sat side by side on a garden bench. She reached over and held my hand.

"You're such a good guy." She looked sideways at me. "So kind, so good-hearted."

I'd lived long enough to know that any sentence a woman speaks that starts with "You're such a good guy" isn't going to end well.

"I'd do anything for both of you," I said, choking up. She looked sad. Somehow, I knew what was coming.

"I know that." She went silent. The garden crickets' song, usually so peaceful, seemed now to be a high-pitched whistle, the kind a coach blows when a player screws up on the field. "That's why I can't let you do this."

"Ani, no." I turned to her. "I meant what I said. I take care of people." Why wouldn't she just let me do that? At least this was something I could do to solve a big problem. From that perspective, the decision was easy and clear. I might feel a sense of dread, but at least I didn't feel the horrible helplessness I did when Liv got sick and the entire world bottomed out.

"I don't need you to take care of me."

I jerked up my head, thrown by her words. But there was more.

"Between my jumping in impulsively and you trying to save me, we could get into this for all the wrong reasons."

I heaved a sigh. She'd stabbed me with the first comment and then finished me off with the last. "So I'm a little reluctant, okay?" I stared straight down at the bricks, noticing for the first time all the little weeds that had managed to grow in between the cracks, and how I'd failed to take care of those. "I'm working through it."

She nudged my arm, gently forcing me to look at her. "I swept you up in this whirlwind. You were the guy on the plane who turned into a Good Samaritan. You helped me through the most difficult moment of my life, and you kept being there. You got pulled into the undertow when you weren't ready."

"I'm the judge of whether I'm ready or not." But inside, the terrible pitching of my stomach told me that what she was saying was spot on. I'd let myself get swept along, and it had been a wild ride. But my head was whirling.

"You're noble and good-hearted, but I don't want to marry someone to keep my baby. I want to marry someone because I love them, and they love me. Marriage is not something you do for any other reason, Adam. I learned that lesson the hard way." She stood up. "I can't marry you."

I was bleeding here. Plus, she'd said *my* baby, not our baby, and that jarred me. "The risk of losing Rosie is too high to stick to the fairy-tale script. I'm sorry I can't give you all sunshine and flowers, but I can work this out."

I struggled to think. I'd tried to give everything I had. Hadn't I?

It was natural to feel a little reluctant under these circumstances, I rationalized. I wasn't like Ani, plunging headlong into adventures. A year ago, I was practically an inanimate object. I'd come a long way, but I didn't know what else I could do not to feel a sense of caution here. I had no idea how to tell her that.

"What do you want from me?" came out instead, all my frustration pouring out into that one sentence.

"Something you can't give," she said flatly. "All of you. Someone filled with joy and happiness at the prospect of spending their life with me." She closed her eyes and blew out a breath. "I deserve that."

She stood up straighter. The moon was shining on her, lighting her up. Even now I marveled at her beauty. And her certainty. It sank in that she was right—she did deserve better than me, someone who had taken every step with extreme caution. I dragged my fingers through my hair. I couldn't figure out how to turn this around. I couldn't stop my sense of panic that things were moving way too fast.

She watched me with an eagle eye, knowing like she always did more about me than I did myself. "From the outside," she said, "we *look* like a fairy tale. A perfect couple, a perfect baby. Rosie is beloved by both of us. But you and I—I can't love us enough for both of us and hope for the best. I won't. It's not fair to either one of us."

She walked over to me like she did when she was ready to jump into my arms. Instead, she stopped and pulled me to her, holding my head against her and wrapping her arms around me.

She was right.

Maybe I simply wasn't capable of fully loving someone ever again.

Ani

I showed up at my mom and dad's house at seven the next morning, Rosie in tow. The truth was, I hadn't slept all night, so when she woke up at six, I decided that I had to get out or I was going to fall asleep on the job. Plus—and I had a hard time admitting this—I needed my mom.

My complicated, interesting, sometimes annoying mom, whom I somehow felt wouldn't have the same reaction to Adam's declaration that my friends had. I hoped she'd understand, because I felt desperate for someone to talk to.

While Arnold intuitively understood that I was out of sorts and would be more than happy to stick like glue to my side for comfort, I didn't have the luxury of breaking down with Rosie to care for.

My mom answered the door, cell phone in hand, wearing cute yoga pants and a blue top that matched her eyes. I'd have to borrow that. I heard a soothing female voice in the background saying, "Inhale space into the tight spots, and as you exhale, let go of any effort that's not serving you right now."

"Ani," she said with surprise. "Did I miss a call from you?"

"No, I just walked over."

"Oh." She sounded surprised. That got me thinking that I never really did walk over here *just because.* Maybe I should start.

She immediately bent over and checked in with Rosie, telling her good morning and how lovely she looked. Then she straightened up. "Did you do an ER shift last night? You look terrible."

I knew she'd call it as she saw it. But then, that's why I was here. She'd assess the situation objectively. I wasn't sure if she'd be comforting, but honestly, I was out of options. As I had this desperate thought, the tears began to roll.

She grabbed my elbow. "Oh my goodness, what's wrong? Come in! Do you need me to take Rosie this morning? I have an art guild board meeting at eleven, but honestly, she'd be a big hit. Come in!" She practically dragged me into the house and immediately set about releasing Rosie from her stroller and grabbing the diaper bag I'd shoved underneath.

I walked into the sunny family room, flooded with morning sunlight. How strange it was to have my parents here, in town, but not in our same old house. It was as if all that history had been erased.

But maybe it was a chance to start fresh. For my mom and me, that was.

"Where's Dad?" I asked as she grabbed a throw off the back of the couch and spread it on the carpet. She then laid Rosie down, jabbering to her all the way while I grabbed a few toys from her bag.

"Golf with the guys and breakfast," she said. Then she ran into the kitchen.

"Mom, come back. Stop fussing."

She handed me a glass of something. The color was just a notch under nuclear, glowing green. And it was loaded with chia seeds. I took note of the eager expression on her face. "What is this?" I asked.

"It's a green protein smoothie. You look like you could use it." She seemed thrilled to see me. Eager to help. As if she'd been waiting for the day when I'd spontaneously seek her out.

That made me a little sad because we weren't the type of mother-daughter combo who lived a few streets away and shared recipes and went to T.J. Maxx together on the weekends. Why weren't we?

"So I had the case worker from hell for my last interview, which was the psychosocial one." I filled her in on everything and told her I couldn't marry Adam.

"Breathe," the yoga lady on TV said. "Visualize your ribs as an accordion, expanding them with every inhale to enhance your flow of oxygen through your body."

I did the opposite—I held my breath. Waited for my mom to say, "Engaged again? Less than a year later?" or "You're *living* with him? Oh, Ani. What are you thinking?"

My mom seemed to purposely *not* look at me. She shook Rosie's cow rattle, echoed back her oooooh ooooooohs. Then finally she turned to me. "Adam loves you. You know that, right?"

Whoa. "Wait. Aren't you going to tell me how ridiculous it is to be engaged again in less than a year? That I have a new job, a new baby, and a new home, and with one more stressor, my life will literally explode?"

"Oh, please, honey." She waved a dismissive hand. "Don't be dramatic."

"I told Adam that I couldn't marry him. Because he was sweating bullets. Because he asked me for Rosie's sake. Because panic is a terrible reason to get married. I've finally learned to listen to that feeling inside of me that's telling me that something is wrong. But what if I lose her? And what if I lose him?"

I buried my face in my hands, trying not to make bad noises that would upset Rosie, which really didn't work very well. The dog, however, was right at my side, pushing up against me, telling me that he was there for me. I patted his head and told him that he was a very good boy because he totally was.

Of course, Rosie started to cry. Maybe she sensed the bad vibes. My mom picked her up and walked around with her, showing her the sunbeams and pretending to catch them. It was sweet. The yoga lady said, "As you hold your body in child's pose, imagine your body melting into the floor like an ice cube on a sunny day."

My mom handed me a box of tissues and said, "Ani, you don't need a man to give you power. You have the power within you, don't you know?" I stopped sobbing and stared at her. Did my mother just give me the Glinda spiel, that *you've always had the power, my dear, all along?*

"And stop hiding your face," she added, a bit annoyed. "It's okay for the baby to see you cry. Crying is normal, for goodness' sake."

"Wait—you-you think I'm *right*?"

"Of course you're right. I mean, it's very noble of Adam. But what you really need to do is to go after that unjust assessment."

My mom sat down next to me and rubbed my back while I regrouped. Of course, I needed to fight Ms. Nelson, who was a real pill. Why *wouldn't* I defend myself—as well as try to prevent this from happening to others whom she prejudged with her own prejudices? Finally, Rosie batted at my head, and we both burst out laughing.

Finally, I got the courage to really talk with my mom. "I'm sorry that I haven't been the daughter you've wanted. I've brought all this turmoil into our lives."

"Oh, Ani." She grasped her chest, a move not unlike one I tended to use when I was really emotional. "You're so much more than the daughter I wanted." She grabbed my hand.

Wait, what?

"Granted, it is sometimes difficult to watch you plunge headfirst into projects. And granted, I always disliked Tyler. That was a hard one. But you became a *doctor*. You opened your heart to give this beautiful baby a terrific life. And Adam...well, he's special."

"You didn't put me on that plane because you were embarrassed by me?"

She heaved a sigh as Rosie now tried to swat at Arnold with Mr. Cow. Except then Arnold grabbed Mr. Cow in his teeth. Rosie laughed. And then I intervened by reaching over, prying it out of his teeth, wiping the dog spit off on my pants, and handing it right back to her. Desperate times. I wasn't sure if she was old enough to miss Mr. Cow if he got eaten, but I wasn't going to take the risk.

"I think at that point, none of us knew what we were doing," my mom said. "I realize now that being alone after what happened was a terrible decision, and I am sorry. I was just trying to get you away from all that wedding wreckage. But look what happened. You met the love of your life."

"I do love him, Mom. But I'm not sure he can get all the way there. Maybe he's still grieving—"

She stopped me with a hand on my arm. "You've always known what you wanted. Not everyone gets to that point at the same time. Some people take the bus; some take the high-speed train. But people do get there eventually."

We sat there like that for a minute, all of us, the baby half on her lap, half on mine, until she got wiggly and bored.

"I have an idea," my mom said, scooping Rosie up.

"What is it?"

"Get letters of support from everyone you know and turn them into the head of Children's Services. Literally flood the agency with high praise from people who know what a wonderful person and capable mother you are." She pulled out her phone. "I'm the president of the hospital board. I'll write you one." She squeezed my hand. "You're very extraordinary. I'm so proud to be your mother."

"I love you, Mom. You're so kickass." I squeezed her hand right back.

"I know. And the apple doesn't fall far from the tree."

Chapter Twenty

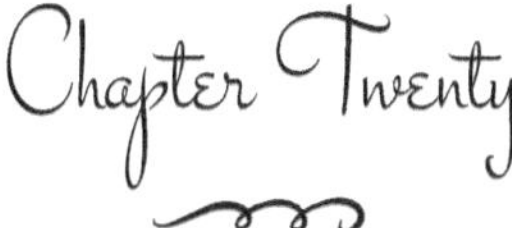

Adam

"Dr. Lowenstein, you've got a patient in Bay 2," Angie said from my doorway. "A seventy-six-year-old woman who fell while walking her dog and can't bear weight."

I was sitting at my desk, tapping Liv's Turks and Caicos postcard against my fingers, thinking about how my time with Ani had begun. How she'd pulled me in like a hurricane. I'd lost my balance, my head. My heart. It had been easy to go along on a wild ride with her, stamping out fires, helping when I could. But this wasn't an adventure game. This was reality, our life—and Rosie's life. For any normal man, it would be justifiable to be cautious, wouldn't it? Ani was a whirlwind, and I wasn't. Was that a crime?

But if it wasn't, why did I feel so bad? Why did I miss Ani, miss Rosie, and regret how I'd ruined the life we'd been building? What had I been I so afraid of?

I looked up and smiled at Angie. "Okay, thanks. I'll be right there." I thought of Mrs. McClellan, who'd been afraid of exactly that same thing, falling with a big dog, and how maybe I'd been a little judgy. Ani and I had relieved her of the worry, as evidenced by our big hairy family member who'd happily entrenched himself into our lives to the point of cockiness, as evidenced by his propensity to think that our bed was his too.

I found myself smiling.

Our family. Until I realized there was no *our* because I'd screwed everything up. And believe me, I was feeling the effects of my stupidity. I couldn't eat, couldn't sleep, couldn't do anything but work, and that only because I kept my head down and forged through a sea of difficulties, counting the minutes until the end of each shift.

As for the postcard, I guess I'd been asking Liv what she thought of all this. But I wasn't getting any answers. So I slipped it into my white coat pocket and went to do my job.

I rolled back the curtain of one of the acute patient bays to find an elderly couple. The man sat in a chair. He had close-cut, white hair and was dressed sharply in a white button-down shirt, black pants, and a black suit coat with a bright red pressed handkerchief sticking out of the pocket. He sat straight as an arrow, holding a polished wooden cane.

In his other hand, he held the thin, veined hand of a woman lying on a stretcher. When she saw me, she hid a grimace with a weak attempt at a smile. Despite her look of frailty, she wore a Nike quarter-zip and running pants with a stripe down the side. The rubber-bottomed soles of her bright white sneakers poked out through the ER blanket.

"Mr. and Mrs. Russ? I'm Dr. Lowenstein." I shook their hands and addressed Mrs. Russ. "Heard you had a fall."

"I was walking our dog, and he spied a darn squirrel." She grimaced again and held her hip. "And please call me Cynthia."

"Okay, Cynthia. You fell on your right side?" I already knew in my heart with ninety-nine percent certainty what the diagnosis was: a hip fracture. I hoped for the best kind, a non-displaced, clean break that would give her the best prognosis.

"That dog is a menace," Mr. Russ said. "He has no restraint. I told you he's too big for you to walk him on a leash."

"Hush, John." She tipped her head toward him. "He was just being a dog." Then she turned to me. "We love our Newfoundland. But I think I did it this time, Doc. Better sign me up for the nursing home."

John looked crestfallen. A shadow fell over his face. He bit down on his lip.

"Hey, I don't think you're ready for *Green Acres* yet." I used the nickname of the local assisted living community, Pleasant Acres. I spied a Kindle sticking out of her purse, which was on the floor near John's chair. "Although I hear they have a fantastic book club there."

I learned that Mrs. R walked five miles every day. That she gardened and read and got around for both of them, as John had bad arthritis.

"I'm worried about John if I'm going to need surgery," she said with blunt honesty. "He hates driving anymore, and he's a terrible cook. And poor Jaxson won't get any exercise." Jaxson, the Newfie, I reckoned. Why did everyone in this town give their dogs people names?

"Don't worry about me," John said. "I know how to do Door-Dash." He directed his next comment at me. "She loves that dog more than me."

"Jaxson's a lot easier to live with than you are sometimes," Cynthia said. "He doesn't talk back."

John made a face.

"I know it's broken," Cynthia said, pointing to her hip. "I heard a crunch. John's right. He can do DoorDash. But I'm going to have to go to rehab and our poor dog is going to suffer."

"Where do you live?" I asked.

Don't do it, Adam. Don't be a savior this time. Haven't you got enough problems already?

"On Hawthorne," John answered. "For the past fifty years."

Old neighborhood, one street away from our—I mean *Ani's*—house. I absolutely was not thinking about helping with their dog. One giant dog was more than enough—except I realized that I wasn't a part of Ani's household any longer, and so I didn't technically have a dog. After my shift, it was back to my sad, gray house. "If you did break your hip, the rehab hospital is close by. Let's do an X-ray and see what we're dealing with. Don't put yourself out to pasture yet."

We gave Mrs. R some pain medicine. Things in the ER were slow, so while she was at X-ray, I checked in on Mr. R, bringing him a cappuccino from the back room, made by the expensive machine my staff had asked for and the hospital board had magically provided. *Thanks, Julia.*

"You married?" Mr. Russ asked after thanking me for the "fancy coffee."

"No." I decided to spare him the sob story.

But maybe my pathetic, depressed expression gave me away. "You love someone?"

I sighed heavily. "Yes." Two someones, actually. And neither of them had been far from my mind for, oh, about fifty-seven minutes out of every hour. And yes, of course I loved them. But I hadn't even said it to them yet.

"We've been married for fifty-seven years," he said. "Even with all the ups and downs, I wouldn't trade even one of them for the world. Best decision I ever made was to marry that woman."

"H-how did you know?" I blurted.

Mr. Russ looked at me with a puzzled expression. No doubt wondering why the ER doctor was asking for a therapy session in the midst of a busy day. "Say that again, son?"

"How did you know that it was a great decision?" What I really meant was that there are no guarantees in life. How do you commit for the long run, knowing you could get your heart ripped out?

"She's the best thing in the world for me. Sometimes she

knows what I'm thinking before I think it. She makes me laugh. Of course, she calls me out when I do something stupid. She's real good at that too."

I wanted to know something else. But it would have been inappropriate to ask. What if something happened? Something you couldn't control? What if you weren't lucky enough to share a whole lifetime together?

That would have been callous and unprofessional. It reminded me that I needed to do my job, not ask patients for advice.

I looked up to find John laughing.

"I know about you and the doctor and the baby. You three are cute together. Why not marry her?"

"I-ah-my wife died," I blurted, my words spilling out. "And I—I—to do it again..." I swallowed.

"Oh, I get it." He waved his hand as if to say *no big deal*. "You're afraid it's going to hurt. Well, sometimes it does. But take some advice from an old man." He waited until I made eye contact and he was certain that I was paying attention. "Enjoy every minute together that you can. You think life will go on forever, but it doesn't. It's short. And precious. Every single minute of it is precious."

A lump got trapped in my throat.

Ani *had* been the best thing in the world for me. She'd awakened me from the dead. Not just woke me up—startled, shook, and stunned me awake. Made me care about—well, everything. And she hadn't been afraid to call me out on my fears. Somehow, she'd known them better than I did.

"I'm near the end of my time with my wife, but I'd still do everything exactly the same." He looked up at me, his eyes watery. "Don't miss out on a beautiful life."

I got up. I squeezed his shoulder, but he was too choked up to talk. Actually, I was too.

If I'd suspected that I was short on brain cells before, this solidified it. I'd been so afraid to love, to be hurt, to have pain—but I'd realized that it was already too late. Because I *was* hurt. I *was* in pain—the pain of being petrified that I would never get to spend my life with Ani.

I found myself desperately wanting two things: one was for Mrs. Russ to have a clean, simple fracture with a great prognosis so that I could deliver this nice couple some good news, and the other was the end of my shift so that I could go and try to make up for all my dumbness.

I was granted my wish on the first count. Mrs. Russ had a non-displaced intertrochanteric fracture, which was fancy talk for the best kind of hip fracture possible. It didn't get her out of having surgery, which Caleb, the orthopedic doctor who saw her, scheduled for the next day. With the right rehab program, she would do great.

At last, my shift ended. Back in my office, I was taking off my white coat to hang it up when I felt the cardboard postcard in my pocket. I pulled it out, staring hard at the pure white sand of Grace Bay Beach, the turquoise water, the pier, the azure sky.

This was where I'd said goodbye to Liv and hello to Ani, when I was so full of sorrow that I could only hold myself together by regimenting every aspect of my life.

I was about to shove the postcard into my desk drawer when I dropped it, and it landed handwriting-side up. I read the back as I put it away. *You've got to see this place! Having a fun time, so don't worry about me. See you soon!*

This time, I noticed something I'd missed before. A little squiggly arrow that pointed to the three tropical flora stamps she'd affixed to the right upper corner. Hmm. I held the postcard up to the light, but I couldn't see anything. My heart began to beat a little faster as I picked off the stamps with my fingernail with all the zeal I'd normally use to rub off a lottery ticket.

I told myself that this was not going to be a message from beyond. Of course it wasn't. But any message from her would be a blessing, even a silly one from years ago.

Finally, I got the stamps off, but not until I soaked the corner of the postcard in some water I'd poured into an old coffee cup. When they finally floated off, I blotted the postcard dry on my pants.

Book that ticket! It said in tiny letters. *It will change your life. ILY4ever, Liv*

She'd signed it the way she signed everything. *ILY4ever.*

I was a little overcome. So much so that I had to sit down, which I did, and read the words over and over.

I tried to pinch my nose when the tingling started, but I just broke down. I heaved a sob. And then another. And then I started laughing. I had to close my door to get myself together.

I wasn't a woo-woo person, but I'd always wanted to believe that Liv was somewhere up there, looking down on me. A star twinkling in the heavens, or a shooting star. A bell ringing when an angel gets its wings. But a postcard?

It wasn't postmarked from heaven, but in my opinion, it might as well have been. I clutched the postcard to my chest and just sat there, thinking. About how love is a funny thing. That you can love someone a lot, but you can love someone else a lot too. Wounds can heal, and you could move forward. Ani was my forward. Ani was the rest of my life. And now I knew that was okay.

I wiped a tear from my face. "Thank you, Liv, for those wonderful years." I pulled open my drawer and ran my fingers lightly over the glass of our photo. "And for looking out for me. I love you, honey." I paused. "I always will." I placed the postcard inside the drawer and quietly shut it.

Then I went to start living the rest of my life.

～

Ani

.   .   .

The next day was Monday, and letters in hand, I walked into a plain brick building near the hospital. Wheeling the stroller with a Rosie dressed to impress in a sweet pink jumper over a little white collared shirt with rosebuds, I'd stopped to put on Cathy's little pink booties with the rosebuds too, but Rosie had already pulled one off and was working on pulling off her sock too.

I'd been talking to myself in the mirror all morning in between getting both of us ready, presenting my case. The fact that virtually everyone I knew had written me a letter so quickly and was so supportive made me even more confident that I could explain to the head of the agency, Hugo Rothstein, that I felt misrepresented.

I was heartsick about Adam, but I couldn't dwell on it. The stakes if I screwed this up were too high. Had I been prideful because I wanted it all—not a half-hearted proposal given in a moment of panic? Maybe I was too much of a dreamer, always shooting for the stars, but I believed that I was a good mother, that I was capable. I wouldn't be intimidated.

Which was all fine and good, but life wasn't a fairy tale, as Adam had said. Bad things happened. Sometimes the truth didn't prevail, and what if I lost her?

He'd texted me good luck this morning, which made me cry. Forget the marriage proposal, I wanted *him* by my side, with his calm collectedness, his staid reassurance that everything would be fine. But I was no longer a runaway bride on an airplane trying to drown myself in Bloody Marys. It was high time I learned to rescue myself.

Step One was struggling to get the stroller onto an old, crowded elevator. Especially when Rosie finally pitched the final sock overboard right before I maneuvered her in and no one held the elevator for me. I scooped up the sock and had to throw my body in at the last second. And put up with dirty looks to boot. Didn't anyone have children here in the Children's Services building?

When the old elevator shuddered up to the third floor and the door opened, I had to blink twice. Adam stood there, dressed in a gray suit, a white shirt, and brown shoes. And a blue tie. Smiling.

I had to blink a few times to make sure he was real.

Here I'd thought that seeing him in the ER in a button-down shirt with the sleeves rolled up, listening to a patient with his stethoscope, was sexy. If being a doctor didn't work out, he could always audition for the cover of books like *Billionaire Boss Hottie* and do just fine.

I just broke down. Right there. People around me quickly flowed around the roadblock of Rosie and me and exited the elevator. Adam jumped quickly into action, tugging on the stroller and then grabbing my arm with his other hand and getting us all out of there before the doors closed. All the while, he was saying hi to Rosie, telling her how pretty she looked. By this time she was a total chaos agent, grabbing her foot and trying to stick her bare toes into her mouth. Still, she lit up on seeing him, smiling, eyes dancing.

I loved seeing him in action. But mostly, I loved seeing him here. Waiting for us. And you know what? It felt like everything I'd ever wanted. I didn't care about a proposal. I cared about someone being there for me—for us—at every turn.

"Why are you here?" I managed, just in case he was here for that cover model shoot or something.

He took a second, scanning my face with intense eyes. Gripping my arms. Turning his full lips up into a slight smile. "I love you," he said. "Both of you."

I let out a sob. I was a camel's hair close to crying anyway, but that did it.

"Life is nothing without you." He reached up and stroked my cheek, resting his palm there. "You're my home. I belong with you —with both of you—if you'll have me."

"I love you too. I'm so glad you're here." I kept sobbing. "But I'm terrified."

I could barely see where I was going as he quickly steered us into a large, paneled room with a neutral-colored couch and uphol-stered chairs labeled Family Visitation Room. I could barely see where I was going.

As we entered the room, he closed the door, took me in his arms, and held me. "We're not going to lose her." I pulled back and looked up into his gentle brown eyes. He appeared calm. Confi-dent. I derived strength from that.

He was here. That was all I needed.

"I'm sorry I was an ass," he said. "Forgive me."

I didn't tell him, *Oh, that's okay. Don't worry about it,* as I might have done in the past. This time, I tried for more honesty. I simply listened. And nodded. And he kept going.

"I realized that I've loved you from that moment on the plane when you barfed into my Santa bag. There was no turning back from it. But I was so terrified to jump in. So afraid of—well, of life. I thought I could protect myself from loving you. But the truth is, I fell a long time ago, and I've been a goner ever since. So it looks like you can't get rid of me so easily."

I was sniffling, my nose was running, and of course I didn't have a Kleenex. So I snagged a baby wipe from Rosie's bag and blew. The fake powdery fresh scent of baby wipe was over-whelming this close to my nose, and at any other time, I might have laughed.

"Adam." I touched his nice jacket. Looked up into his nice eyes. Kept crying. "Somehow in my heart, I always knew you loved me. But right now, I'm so afraid."

"Don't be. I brought reinforcements." He made a hand gesture like a traffic cop motioning cars through a blockade. "I thought it would be great to not only bring the letters, but also to bring all the people who wrote them."

I looked up in shock. In the doorway, people had gathered. My people—our people. Daria, my mom and dad, Mia and Sam, Brax, Caleb, Helen, Penelope, and Dylan. And guess what? Dylan and Pen were holding hands. Imagine that.

Angie, Cathy, Tom, Ivy, and BethAnn came from the ER. Even Adam's sister Anita was there. *Everyone.* They all came flooding in, surrounding us, surrounding Rosie. And they all waved and cooed and made faces at our baby.

Our baby. Thinking that choked me up and made me realize that I would fight with all my might to keep her. Whatever it took.

Angie gave me a big squeeze and said, as if she'd read my mind, "We're all here for you."

I hugged her back, managing only a nod.

Cathy walked up with a special pair of bright green booties with daisies on them. "You're never too young for power shoes," she said, putting them right on Rosie's now-bare feet. Then she grasped both my hands. "Knock 'em dead in there."

Dylan and Pen walked up together, arms linked, smiling. I blinked. Did I hallucinate that? I didn't have time to wonder, because Pen immediately hugged me. Dylan said, "Breathe and be present." This was accompanied by some arm movements like laying on of hands. "Be like water," he said in a serious tone.

"Like water?" I frowned, uncomprehending.

"Fluid, adaptable, and calm, regardless of the container you're in." Then he smiled and gave me a kiss on the cheek.

Adam was watching from across the room with a slightly testy expression. I shrugged and smiled, and then he smiled back. He had nothing to fear from Dylan.

"Give 'em hell," Helen said, giving me the closest approximation of a smile I'd ever seen from her.

Rosie, clearly an extrovert, just kept smiling and being theatric —she kept tossing her cow, and a different person would pick it up each time. When Tom did it, she let out a laugh.

Great. An extrovert, and a flirt to boot.

Then someone else walked in. A tall guy with blond hair, dressed in a white shirt and a tie and a lab coat. He was holding a brown shopping bag.

"Tyler?" My jaw dropped open as he crossed the room and stood in front of me. "I thought you were in New York."

He shifted his weight and looked uncomfortable. "I got your voicemails, Ani. I'm sorry I didn't call you back."

Wait. Stoic, proper, country-club-raised Tyler, who'd wanted me to bend to his way of life. Who could be so callous and self-serving and unemotional—was *sorry* about something?

"A cardiologist friend of mine told me about the baby," he explained. "When I heard what you did, I just—couldn't hold on to my anger anymore."

He sounded...human. Vulnerable. Where was the real Tyler? As I gave him a giant hug, I noticed that he looked a little thinner, acted a little nicer. I briefly wondered who or what was responsible for the transformation.

"I'm glad you're here." Touched by his show of support, I looked him in the eye. "I'm sorry for breaking things off the way I did." I was finally saying my piece. "I should've never let things get to that point."

"I know you're sorry." That sounded more like the Tyler I knew. "But I don't want you to be. You were right about a lot of things, and that was one of them." He held out a bag. "I brought the baby some medical books."

I peered into the bag. "Medical books?" Rosie was clearly a genius baby, but I wasn't sure she was ready for that.

"Yeah, you know. Board books that teach you anatomy. They're...fun. And I wrote you a letter." He gave the slightest, maybe a little sad, smile. "Nice to see you, Ani. What you're doing is incredible. But then, I always knew you were amazing." Then he kissed me on the cheek.

I felt relief. Resolution. I even felt charity toward him. Until he spoke. "By the way, I'll be seeing you around. I just got hired into the cardiology group here."

Oh dear.

"Do all your exes move to Oak Bluff?" Adam asked, standing

at my side before I could even process that. He wrapped an arm around me and grinned, which made Tyler and everything and everyone else fade into the distance.

His broad shoulders that were strong enough to help carry the burden of everything that was happening right now. His calm presence and warm humor made me more certain than ever that together we could make this happen—make anything happen, actually. Not to mention that he was the most gorgeous man I'd ever seen in that suit. And I could barely dare to think it, but he was mine.

He reached down and pulled Rosie out of her stroller and set her in the crook of his big arms, a flowery pink rosebud—well except for the green and yellow daisies, but hey, at least she had booties on.

He smiled a big, confident smile and held out his other hand to me.

"I love you," I said a little breathlessly. As I looked into his eyes, I felt that no one could stop us.

"I love you too," he said as he squeezed my hand.

And together we led the way into Mr. Rothstein's office.

Epilogue

Eight months later

Ani

"Have you seen my sock?" Adam asked as he trailed a wobbly Rosie who was wide-legged-tightrope-walking her way across the family room while I stood capturing it all on video. Arnold and Jaxson stood right near her too, sentinels to protect her from falling.

"I don't think Jaxson ate any today," I said, trying to recall if I'd caught him sneaking one away from the laundry basket. He was very good at sorting through things to find exactly what he needed to support his habit.

"Yet," Adam added. "I'd really love to find a sock to wear to work, though."

The sock was quickly forgotten as Rosie's first few steps turned into her first big walk. She left the couch behind and entered uncharted territory. So exciting.

On hearing his name, Jaxson's ears drooped. Guilty as charged. He was an in-and-out visitor to our home, often staying over. Arnold, a genuinely kind spirit, took right to having him as a doggie pal. The Russes genuinely loved Jax, even Mr. Russ did, it turned out, and we made sure to walk him every day. And the Russes enjoyed our little family. Win-win.

Adam had his shirt rolled up to the elbows as he bent over, ready to stabilize Rosie if she needed it, which, despite one-sock-on, one-off, had to be the sexiest look on a man I've ever seen. The forearm muscles, the watch, the beautiful hands. I was done for.

But then I had to put down my phone because I had to get to work.

"Whose mom is coming today?" Adam asked. He was scanning everywhere for that missing sock.

"Mine, I think." Lucky us—our moms had each begged to babysit a day a week, and Adam often watched Rosie when he had days off.

I was back at work three-fourths time. Dylan had stayed on, which was a good thing because Pen had started working in hospital administration while pursuing her MBA. And she'd begun teaching new mom classes at the hospital. Helen had finally admitted that she wanted to retire, and we were currently looking for another associate.

Pen and Dylan were a thing, and I believed that both of them were truly smitten. They meditated together daily. The best part, in my opinion, was that Dylan had helped Pen get into therapy, which had reduced her anxiety and helped her to make some hard but good life decisions.

But I'd warned Dylan that if he hurt Pen, I'd personally make sure he had no Zen for the rest of his life.

Rosie crossed the room and pulled herself up to the couch. "Dada," she said, pointing at Adam.

"I'm your favorite," he said in a smug tone, making her laugh. But when he went to pick her up, she cried and held out her arms for me. It was a game she played, sometimes Mom, sometimes Dad, but honestly, she secretly did prefer me. For now, anyway.

After all, I was her mother.

I kissed her on the cheek and told her how smart and beautiful she was, as I always did. I thought of her birth mother, as I often did, and hoped and prayed that she was okay, and that one day, if she ever returned, she might learn what happened in this town to her beautiful daughter and understand that I'd kept my promise.

A feeling welled up inside of me. That I was the luckiest woman on the planet to claim this man and this baby as my own. My heart was overflowing with happiness and relief—times two. I felt that my life was truly beginning right now, that everything up until then had been a rehearsal. This was the real show, and I was loving every minute of it.

Later that night, we were enjoying a glass of wine, both dogs on the rug in front of the roaring fire, wrapped up in the Packers blanket, the lights dim.

All was silent except for the occasional pop of the fire, crackling and lively.

My ring sparkled in the firelight. My grandma Rosalie's diamond, with a tiny vine pattern and two little diamonds on either side, symbolizing our ready-made family. Woven together forever. Adam had given it to me in a Santa bag, of all things.

We'd gotten married at the courthouse a few weeks after I was officially named Rosie's foster parent. I'd told Adam that I was fine with taking things slow, but he'd said *the hell with slow*. He'd wanted to be Rosie's adopted father, not her stepfather, which he would have been if we were unmarried at the time the adoption was official.

We were planning another (but still small) wedding for the coming summer, officiated by a Christian minister and a rabbi, blending both of our traditions. Meeting halfway, as we always did.

All was quiet, an unusual moment. I think we both got lost in the magic of it, with the flickering fire, the soft snores from the dogs, Rosie's occasional stirring. Adam's soft brown eyes lit up with the firelight. "I loved you on that plane, I love you now, and I will always love you."

"I love you too." I met him halfway now, tumbling into his arms, kissing him thoroughly, wrapping my arms around his neck. I tangled my hands in his hair, feeling the familiar softness of his lips moving over mine in a way that sent warmth flooding everywhere, leaving me breathless and dizzy. As he always did.

A log on the fire suddenly popped extra loudly, causing us to stop kissing. Nothing was amiss. Rosie was still fast asleep, the dogs dreaming no doubt of chasing squirrels (or whatever dogs dreamed of).

"I feel so peaceful," he said. "Like everything has finally settled down."

"There's just one thing," I said as the fire softly crackled and popped. "I mean, it's probably not anything."

"What is it?" He looked at me with concern.

"I'm probably not pregnant." His entire body stiffened below me. "I mean, the morning nausea is probably from the stress. Going back to work thirty hours a week, balancing everything, yada yada."

His expression was one part, *What have I just gotten myself into?* And another part, *This is what life is like around here.*

"I'm kidding," I said. At least, I thought I was.

And then he tackled me down on the couch. Between laughs, I looked tenderly into his eyes. "But you do want more, right? I mean, maybe not right away, but...down the line?"

He kissed me solidly and said, "I can't wait to spend my life with you. Have babies with you. Do all the things with you. But for right now, maybe we can just shoot for that slightly peaceful thing for a little while."

I was more than okay with that. We could always negotiate what *a little while* meant, right? Like maybe next month, when we were headed back to Turks and Caicos for a long weekend. Either way, I was certain we would negotiate it, because I was getting really good at telling people what I wanted.

Then he kissed me again, deeper and more seriously. One of the dogs might have twitched a time or two, and Rosie sighed in her sleep, but then I missed anything else because I got very busy focusing on him and me.

Acknowledgments

Twenty-one books ago, I wrote a story about a professional woman who works eighty hours a week, knows nothing about babies, and suddenly finds herself responsible for one. That book won the Romance Writers of America Golden Heart Award for Unpublished Contemporary Romance and launched my career.

A decade later, after I learned a thing or two about writing, I wanted to come full circle and do another baby story. But this time, I wanted my main female character to *deliver* the baby.

I could not leave Ani Green standing at the altar, as I did in *Take Me to the Wedding*. But she is a force, and not just any man would do! I hope you've enjoyed her hard-earned happily ever after as much as I did.

I wanted to give a shout-out to two talented professionals, my editor, Patience Bloom, and my cover artist, Kim Killion, both of whom helped to bring this story to life.

With this series, I've tried my best to honor the selfless people who serve in health care. Thank you for all you do for us.

Ani lives big and is unafraid to make bold, courageous decisions. She's my hero! The rest of us might take comfort in remembering that starting small still counts:

"The best portion of a good [person's] life is [their] little nameless, unremembered acts of kindness and love." ~ William Wordsworth

Thank you as always for reading my books, reviewing them, and writing to me. I love to hear from you!

xo,

Miranda

About the Author

I am a former pediatrician and an Amazon Top-Five best-selling author who writes about the important relationships in women's lives. My heartwarming and humorous romances have won numerous accolades and have been praised by *Entertainment Weekly* for the way they "deal with so much of what makes life hard... without ever losing the warmth and heart that characterize her writing." I *always* believe that we can handle whatever life throws at us just a little bit better with a laugh—it's the best medicine, after all!

A proud native of Northeast Ohio, I live in a neighborhood of old homes that serves as inspiration for my books. I'm very proud of my three now-adult children. When I'm not writing or enjoying books, I can be found biking along the old Ohio and Erie Canal Towpath trails in the beautiful Ohio Metro Parks.

I love to hear from readers! (See next page for where to find me.)

Learn more at:

MirandaLiasson.com

Facebook.com/MirandaLiassonAuthor
   (my Author Page where I hang out daily 🤍)

Instagram @mirandaliasson

X @MirandaLiasson

🤍Find all my books and sign up for my newsletter on my website.